PRAISE FOR JULIA GABRIEL

"A compelling romance supported by nuanced characters ... heartbreaking and sensitively drawn ... a well-crafted contemporary romance." —*Kirkus Reviews* on *Hearts on Fire*

"Julia Gabriel does an amazing job with this devastatingly, heartbreaking love story." —*RT Book Reviews, Top Pick* for *Hearts on Fire*

"A heart-wrenching and emotional read, with a sweet payoff that will leave readers smiling" —*InD'Tale Magazine* on *Hearts on Fire*

"A bittersweet story about perseverance and adversity. Julia Gabriel does an amazing job of conveying the characters' feelings. The writing style is flawless, and the characters are both multifaceted and dynamic." —*RT Book Reviews, Top Pick* for *Next to You*

"The second novel in the Phlox Beauty series, *Back to Us* is an intimate look at an unforgettable, albeit imperfect, love. Ms. Gabriel's deeply moving storytelling evokes every facet of emotion from the reader. Not only does this book have standout characters, the city of New York shines in this tale. All in all, between the beautiful settings and the sweet and satisfying ending, this book is a winner!" —*InD'Tale Magazine* for *Back to Us*

"*Back to Us* is a unique romance about falling in love all over again. Colt is a great character that readers will be rooting for throughout the book. Suffering from memory loss, he needs to recall his past in order to move on with his future. The alternation between past and present timelines works well and while the story can be enjoyed as a standalone, it is further enhanced by the inclusion of all the characters from Next to You, the first book in the Phlox Beauty series." —*RT Book Reviews*

HEARTS ON FIRE

HEARTS ON FIRE

ST. CAROLINE SERIES BOOK 1

JULIA GABRIEL

SERIF BOOKS

Published by Serif Books

CHAPTER 1

The smell of smoke tickled Becca Trevor's nose. *Not again.* There was no smoking allowed in the bar but the jerk down at the end seemed to believe he was above the law. Just like Brandon had thought he was, right up to the minute he was arrested for embezzling money from the custom motorcycle shop he worked for. That was last week and hell would freeze over before she borrowed money to bail him out.

She sauntered down to the end of the bar. She wanted to be casual about this, non-confrontational. She paused halfway down to wipe up a non-existent spill on the bar top.

"Sir, there's no smoking in here." She smiled prettily at him.

He waved his lit cigarette in the air. "You don't have an ashtray."

Of course we don't. It's no smoking.

She pulled another bar glass from beneath the counter and filled it halfway with water. She set it on the bar in front of him. Water splashed out of the glass when he rammed the cigarette into it. She calmly wiped it up and took away the glass. This was the second time tonight she'd done this; a third time and it would be a comedy routine.

"Can you at least get me another beer?" he growled at her.

"I sure can." She pulled another draft of what he was drinking and slid it in front of him. After all this trouble, he wasn't going to tip anyway. The troublemakers never did.

She tried her best to ignore him for the next fifteen minutes, until a young woman climbed up onto a stool two seats away from him. It was the only empty spot at the moment or Becca would wave her elsewhere. The bar was busier than she had expected for Memorial Day. From what she could glean from snippets of conversation here and there, the baseball game at the stadium a few blocks away had been called for rain in the fourth inning. It looked like a lot of people had come here instead.

"What can I get you?" Becca asked the newcomer. She wasn't a regular. After three months working here, Becca knew all the usual folks.

"Just a sparkling water with lemon, thanks." She glanced worriedly at the door every few minutes. Clearly, she was waiting for someone. Maybe a blind date.

Somehow Becca wasn't surprised when the smoker leaned around the man sitting next to him and tried to strike up a conversation with the young woman. "They don't let you smoke in here, you know."

The woman nodded and gave him a weak smile. "I don't smoke anyway."

He dropped down off his seat and squeezed into the narrow space between her and the next patron. Becca could see the woman's posture tense. "Let me buy you a drink. What's that, soda? You need something better than that." His words were beginning to slur. He waved at Becca.

"No thanks," the woman said firmly. "I'm waiting for someone."

"Well so am I, sweetheart. Don't mean we can't enjoy a drink while we wait." He waved at Becca again. "Two more beers down here, barkeep."

Barkeep? How about wench while you're at it? Becca pulled another draft and placed it in front of the man.

"I'm fine," the woman said, holding up her barely-touched water. "I don't want one."

"Just one, sweetheart. Your date will thank me later."

Out of the corner of her eye, Becca saw a businessman-type vacate a seat at the other end of the bar. "Why don't you sit down there?" she said quietly to the young woman.

"What the hell!" the man shouted. "Can't you just mind your own business and pour drinks? That's what you're being paid for."

The young woman slipped off the stool and practically ran to the empty seat. Becca watched her until she heard the sound of breaking glass and then a sharp prick on her upper arm. She spun around. The entire room was still now, every conversation in the place paused.

"Look what you made me do now, bitch!"

People were backing away from the bar quickly, leaving Becca and Asshole Man in a standoff. The man had slammed his empty glass onto the bar, shattering it. Shards were scattered every-where. That was what she'd felt prick her arm.

"Joe!" Another voice broke in.

"About time you got here. Your bitch of a bartender won't pour me the drink I ordered."

Your bitch of a bartender? Becca looked at the large man walking down the length of the bar. *Shit.* It was the owner, a man she'd never been introduced to but knew by sight. The sight right now was not that of a happy man. There was also, for Becca's immediate prospects, an unhappy familial resemblance between the owner and the asshole grinning ear to ear at her now. Across the room, the assistant manager hovered by the hostess station, too chickenshit to intervene.

Becca knew what was coming. She could see it unfolding in the minutes ahead of her like a slow motion scene in a movie. She was going to be unceremoniously fired in three … two … yep, one. Strangely, all of a sudden, she really didn't care. First Brandon. Now this. She calmly grabbed her purse from beneath the bar. Right as she pushed open the heavy door to the street, she heard the owner say, "We can manage with just the other bartender tonight."

What other bartender, idiot? He was too cheap to have more than one per shift. But whatever. She was out of there.

Outside the bar, it was raining cats and dogs. Becca raced to where her car was parked down the street. Inside, she let her body sink into the cloth seat and closed her eyes against the sight of rain sluicing down the windshield. *No good deed goes unpunished. Story of my life, starring Becca Trevor.* Once again, she was unemployed. Her boyfriend—well, ex-boyfriend now—was in jail. *Also story of my life: poor choice in men.*

She opened her eyes, inserted the key into the ignition and pulled out onto the rain-glossed street. She had packed a lot of mistakes into twenty-five years on this earth. What was one more? She'd go home, heat up a package of ramen noodles and fall into bed. Plenty of time to worry about her lack of gainful employment tomorrow.

She turned the final corner into her neighborhood—and slammed on the brakes. There was trash strewn all over the street in front of the apartment building. She glanced at the beige brick building's tiny lawn. Boxes and furniture sat on the swampy grass. A television. Piles of soggy clothes and … Becca killed the ignition and burst from the car.

… and quilts.

All of her quilts had been dumped onto the lawn. *In the freaking rain!* And the television … that was her television, and the furniture too. She'd been evicted. *Shit!* Brandon always paid the rent. She gave him her half in cash, he deposited it in the bank, and then wrote a check to the landlord. She was going to have to do that now since Brandon was in jail, but the rent wasn't due for another two weeks. Unless Brandon hadn't been paying the rent. And why did that idea not surprise her?

She gathered up an armful of her clothes and ran it back to the car, dumping it all into the back seat. They'd have to be washed later, but no time to worry about that now. She raced back to the grass, her sodden shoes squishing with each step. They'd been evicted! *Damn him!* She picked through the mess on the ground, searching. Most of it was ruined. The television, certainly. The toaster. The box of now broken dishes. She picked up the book she'd been reading to relax and decompress before bedtime, then let it drop from her fingers. It, too, was soaked clean through.

She kicked at a mound of fabric, Brandon's favored brand of boxer briefs and athletic socks. *Laundry done!* A bitter laugh escaped her lips before she remembered the one thing she absolutely needed to find. Her breath caught in her throat as she leaned down to dig frantically through piles and boxes. She owned nothing of value in the first place. Even if she did—and even if it weren't totally waterlogged by now—there wasn't enough room in her compact car to fit everything.

But the quilt. She needed to find the quilt she was making as a thirtieth wedding anniversary gift for her parents. She was so close to having it ready, and the anniversary party was in two weeks. Only a third remained to be quilted, then the binding sewn on and it was done. Not that Becca was planning to go to the party. She couldn't afford to take the time off, but she could spring for shipping it.

She wasn't finding it here in the mess on the lawn, though. She ran into the building and took the stairs two at a time, not caring about the noise she was making. It didn't really matter now if other residents complained to the building manager.

Damn it all. The locks on the apartment had already been changed. She leaned her forehead against the cold steel door. She'd never be able to get another quilt done before the party. It took her eighty to a hundred hours to complete one. She slumped down onto the floor and buried her face in her palms. When had this happened? They must have been waiting around the corner for her to leave for work that morning.

She sat in the hallway, listening to the rain pound the sides of the building and considered her options. No job. No apartment. No boyfriend. No reason to stay in Ohio. She pushed herself up from the floor. It was just after two in the afternoon. If she hit the road now, she could be home in St. Caroline before midnight.

JACK WOLFE HAD no sooner accepted the mug of coffee from his father's hands when the fire station erupted into choreographed chaos all around him. Suddenly everyone was dashing about, grabbing gear, getting into their trucks.

"Gotta' go, Jackie. We'll see you at home later, okay?" His father clapped a broad hand on Jack's shoulder, then followed his crew.

Jack watched longingly as the trucks pulled out of the bays and disappeared into the muggy night. Just like that, he was alone. Fireflies glittered in the dark outside the station. The ticking of the ancient clock on the station wall was loud in his ears.

The bay doors to the station began to lower automatically and he stood to leave. No point sitting in an empty firehouse, even though he had spent plenty of hours by himself in this very room, reading and doing homework. The station was like a second home to him. The Wolfe family—the Wolves, as they were called around St. Caroline—were firefighters across generations. His father had risen through the ranks to become the chief. His two older brothers were captains. His uncle Jack—twin to Jack's mother—had died in the line of duty before Jack was born.

At Jack's birth, his mother had put her foot down. Her

youngest was not going into the family business. Little Jackie was the one who would leave town, go to college and become a doctor or lawyer or schoolteacher. Spend his life in a nice, safe job instead of rushing headlong into burning buildings and causing his mother years of worry. Finding out that Jack had dropped out of Berkeley Law, gotten a job as a security guard, and was a volunteer firefighter in California would kill her.

And she was dying already.

He went outside, got in his car and began to drive. He'd heard the address of the call when it came in from the county central dispatch. It was Michelle Trevor's quilt shop, closed at this hour obviously—just before eleven—so no one would be there. But his mother was a long-time customer of Quilt Therapy, so he drove out to see what was what.

He parked his car in the small shopping center parking lot across the street and jogged over to Michelle Trevor's shop. In the dark, it was hard to pick out his dad and brothers among the identically-suited figures aiming water at the small cottage that had housed the quilt shop for years. The structure would probably make it, but everything inside was going to be ruined. He noticed a car sitting in the small parking area off to the side of the house. It was a white four-door compact, nothing out of the ordinary. Not brand new, but not ancient either.

"Whose car is that?" he shouted into the din of the truck engines and noise of high-powered streams of water hitting the roof.

A figure turned. "What?" It was his oldest brother, Oliver. "What are you doing here?"

Jack cocked his head toward the small white car. "Whose car is that?"

Oliver looked at it like he was seeing it for the first time. "I dunno."

Alarm bells went off in Jack's head. "Did you check to see if anyone's inside?"

"Shop's closed."

"Owners have been known to come back after hours."

"Michelle and her daughters are in Chicago for some big trade show. They won't be back until later in the week."

"So you haven't cleared the building?"

"There's no one in there." Oliver turned back to the fire.

Jack began running toward the back door. His hand was turning the knob—strangely unlocked for a shop that was closed for the week—when a big hand clapped him on the shoulder and yanked back hard.

"What the hell are you doing?" It was Matt, his other older brother.

"There's a car parked over there and no one seems to know who it belongs to. Hasn't anyone checked for someone inside?"

Matt frowned. "Who'd be inside? The whole Trevor family's out of town."

"Hell if I know! But there's a car there!" Jack was right in Matt's face now.

"Fine. I'll go in," Matt said.

"I'll go with you." The pull of the fire was too much for Jack. He wanted to be working this call, too.

"You sure as hell will not. If dad doesn't kill me, mom will." He shot a fierce glare at his younger brother. "You will wait out here."

Jack took a deep breath. Mattie was right. He was a Wolfe, but not a member of the St. Caroline fire department. He didn't belong here. He watched as his brother grabbed another fire-fighter and headed into the building. Two in, two out. Jack strode over to the car and cautiously touched the door handle. It was warm. If the fire got worse, it would be too hot to touch. He tried the handle, but the car was locked. No moving it now. He peered into the back seat, and recognition hit him like a backdraft.

There was a brown sock monkey hanging from the driver's side seat, its short arms clinging to the metal prong of the headrest. A memory he hadn't given a minute's attention to in years flared in his brain.

This was Rebekah Trevor's car.

He spun around at the sound of yelling behind him. Matt and the other firefighter were out of the building—and between them stumbled a woman, coughing and choking.

CHAPTER 2

From the parking lot across the street, Becca watched the firefighters wrap up their work. The small crowd of onlookers was beginning to disperse. She needed to call her parents but undoubtedly they already knew. St. Caroline was a small town, even when you added in the summer residents. It was part fishing village, part quaint vacation town for the rich and powerful in the mid-Atlantic. The Trevor family could trace their residence on the eastern shore of Maryland back to the early eighteen-hundreds. They were as historic as the buildings on Main Street.

She sat down on a narrow cement parking curb and crossed her ankles in front of her. Probably dozens of people had called her parents by now to give them the bad news. Both parts of it, in fact. One, Quilt Therapy was basically gone. Everything inside— from bolts of fabric to the sewing machines in the tiny classroom —was a total loss. And Bad News Part Two, the black sheep of the family was back in town—and within hours of her arrival, the family business had burned down.

Everything she touched turned to ashes. All her life, that had been the case. She often wondered whether Michelle and Daniel

Trevor ever regretted adopting her after her mother, Michelle's younger (and wayward) sister, died young of a drug overdose. If they didn't regret it before, they surely would now.

From inside her canvas purse came the sound of her phone ringing. She took a deep breath. *Time to face the music.* She should be good at this by now. She dug out the phone and tapped the screen.

"Hi mom," she said glumly. Should she launch into abject groveling immediately? Or let her mother say her piece first?

"Bec! Where are you, honey?" Her mother's voice, soft with genuine concern, washed over her like a balm. She didn't deserve this family. Nor had they ever done anything terrible enough to deserve her.

"I'm in the parking lot across the street." A hiccup seized her lungs and the sharp bite of pain unleashed the tears she had held back for the past hour. "I'm sorry, mom. I am so sorry."

"Are you okay? You didn't get hurt, did you?"

"No. That's the least of your worries now."

"That is the absolute most of my worries, Becca." Concern was replaced by sternness. "Why didn't you go to the house?"

"I did." She wiped her eyes on her forearm. "When I got there, I realized that I didn't have a key. But I remembered the security code to the shop, so I just came here. I was asleep on the couch …"

"Where's your key to the house?"

"I lost it." It had been in the nightstand next to her bed. She couldn't remember even seeing the nightstand outside the apartment. Maybe someone had already made off with it by the time she got there.

"Okay. Well, we'll go to the hardware store and make a new one. I thought you didn't have enough time off to come home."

"I do now." She didn't need to elaborate further. No one in her family would be surprised that she had lost yet another job. Another apartment. Another boyfriend.

"Maybe we should talk about this when I get home. Daddy's online now, looking for a morning flight tomorrow. Your sisters and I will be back Wednesday."

"He doesn't have to come home—"

"Sweetheart, you know how much he loves these quilt shows. He's happy for a reason to leave."

Becca couldn't argue with that. Dan Trevor was a popular pediatrician in St. Caroline. His sole purpose in traveling to the big quilt expos with his wife and daughters was to serve as a pack mule, to help lug home the samples and books they collected. She heard muffled conversation in the background, then her mother returned.

"Alright, Daddy's found one. He's flying into Baltimore."

"I can pick him up at the airport."

More muffled background conversation.

"He said he'd love for you to do that."

"Then it's a date," Becca said, gamely trying for a lighter note before hanging up the call.

Across the road, one of the fire trucks was pulling out of Quilt Therapy's small parking lot. She watched as it disappeared in the direction of the fire station. It looked as if one of the crews was planning to stay and watch the shop for awhile.

"With my luck, it'll burst into flames again as soon as everyone's gone," she muttered.

"Probably not." Someone sat down on the curb next to her. "It's pretty much out." A man's hand held out her car key. "I moved your car for you."

She took the key and turned to him. One of the firefighters who had helped her out of the house had asked for the key, but this wasn't him. This was Jack Wolfe. She had gone to school with him, though that overstated the matter a bit. They weren't in any classes together after elementary school. Jack was one of the smart kids and Becca was ... well, not.

He was staring at her closely. *Please don't remember. Please*

please please. His eyes gave away nothing. That was always her impression of Jack Wolfe—that he was intense, serious, quiet. Kinda' skinny. Although that last wasn't the impression he was giving off now. She resisted the urge to drop her eyes to his chest. It was bad enough that she could see his long, tanned legs in her peripheral vision.

"Thanks," she said, giving the key a little shake.

"Don't mention it."

For an instant, she thought he was referring to something else. Something she definitely had no intention of mentioning. Zero intention.

"Are you okay?" he asked. "I can get you a bottle of water from the truck."

Her mouth was parched, but she shook her head. "I'm fine." She let out a rueful laugh. "Well, as fine as I can be." She looked over at the charred building that used to house her mother's business.

"Why weren't you staying at your folks' house?"

"I lost the key. So I came here. The shop is locked with a security code. I've known that all my life, practically."

He smiled. "Yeah. I know what you mean. I could probably get into the firehouse with my hands tied behind my back."

She stood and looked around for her car. It was parked about twenty feet away. "Well, thanks." She looked across the road and grimaced. "At least there's something left."

He stood too, and walked with her to the car. Jack Wolfe would be a gentleman that way. With Angela and Tim Wolfe as parents, that outcome was never in doubt. She put her hand on the door handle, then stopped. Where was she going? It was almost two in the morning.

"What's the matter?" Jack asked.

She sighed. "Oh, I just realized that I'll have to go back to my parents' house. I should have just stayed there, then this wouldn't have happened."

He leaned against her car. "What do you mean it wouldn't have happened?"

"I mean if I hadn't been sleeping here, the shop wouldn't have caught on fire."

A puzzled look slid down his face. "You didn't set the fire, did you?"

"No, I didn't do it on purpose."

"Were you smoking?"

"No. I don't smoke."

"Then what's the connection between you sleeping there and the fire?"

"I'm bad luck." She resisted the urge to roll her eyes. Jack Wolfe was from St. Caroline, born and bred. Their parents were friends. He knew her story. "Maybe I shouldn't go back to my parents' house, after all. Destroying one property is probably enough for one night."

"Thought you didn't have a key."

"I can sleep on the patio." She looked up at the cloudless night sky. "Doesn't look like rain."

"Bugs will eat you alive"

Becca laughed bitterly. "That's the least of my worries tonight."

JACK WATCHED until Becca's car pulled out onto the road and disappeared into the night. Then he jogged back across the street to where Matt and Oliver were packing up their truck, the last one to leave the scene. Matt's face was streaked with soot and sweat.

"You following us back to the station?" he asked.

Jack shook his head. "I'm headed to the house. Been driving all day. I'm beat."

"Alrighty then. You can crash at my place too, if you want."

"Thanks. Appreciate the offer."

Matt climbed into the cab. Oliver was already in the driver's seat, waiting. He hadn't said a word to Jack and Jack knew why. He had called Oliver out on a mistake and been right about it. Oliver did not handle being wrong well.

Whatever. He was in St. Caroline to spend time with his mother, not deal with his brothers' miscellaneous varieties of bullshit.

The red truck's headlights flashed on and then it was gone too, down the road in the opposite direction Becca had taken. Jack was alone now in the dark. He looked around. This part of town was rather desolate late at night, after the shops and small business offices were closed. It wasn't dangerous—no part of St. Caroline was—but no one really lived out this way. The houses that were around had been converted into retail spaces, like Quilt Therapy.

He turned and looked back at the dark cottage. The fire was out. Everyone was gone. In the morning, his father would be back to take a look at the building in the daylight, try to ascertain what had started the fire. Jack wondered whether Becca had been lying about not smoking.

His feet began moving, carrying him across the small dark parking lot and toward the cottage. He kept walking until he stood at the back door, which was still open a crack. He tested the doorknob. Warm but not enough to burn his hand. He pushed gently at the door.

He shouldn't do it. He should not go inside, and definitely not by himself. He'd told Becca the fire wouldn't reignite. But it could. The structure could be weakened. Who knew what kind of shape the building was in before tonight? He could fall through a floor. He had seen it happen.

But the pull was too great. He had fire in his blood. His father was a firefighter and both of his brothers, too. He was the namesake of a firefighter, his uncle. He had grown up with the rhythms of the station, could identify materials by the way they smelled when they burned.

To be a Wolfe was to fight fires.

He pushed the door open all the way and stepped inside. His last call in California was over a week ago and already he missed it. Not just the sense of doing something useful for people, but the camaraderie, the teamwork, the immediate satisfaction of fixing a problem ... something he had known almost immediately that he wasn't going to find in the practice of law. He stuck out law school for two years until his bored mind and idle muscles just couldn't take it anymore.

He climbed the stairs to the second floor. That's where his brothers had found Becca Trevor. The smell of smoke and burnt wood was still strong, but the smoke had cleared and it was easy to see where she had been sleeping. The second floor was an office with a desk, a table stacked with folded quilts, and a sofa.

Becca Trevor. He hadn't thought of her in years. He had pushed her and that one night totally out of his mind. It hadn't been his finest moment, by any measure—hence his interest in not remembering it. That stupid sock monkey in her car had brought it all back. A stupid high school graduation party he had gone to only because he had caved into peer pressure. He was never much of a partier in high school—still wasn't, for that matter—but he had stepped out of character for one night ...

Jackie Wolfe gulped down another bitter swallow of beer and eyed the goings-on at the graduation party. Some of these kids he might never see again. He wasn't the only senior planning to leave St. Caroline and not come back. Not that he disliked his hometown, but St. Caroline only needed so many lawyers and none of the ones it had were near retirement age yet.

A hand clapped him square between the shoulder blades and he snorted beer through his nose. Raucous laughter surrounded him.

"We need to get Jackie here laid before dawn," Ian Evers said.

"No, we don't," Jack answered. None of the girls in school had

evinced much interest in him up to now. They were always more interested in his brother, Matt—one year older and a hell of a lot better looking.

"We can't send you off to Cornell a virgin." More beer-fueled laughter. "The girls of the Ivy League would never forgive us."

"Well, good luck with that," Jack retorted.

But shortly after midnight, Jack found himself walking to Becca Trevor's car. Improbably enough, she had come onto him. Between the beer and his friends' enthusiasm, Jack's better judgment fell by the wayside. They were right, he told himself. He was leaving town, even sooner than most of his classmates, since he was taking summer classes at Cornell. And it wasn't as though he was about to do anything dozens of other guys in school hadn't done already. Rumor had it Becca Trevor had slept with half the senior class. Why should he be the only one heading off to college a virgin? God knew, Mattie razzed him about it all the time.

So they'd had sex in the back seat of her car, Becca riding him, her blouse unbuttoned and her amazing breasts bouncing right before his very eyes. For fifteen window-fogging minutes under the watchful gaze of a silly stuffed monkey, he had been in sweet, sweet heaven.

He'd been a little drunk. She'd been a little drunk. It should never have happened. He turned and headed back down the stairs. Nothing about his performance that night had been memorable. Of that he was certain. He pretty much just sat there and let her do all the work.

Outside, he took a deep breath of fresh air. The odds of her remembering it were slim and none. Right?

CHAPTER 3

*J*ack stopped just outside the doorway to the kitchen, surprised to see his mother awake this early. She was sitting at the big oak table, the one that had hosted years of family dinners and late night homework sessions. A puddle of morning sunlight spilled across the wooden top. Her thin fingers wrapped loosely around the handle of a coffee mug, her head bent to a magazine.

His heart felt suddenly huge in his chest, his shoulders bucking with the force of its beating. His father told him her condition had been downgraded to terminal, but that fact hadn't been real until he saw the dark shadow of stubble covering her head. The last time he was home at Easter, she was wearing wigs or scarves to cover the chemotherapy-induced hair loss. Her hair was growing back in now, which meant only one thing. No more chemotherapy.

They had given up.

Her face lifted. She smiled at him and he wanted to scream, rage at the world, hurl things.

"Morning, Jackie. I didn't hear you and dad come in last night."

That was as bald-faced a lie as the smile on her grey, gaunt cheeks. For most of her life, she'd been sister, wife, and mother to firemen. He knew she never dared fall asleep until they were all home or back at the station safely.

"Coffee's ready," she added, nodding toward the coffeepot on the counter.

He poured himself a cup, then carried the pot to the table to top off hers. Then he pulled out a chair and sat down.

"How was your coast-to-coast drive? Check that off your bucket list now?"

He nodded dumbly. How could his mother sit here and calmly talk about bucket lists? Driving cross country had never been any sort of goal for him. He'd done it simply because he wanted his car here, if he was going to be in St. Caroline for awhile. Not to mention, he had no idea if he'd be going back to California afterward. He had no idea what he was going to do in six months. Right now, he didn't particularly care what the future held for him. His mother was going to miss all of it.

His wedding. His children. Birthdays. Holidays. All of it, gone.

So the future? Yeah, he couldn't find it in himself to care.

"Your father said Michelle's shop is probably a total loss."

He nodded. "Looked that way," he agreed. His mother and Michelle Trevor were lifelong friends.

"Was the fire quilt still in there, I wonder?"

"Don't know." The fire quilt was made by the shop's customers every spring, to be auctioned off at the annual fireman's carnival.

"Let me know if you see it tonight."

"I thought I'd stay here with you," he said.

"Nonsense. I don't need a babysitter, Jack."

"Didn't say you did. Just thought you might like the company." That's why he was here, to spend time with her before she was gone. "Did you help with the fire quilt this year?"

His mother stretched her bony fingers in front of her and wiggled them weakly. "I donated my stash to the shop."

"You mean the entire contents of the guest room."

She laughed quietly. "Yes, there's finally room in the guest room for a guest." His mother had used the spare bedroom as a sewing room since Jack was a child. Her stash was the ever-growing supply of fabric she collected. "It was a Thousand Pyramids quilt this year, so all my scraps came in handy."

"What does that look like?" He thought of the stack of quilts upstairs in the Trevors' shop. Not that he could mention being in there to his mother.

"A lot of triangles sewn together."

He couldn't remember seeing one like that. "And were there a thousand pyramids in it?"

"More like fifteen hundred." She waved her empty mug at Jack and he got up to refill it. "Dad said Becca was sleeping at the shop."

"Yup. She said she didn't have a key to the house."

"That's odd," his mother sipped from the fresh cup. "I'm certain Michelle said Becca wasn't coming to the anniversary party."

"I guess she changed her mind."

"I guess so. Well, Michelle and Dan will be happy that she's here."

Despite the friendship between their parents, Jack and Becca had not been similarly close. Not even friends, really. They had always been in the same grade but Jack Wolfe and Becca Trevor were about as different as two people could be. A veritable tornado of trouble versus the straight A student.

"How did she look?" his mother asked.

"Becca? Good, I guess. I didn't spend much time with her. Moved her car for her. That was about it." She had looked *normal* is what he wanted to say, but his mother wouldn't countenance such snark. Becca hadn't been like her sisters in high school, that was for sure. She'd been one of those kids who wore all black, dyed her hair black then blonde, played at being one of the tough kids. It wasn't like she was getting suspended for smoking behind the maintenance facility or defacing public property or anything … he thought for a moment. Well yeah, actually she had done those things. It was almost as if she was always trying to make sure everyone knew that she was adopted, that she was a little different from the rest of her family.

But she had looked normal last night, as much as he could remember. A little plain, probably. It was dark and he'd had other things on his mind. His own problems.

Like the fact that his mother was dying from ovarian cancer. Like the fact that she and everyone else believed he had finished law school and was working in the legal department of a tech company in Berkeley. Like the fact that she believed he was her one son who didn't feel compelled to rush into burning buildings to save life and property.

Of those three facts, only the first was true. His mother was losing a valiant battle against one of the deadliest cancers there was. But he had dropped out of Berkeley Law after two years. And while he *was* employed by a tech startup, it was as a security guard—not an attorney. Then there was his service as a volunteer firefighter in California.

In other words, basically nothing anyone believed about him was true.

"Michelle worries about her," his mother said.

And my mother doesn't. Because I lie to her so she won't.

BECCA'S HEART sunk as she looked around the main room of her mother's shop. Quilt Therapy was her mother's *life*. And what the fire hadn't destroyed, the water and smoke had. She took in the rows of fabric bolts, hundreds of them in every hue and print. All ruined. The sharp odor of smoke would never come out of the fabric.

Her father was alternately taking pictures with his phone and making calls to the insurance agent. When he hung up for the last time, he stood next to her and pulled her into his chest.

"I'm sorry, dad."

"Sweetheart, it wasn't your fault. It was probably the wiring that caused it. Chief Wolfe is coming by later to take a look. This house is old. I've been telling your mom for the past year that she should look for a new location. She's always complaining that she needs more space."

"I'm sure she didn't want to be forced into it like this."

"I'm sure she didn't. But it is what it is. This is why we have insurance."

They both turned when the front door opened behind them. It was Jack Wolfe, dressed in long athletic shorts and a tee shirt.

"Hey, Jackie." Her father walked over and pumped the younger man's hand. "Good to see you again. How's your mother?"

Jack shrugged. "She's back home now. Her spirits were up this morning."

"Good to hear. Anything you guys need, you know you can call me or Michelle."

"Thanks, Dr. Trevor."

Becca remembered her mother saying that Angela Wolfe's cancer had spread, and that it wasn't looking good.

Jack's gaze skipped over to Becca briefly before returning to her father. *Please let him not remember.* They had both been drinking that night. They'd been kids. Dumbest mistake of her life, and that was saying something. She had at least a zillion dumb mistakes under her belt.

"I, uh, just stopped by to see if the fire quilt was in here. Or if perhaps Mrs. Trevor had taken it home?"

Dan Trevor looked around the shop. "I know the ladies finished it."

"What kind of quilt was it?" Becca asked.

"A Thousand Pyramids? Lots of triangles, mom said?"

Becca nodded and held her breath as she turned to look around the shop. Every year, her mother's customers spent months making a fundraising quilt that got raffled off at the fire department's annual summer carnival. Dozens of people chipped in to piece and quilt it by hand. She walked over to where the big quilting frame lay in charred pieces on the floor. There was no evidence that a quilt had still been on it when the fire began.

"Is this it, maybe?"

She turned toward the sound of her father's voice. He was holding up a blackened and burned wet quilt.

"That's the right pattern," she said quietly. *Hundreds of hours of work, down the drain. Add that to the list, too. Destroying the fundraising quilt mom's customers—and her dying friend—spent months making.* "When does the carnival start?" Maybe there would be time to make a new one. A Thousand Pyramids quilt was easy to piece.

"Tonight," Jack and her father said simultaneously.

Well, there went that idea. She was a good quilter, but she couldn't piece and quilt one by then. She bit the inside of her cheek to stem the tears that threatened, and wished Jack Wolfe would stop looking at her. Even setting aside the night of the graduation party seven years ago, he thought she was an idiot. Of course he would. He was the golden child of the Wolfe family—smart and ambitious. Ivy League. Law school. Working in California at some hip technology company, according to her mother. Everyone looked like an idiot next to Jack Wolfe.

He was also gorgeous. Had he been that handsome in high school? Becca's recollection was that he was skinnier than he looked now, and with a worse haircut. That had been the *only* consolation with Jack—he might have been perfect in every other way but his brother, Matt, was better looking. Maybe not anymore, though. She hadn't seen Matt in years either but Jack was ... damn. His hair was blonder—from all that California sun, she imagined—and cut short. His face, too, was more sharply defined than she remembered it. No way he had that chiseled jaw in high school.

And his body? *Double damn.* Either he'd been working out or he was lifting some seriously heavy law books all the time.

Finally, he looked away from her and back to her father. "Oh well, Mom was curious, that's all," he said.

"Tell her we're sorry. We'll see you at the carnival tonight."

We will? Becca had loved the annual fireman's carnival when she was a kid. The carnival and the fourth of July fireworks over the bay were always the high points of the summer for her. But it was the last place she wanted to go now. Everyone would be there, and she was sure there wasn't a soul left in St. Caroline who hadn't heard that she'd been sleeping in the shop when it caught fire. To say that Quilt Therapy had a loyal following would be understating the matter. A rabid following was more like it. And it was almost July. The peak summer season was bearing down on them. With the shop closed, her mother would lose a lot of money.

And the idea of seeing Jack Wolfe again? Not at all appealing. Even if he was double damn good looking now. In fact, if she had known he was in St. Caroline she wouldn't have come back.

Her father and Jack were trying to wring the water from the burned quilt. She turned away. Their efforts were pointless. The quilt was ruined. That was Becca, always leaving a path of ruination behind her. That's why she left St. Caroline seven years ago —so she wouldn't ruin Jackie Wolfe's life. Angela and Tim Wolfe would have pressured him to marry her. Then he would have gotten stuck in St. Caroline, ended up taking classes at nearby Talbot College, and probably gone to work for his dad at the fire department—which everyone knew his mother was dead set against.

Unlike Becca, Jack Wolfe had prospects and she hadn't wanted to take those away from him. So she packed up her car and drove until she got to Ohio, where her biological parents had lived before they died and where she had been born. She worked her way through a series of temporary jobs while she was pregnant, and made arrangements for the adoption to a woman in her forties who struck Becca as perfect in every way. Stable, professional, kind. Shari Weber had held Becca's hand in the hospital. A friend of Shari's claimed paternity so that Jack wouldn't have to be notified. Becca assumed money was involved in it. Or maybe Shari just had really good friends. Becca knew better than to ask questions she didn't want the answers to—or to throw people into situations they didn't want to be in. She didn't throw Jack Wolfe into marriage, fatherhood, and a life in St. Caroline cobbling together a full-time income from part-time jobs. And wondering how much better his life would be if he hadn't made the stupid mistake of hooking up with her.

Behind her, a phone rang and she turned. Her father was rummaging in his shirt pocket as Jack waved a hand in goodbye. Becca watched him leave. Maybe he didn't remember the night of the graduation party, or didn't remember it clearly enough to remember her. They had both been a little drunk. Otherwise, neither of them would have ended up in the back seat of a car together.

Becca's own memories of the night were fuzzy. That was what gave her hope in regards to his. Nonetheless, it was a night she would never forget. She thought about it every time she looked at her body in the shower. Heaven knows, Brandon never let her forget about it, though she had intentionally kept him short on the details. Every time they had sex he would run his finger along the silvery stretch marks on her lower abdomen, and the pale scar.

How many times had she rued the awful choice she made at that party? Why did she do it? If she had said no, Jack would have slunk away, embarrassed by her rejection. His friends might have made fun of him for striking out. But no big deal. He would have left St. Caroline as planned and never given her another thought. She could have stayed in St. Caroline, worked with her mom and sisters, taken classes at the college, maybe even had Jack's mother for a professor. It was hard to see a way that her life wouldn't have turned out immeasurably better if she had been able to stay here.

"Hi, love," her father answered his phone.

She watched as his face softened right before her eyes. Even after thirty years of marriage, her parents were crazy in love with each other. The pediatrician and the quilter, high school sweethearts, parents to four beautiful daughters and … Becca. The adopted child, the child they took in out of the goodness of their hearts after Becca's mother died. Michelle and Dan Trevor had hired an investigator to track down her father, who'd never had anything to do with Becca as a baby anyway. He was only too happy to sign over his parental rights to the Trevors.

She walked toward the long cutting table that ran the length of the fabric section, the years of nicks and scores from the rotary cutters now filled in with ash and water from the fire hoses. She plucked a fat quarter bundle from one of the wicker baskets on the table and squeezed it, wringing the water from the layers of fabric. As a little girl, she used to think that the fat quarter baskets looked like bouquets. The colorful bundles of fabric tied 'round with shiny satin ribbons were flowers blooming around the shop, each one begging to be picked.

Now every basket was filled with soggy, wilted flowers.

Becca couldn't even begin to fathom how much money had been lost here. Twenty-four hours ago, Quilt Therapy was intact and her entire family was in Chicago, attending a giant quilting trade show. And then she blew into town like a hurricane.

She tried not to eavesdrop on her parents' conversation, but it was impossible not to overhear.

"Yes, it looks bad," her father was saying. "No, I wouldn't bother renovating this place. This would be the perfect time to move to a better location ... I know, sweetheart, but you'd get better traffic during the summer if you were closer to downtown. And if you're going to do quilting retreats at the inn, it'd be easier for those folks to come shop with you afterward." Her father listened patiently for several minutes, then spoke again. "I already spoke to the insurance agent. Yeah, the deductible is ten thousand ... I know, baby, but we have that in the bank ... that's not a problem ... yes, love, we'll see you guys on Thursday."

Ten thousand dollars out of pocket before the insurance even kicked in. Becca's heart sunk. *I'll repay them, every penny. Everything I touch ends in disaster.* Even when she tried to do a good deed, things still blew up in her face. Trying to help a woman in the bar ... trying to get Brandon back on the straight and narrow ... even trying to help Jackie Wolfe lose his virginity.

CHAPTER 4

*J*ack closed his eyes for a moment and let himself disappear into the sounds swirling around him. Screams and shrieks from the rides. The periodic splash from the dunk booth. Tinny music from the carousel. Laughter and cheers as people won giant stuffed animals. And the smell of food … barbeque, funnel cakes, french fries, cotton candy. As a kid, the annual fireman's carnival had marked the true start of summer for Jack—and been a rare chance to cut loose for an otherwise buttoned-up child.

Jack's mother used to give him and his brothers some "walking around money" and set them loose every evening. The freedom of it was intoxicating. Even today, Jack could remember that feeling, that sense of being off the grid, off your parents' radar.

He heard another splash and a loud cheer. He opened his eyes and strolled toward the dunk booth. Eventually, Oliver would do some time in the dunk booth; he did it every year. But Jack chuckled to see Ian Evers in there now. Ian had gone to Talbot College, studied business, and then opened his own landscaping company in St. Caroline. According to Matt, Ian was doing pretty well for himself. The wealthy summer residents were willing to pay someone else to take care of their lawns, and willing to pay well.

Jack felt a little twinge of jealousy. Who would have thought Ian Evers would be established and successful before Jack Wolfe? Jack was supposed to be a lawyer by now. Instead, he had no career and no idea what he wanted to do.

Well, that wasn't exactly true. He knew what he wanted to do, but it would break his mother's heart if he went down that path.

He sidled up to the dunk booth and recognition lit up Ian's dripping wet face.

"Hey, it's Jackie Wolfe! Esquire!"

Out of the corner of his eye, Jack saw Becca Trevor on the other side of the booth.

"Got any tickets left, Jackie boy?" Ian was taunting him. "Not that it would matter. You can't dunk me."

Jack resisted the urge to roll his eyes. The dunk booth was always set easy so even kids could successfully dunk their teachers, their dentist, their parents. But a slow ball glancing off the lever meant a slow motion style dunk. A line drive propelled by a good arm dropped a person into the water before they had a chance to even hold their breath.

Jack Wolfe had a good arm these days.

He was suddenly annoyed with Ian. If it hadn't been for Ian, he would never have slept with Becca Trevor at the graduation party. That was an idea he wouldn't have come up with on his own, not back then anyway. And yes, she had been a willing participant, but he should have been the gentleman his parents had tried to raise him to be and said no.

He pulled a strip of tickets from his pocket and made a show of counting off three. He handed them to the attendant, a high school kid Jack didn't recognize. Becca was still watching. She was quite pretty, actually. He noticed that when he stopped by her mother's quilt shop that morning. It was true, she didn't look like Michelle and Dan's biological daughters, who were all various shades of blonde and tan. Becca's hair was ... well, it wasn't brown exactly, and it wasn't red exactly either. It was sort of ... cinnamon-colored. And where her sisters all looked healthy and athletic, Becca gave off an air of fragility.

"Yo Jackie! I'm drying out up here!"

Jack tore his attention away from his peripheral vision and Becca Trevor. He took the ball from the attendant and stepped up to the booth. He tossed the ball from hand to hand, looking Ian right in the eye. He'd taken advantage of the pretty cinnamon-haired girl, and it was a fact he wasn't proud of. He cocked back his arm and in the instant before the ball left his fingertips, he saw the shock of surprise in Ian's eyes.

Jackie Wolfe wasn't the skinny, scrawny giant he'd been in high school. At twenty-five, Jack was six feet five inches of well-coordinated muscle. And not afraid to use it. Ian Evers hit the water before he even had a chance to hold his breath.

THE GUY RUNNING the ferris wheel was about to pull down the metal restraint bar when Jack Wolfe ran up, thrust some tickets at the guy, and slid into the car with Becca.

Becca was more than a little annoyed.

Over the past three hours, she'd spoken to every single person who lived in St. Caroline. Felt that way, anyway. Everyone wanted to know where she'd been living, what she had been doing, how long she was home for. People who wouldn't have given her the time of day back in high school now acted like they'd been friends forever. She needed a break from people for a few minutes. The ferris wheel was the perfect escape, until Jack showed up.

Why was he here anyway? To talk to her about the fire? To remind her that she was a walking disaster? *Believe me, I am well aware of that fact. As is everyone else.* The car began to rise into the air, above the lights and noise of the carnival below. Up here, the silence was awkward.

"I'm sorry about your mom," she said.

"Thanks. It's hard." A pause, then he added, "you know."

Becca nodded. She didn't know, actually, so she clamped her mouth shut to keep from saying something stupid. She lost her own mother when she was a year old, but she had no memories of her. Michelle Trevor was the only mother she could remember, and she couldn't fathom losing her even though she was sure her parents and sisters all breathed easier when Becca wasn't around.

Their car was descending the back of the ferris wheel now, the breeze lifting up her hair as they dropped. "So how long are you home for?" she asked.

"I don't know. Until …" He let her fill in the rest of that sentence. "I just got in last night. Probably around the same time you did."

She turned her head to look at him, her long hair floating between them like they were underwater. "You just came home yesterday?"

"Yeah. I just stopped in at the station and then the call came in. Thirty seconds later everyone left. So I tagged along."

His eyes were beautiful, a rich brown shade and fringed with long lashes. How had she not noticed that in high school? How had anyone not noticed it? Sure, he had been skinnier back then … and quiet and, well, kind of nerdy. But he couldn't have looked that much different, could he? His eyes would have been the same, surely?

"Your dad said it was probably an electrical fire." Chief Wolfe had swung by the shop after lunch to talk to her father and the insurance agent.

He nodded. "That's not unusual around here, especially with the older structures, and the salt in the air."

Of course, that still didn't explain why the wiring chose to burst into flame the very night she arrived. She was bad luck, that's why. That was a well-established fact. But she nodded agreement, anyway.

"So how long are you back in town for?" he asked.

"I don't know. Probably depends on how long everyone can tolerate me."

His hand slid over to cover one of hers. His skin was warm in contrast to the coolness of the restraint bar.

"I'm sure everyone is happy to have you home."

The palm of his hand felt rough on her skin. Like Brandon's had. The hands of a man who worked with them for a living. Only Jack didn't work with his hands. He was a lawyer. But the thought didn't stick in her mind. The feel of his warm skin on hers pushed away any rational thought.

"Only until they find out how badly I've screwed up again."

"Hard to imagine how bad that could be."

Was that his thumb rubbing lightly over her skin? Yes, it was, and it was interfering with her breathing for some reason.

"I lost my job, got evicted from my apartment, and my boyfriend's in jail. Ex-boyfriend now." She pulled her hand out from under his. "Bad enough?"

"I dropped out of law school last year."

She squinted harder at his hands in the dark. *Not lawyer's hands.*

"Oh. I hadn't heard that."

"No one has. Well, except for you now. You're the only person who knows."

"Why would you tell me?" She looked over at him, suddenly aware of how little room there was between the two of them. From the expression on his face, she could tell he was puzzling out the *why* behind his impromptu confession, too. Jack Wolfe had dropped out of law school? Her mother definitely would have mentioned *that* if she knew.

"I mean, I won't tell anyone," Becca hurried to clarify, because no one in their right mind would share a secret like that with her. Not that she would ever rat out Jack Wolfe, but her reputation in town wasn't exactly sterling. "You know, what happens on the ferris wheel stays on the ferris wheel," she joked lamely, trying to allay his fears. He was probably kicking himself for telling her that—or entertaining the idea of jumping off the ferris wheel altogether.

In reality, Becca was extremely good at keeping secrets. The man sitting next to her was proof of that. If he knew her secret, he'd be pushing *her* off the ferris wheel.

"I'm sorry about what happened. That night," he said. He touched her shoulder, then pulled his hand back as if he'd just gotten burned. "The graduation party. I took advantage of you and I shouldn't have."

Wait … he was apologizing to *her*? She had taken advantage of him. Or taken pity on him, which wasn't much better. Worse, really.

"I've never talked about it to anyone," Jack said. "Honestly."

No kidding. Hooking up with Becca Trevor wasn't exactly something a person would brag about. Brandon had made that clear a time or two. Jack Wolfe telling someone was the last thing on earth she was worried about.

The ferris wheel began to slow. Their ride was almost over, and not a moment too soon. She and Jack didn't know each other well enough to trade confidences, let alone confessions. What she had told him about her job, apartment, and Brandon wasn't widely known at the moment, but she would have to tell her parents when her mother got home. Nor would it be widely surprising to anyone.

But that was all she would ever tell Jack about her life. What happened in Ohio would stay in Ohio. Forever.

CHAPTER 5

"$\mathcal{M}$mm, these look amazing, Becca." Natalie picked up the platter of shrimp and chicken kebabs, then opened the door leading from the deck into their parents' house.

"Thanks. Still surprised dad let me touch his brand new grill."

Natalie's laughter was like church bells, proper and feminine like everything about her twenty-four-year-old sister. All of the Trevor women were blond and brown-eyed, tan from Memorial Day until Thanksgiving, and possessed of an innate grace and sense of propriety. In the family unit, Becca stuck out like the proverbial sore thumb. Proverbial black sheep. Proverbial everything.

"Well, mom and dad were apart for what? Twenty-four hours? The grill was definitely not foremost in his mind today," Natalie added.

This time, Becca joined her younger sister in laughter. "Remember how embarrassed we were by that when we were kids? Like what would people think if they knew our parents were—" Becca faked a gasp. "—sleeping together?"

She turned off the grill and followed Natalie inside. The entire family—save Lauren, who lived in California—sat around the large dining room table. Her parents, younger sister Charlotte, and Cassidy, Lauren's twin. Charlotte was twenty-one. Lauren and Cassidy were twenty-seven. Becca sat down next to her father.

"I went ahead and brought the wild rice to the table," her mother said, nodding toward a large bowl in the center. Natalie set the kebabs down next to it.

"This looks delicious," her mother added. "Thank you, Becca."

Becca had insisted on making dinner for the family. It was the least she could do. Besides, her mother and sisters had just arrived home from Chicago that afternoon after an exhausting week at the trade show.

"Let me say grace." Daniel Trevor bowed his head and reached out his hands to his wife on one side, to Becca on the other.

Her father's soothing voice was as much a balm to the tumbling emotions inside Becca as it was to the worried parents who brought their children to his pediatrics practice. For a moment, she wished she could just stay here like this—listening to her father give thanks for their family, his hand warm and comforting around hers, the fragrance of the meal they were about to eat enveloping them all.

But it ended, as all good moments do.

"Amen," her father concluded. A chorus of "amens" echoed around the table.

"Well, dig in," he said.

Becca ate and listened as her mother and sisters relived their week in Chicago. New products and fabrics. Which trends were emerging and which were fading. Old friends they'd caught up with. The last time Becca had gone to the trade show, she had been in high school. She remembered it as a whirlwind of people and noise. She hadn't enjoyed it. Her mother, Natalie, and Cassidy thrived on the activity, but to Becca it was the complete antithesis of what she liked about quilting.

For Becca, quilting had always been a solitary activity. Just her and the fabric, her needle and thread. Her mother was an accomplished traditional quilter, but Becca had never had the patience for traditional quilt patterns. She preferred to just start cutting and see where the fabric and her imagination took her.

On the wall behind her mother hung one of Becca's quilts, a large abstract design for which she had hand-dyed the fabrics herself. She should have donated that to the carnival to replace the Thousand Pyramids quilt that had been lost in the fire. In typical Becca fashion though, the idea didn't occur to her until just now.

And the anniversary quilt she had been making for her parents? She suppressed a sigh of anger. Of all the quilts for someone to take, it had to be that one. It wasn't even finished yet! Nor was Becca sure she could recreate it exactly. Because her quilts were so improvisational, each one was a little different.

"Angie's home from the hospital." Her father's words pulled her from her own thoughts. The conversation had continued around her while she was spaced out. "We ran into Jackie."

"Oh? We should go over tomorrow and see her," Michelle replied. "Did Jack say how she's doing?"

"She was in good spirits, he said."

Becca watched as her mother processed all the possible implications of that statement. Jack hadn't said his mother was doing well. Or better, even. Just that her spirits were good. Becca was tone deaf when it came to other people, she freely admitted that, but even she recognized a bald-faced euphemism when she heard it. Sometime in the near future, her mother was going to lose a friend she'd known all her life.

Then the moment Becca knew was inevitable happened. Cassidy sat up straight with a start. "What about the quilt for the carnival? Mrs. Wolfe donated all her fabric for that."

Her parents were silent.

"Don't tell me that got destroyed!" Cassidy's voice rose an octave.

"No, but not fixable before last night," their father said.

"It can't be restored," Becca said quietly. "Not well enough to auction off."

"All that work!" Cassidy's fork and knife were trembling in her hands. "We've never not donated a quilt to the carnival."

"Let's not talk about this tonight," their mother said. "There's nothing to be done about it right now. We'll all go look at the shop tomorrow."

"You didn't stop on your way into town?" Becca asked.

"I wanted to." Cassidy waved her fork in the air until her mother reached over and gently pushed her arm down to the table.

"We're all too tired today," Michelle said. "We'll inspect the damage in the morning, then set about looking for new space to lease."

"It's July," Cassidy said. "No one gives up their lease until the end of the season."

"I've already called a realtor," their father cut in. "There's a place on Azalea that's still empty."

Cassidy rolled her eyes. "That place? That building is cursed. There's a new business in there every summer. Half the time, they don't even last until August."

"I'm sorry," Becca said. Her older sister was right. Finding available retail space in the middle of the summer was going to be difficult. Anything open was likely problematic—too small or weirdly configured or too little foot traffic.

Or just plain cursed.

Every town had those retail locations, the ones that were a revolving door of failed cafes and boutiques. Every summer, a new set of dreams dashed by reality.

She had prevented Jack Wolfe's dreams from being dashed by reality. She had dashed her own, instead.

～

A LIGHT KNOCK sounded on the bedroom door, then her mother's tired but smiling face appeared.

"Mind if I come in?"

Becca slid over on the bed to make room for her mother. "I like what you've done with this." She waved her hand at the four walls of her old bedroom; she had given her mother permission to do it over as a guest room. Not that her mother needed permission, seeing as it was her house.

Gone was the border of black skulls a teenaged Becca had stenciled around the room, just below the crown molding, and the "artfully" ripped curtains on the windows. Even the inside out quilt she had made, the one with the seams exposed, was gone. Well, probably just packed away somewhere, knowing her mother. Her mother would never throw away a quilt, even one made by a teenager who'd thought she was so clever.

"Do you?" Michelle bounced gently on the bed. "We replaced the mattress, too. Let me know if it's too firm. You can always sleep in Natalie's old room."

Downstairs, the house was quiet. Dinner was—blessedly—over. Her father was reading in his study. Cassidy and Natalie left for the apartment the two of them shared near the college. Charlotte had gone out to meet a friend for an after dinner coffee.

"I'm sure this will be okay, mom." She thought of the mattress lying on the lawn of the apartment building in Ohio, soaked with rain. She wondered if all that had gotten cleaned up. *Probably I was supposed to do it.* Too late now. None of her sisters would ever get evicted. She'd bet her last dollar on that, and her last dollar was in her wallet right now.

She felt her mother's arms wind around her shoulders and she gave into the tight hug. Her mother was a softer version of Becca's sisters, her body widened and relaxed by middle age and childbearing. She inhaled her mother's perfume and was immediately transported back to earlier days in this room, days that had always ended in a hug—even if it was yet another day when Becca had gotten suspended from school or caught drinking beneath the bleachers or failed an exam.

"I'll pay you and Daddy back for the insurance deductible."

Her mother pulled back and frowned. "What? Nonsense. You didn't cause the fire."

"I might have. By turning on the lights upstairs, I might have stressed the wiring."

"If that stressed the wiring, the wiring was ready to go."

"I'll get a job and pay you back. Every penny. I promise."

Michelle studied her daughter's face for a moment, then shook her head. "Your father and I have more than enough money to cover the deductible. That's not even a worry of mine." She tucked a lock of Becca's hair behind her ear. "What *is* a worry of mine is why you blew into town late at night without telling anyone you were coming. Not that Daddy and I aren't happy to have you, but two weeks ago you weren't able to get off work and now here you are."

"I lost my job."

"Okay …" Her mother's expression was guarded, but calm.

"And got evicted from the apartment."

"And …?" Her mother knew her well enough to know there was always an "and."

Becca took a deep breath. "And Brandon got arrested."

Her mother's eyes widened in alarm.

"I wouldn't bail him out." *This time.*

"I should hope not." Michelle pulled Becca into another hug. "Oh, Bec. I'm glad you came home. You need to get away from all that."

"I got fired, actually."

"It doesn't matter."

Hot tears burned the insides of Becca's lids. "I was trying to help someone. There was this ass- jerk—"

"Asshole," her mother completed Becca's aborted word.

"He was harassing a patron and I was trying to intervene. He got mad and smashed a beer glass on the bar."

"Why would you get fired for that?"

"He was the owner's brother, it turned out."

"I'd say you're better off not working for someone like that, then."

She felt her mother's hand smoothing her hair, and the familiarity of the gesture shamed Becca. How many times had her mother done this with her? More times with Becca than with all her sisters combined.

"And I lost the quilt I was making for your anniversary."

The hug loosened and then her mother was thumbing away the tears on Becca's cheeks. "Daddy and I weren't expecting any gifts. Don't worry about it."

"I'll pay you back, mom. I really will."

"You know how you can pay me back, sweetheart? Spend the summer here and let daddy and I help you get your life back on track."

"I want to pay you back in—"

"Then work at the quilt shop with me. I'm losing Charlotte as soon as she finds a job in Washington."

Work at the quilt shop that currently doesn't exist. "That's hardly paying you back. That's just taking your money and giving it back to you."

Michelle laughed softly, her brown eyes lighter now behind her tortoise-colored glasses. "Reopening the shop in a new location is going to be a lot of work. Plus, we have our first-ever quilter's retreat at the Inn coming up." She stood to leave, but turned back at the door to look at Becca again. "Don't worry. I'll get my money's worth out of you."

CHAPTER 6

he morning sunlight glinted off the pond behind the cabin Matt Wolfe rented, and Jack let the glare and shine dazzle his tired eyes for a few minutes. He'd been awake since three. Thanks to his overnight security job in California, his internal clock was all shot to hell. He stepped out onto the narrow back porch and knocked back another slug of coffee.

He shuddered at the taste. If he was going to stay with his brother he needed to lay in a better class of provisions. But Mattie had always been that way. One step up from a caveman. Matt was a year older than Jack and as kids, they'd been treated almost like twins. In reality, Mattie and Jackie Wolfe couldn't be less alike—even physically. If a person were to spot the two of them standing together on the street, they'd have to squint to see a family resemblance. Where Jack was tall and lean, Matt was shorter and stockier like their father. Jack had blondish hair and eyes the color of milk chocolate. Matt's hair was dark and his hazel eyes were flecked with gold.

Jack wasn't sure how long the two of them would be able to stand each other, living in this small cabin, but his father had suggested it. Jack had gotten the distinct sense that his parents wanted to be alone in their house, that Tim Wolfe wanted his wife's remaining weeks mostly for himself. Not that Jack blamed him. His parents' marriage, like Michelle and Dan Trevor's, was the envy of St. Caroline.

The screen door behind him wheezed open and he felt a broad hand land on his shoulder.

"What a view, eh?" Matt snorted.

Scrubby grass that could use a good mow stretched from the porch to the pond's edge. Jack imagined that the small pond held more snakes than fish.

"What was this, someone's duck hunting camp?"

"Once upon a time. Too close to town now for that." Matt let his hand fall from Jack's shoulder. "What are your big plans for the day?"

"A late lunch with dad, after the nurse comes over. Then spend the rest of the day with mom. What about you?"

"Going into the station. I got to finish up the report on the Trevors' fire. I don't get too many days off anymore. We were down two guys to begin with and then Heath busted his arm two weeks ago playing football."

"That's still not a reason to cut corners." Jack watched as a bird swooped down and skimmed along the surface of the pond before taking flight again.

"What are you talking about?"

"Not clearing the quilt shop right away."

"There wasn't supposed to be anyone in there."

Jack bit back a sigh. What kind of fire department was his father running? "That's exactly why you're supposed to do it." If he had decided to go home that night instead of going to the fire … "Becca Trevor could have been hurt."

Or even worse. A fact that had occupied way too many of his thoughts in the week since the fire and the carnival. Lots of thoughts about her had occupied his mind. Why did he tell her about dropping out of law school? He had no reason to trust Becca Trevor. He barely knew her when they were kids. He knew her not at all now. The one thing he did know was that her parents were close friends with his parents. If Becca told her mother then it was only a matter of time before his mother found out.

Why did he even hop onto the ferris wheel in the first place? To apologize for his behavior at the graduation party, sure. Although she probably wanted to talk about that as much as he did. Which was to say, not at all.

"Well, aren't we the expert on firefighting?" Matt turned and stalked back inside.

Great. Piss off your brother. Then where will you stay? He could show up on Oliver's doorstep but Oliver was married and had two kids. He'd wear out his welcome pretty quickly. He followed Matt into the cabin.

"Hey, man. I'm sorry." Jack wasn't as clueless about Matt's job as Matt thought he was, but that was an inconvenient fact at the moment—and one he couldn't disclose. "Nobody was expecting her to be there. Not even her parents, apparently."

Matt refilled his coffee mug, then held out the pot to Jack. Jack took it and poured the dregs of the pot into his mug.

"Have to say," Matt said, "I never would have recognized her on the street. Looks totally different now. Guess she'll be at her parents' party. I might want to talk to her." He winked theatrically at Jack. "Since she's all grown up now."

"She doesn't strike me as your type."

"All women are my type, mate. I believe in equal opportunity."

"You just can't stand the idea of there being a woman within a fifty mile radius who hasn't gone out with you."

"Not just gone out with me, Jackie boy." Matt winked again. "You need to take some lessons from your older, more experienced brother."

"Yeah, maybe."

"No maybe about it. I'll show you how it's done with Becca Trevor."

Like hell you will. Jack felt suddenly protective of Becca and he hadn't a clue why. She was no shrinking violet. She could fend off his brother just fine. Unless she didn't want to fend off Matt. Who knew? Matt was right about his appeal to the opposite sex. Women generally did welcome his interest.

Still. Jack hated the thought of Becca becoming another notch on his brother's bedpost, which made no sense at all. She was already a notch on his own, so why not Mattie's too?

∾

"SON, ARE YOU GAY?"

Jack nearly choked on his crab cake, then looked to his father for confirmation that he was merely joking. Tim Wolfe's face was perfectly composed.

"I mean, it's okay if you are," his father clarified. "But you know, your mother is ..." Tim glanced away from his son's face for a split second. "... trying to put things in order. She'd like you to come out of the closet before she goes."

Jack carefully set his sandwich back down on the grey stoneware plate of Skipjack's, the bar and casual restaurant at the Chesapeake Inn. Thirty seconds ago, he had been contemplating the change in decor at the restaurant. Gone was the slightly kitschy decor he remembered from his childhood—fishing nets and brightly painted lobster buoys. All that had been replaced by black and white photographs of actual skipjacks, a nod to the races held every summer on the bay.

"Um. No?" he answered his father's question.

"You know it doesn't matter to us," his father went on. "To any of us."

"Why would you think I was gay?" Jack lowered his voice. From the corner of his eye, he noticed Becca Trevor looking over in the general direction of their table. She was behind the bar with the bartender, Mike. Apparently she worked here now, which meant she was planning to stay. For awhile, at least. She was dressed in a crisp white blouse and navy skirt that mirrored Mike's white shirt and navy pants. Did she have nice legs? They were hidden by the big, old-fashioned wooden bar at the moment. For a second, he forgot about his father's inquiry into his sexual orientation.

"Mattie mentioned once that he thought you might be." His father's words tugged his attention from behind the bar.

He was so going to kill his brother when he got back to the cabin.

"And you've always been a little different. Not like your brothers, you know."

I'm not like them because you and mom won't let me be like them.

"Not that it's a bad thing," Tim Wolfe added.

"Just because I don't have a girlfriend at the moment doesn't mean I'm gay." The food on his plate looked unappetizing all of a sudden.

"Well, okay. It's just that your mother wants everyone to come clean before …"

Before she dies. Great. Jack had plenty of things to come clean about, but his sexual orientation wasn't one of them—as evidenced by the fact that he couldn't keep himself from glancing over toward the bar.

His father followed Jack's gaze.

"Dan says Becca's home for the summer. He said Michelle's happy about that."

Great. Jack was happy for the change of subject, but he doubted Becca's parents would still be happy once Matt was through with her. Not that it was Jack's problem. He wasn't his brother's keeper. Nor Becca's. But Matt and Becca together? That wasn't going to end well.

"Mattie's interested in asking her out," Jack said.

"I'm sure Dan and Michelle will find a way to head that off at the pass."

Jack wasn't so sure. Becca Trevor had always seemed like one of those people whose behavior wasn't much governed by other people. But that wasn't his problem, he reminded himself again.

"Matt also said you're down three men at the station."

"Yeah." His father's phone buzzed in his shirt pocket. Tim Wolfe pulled it out partway, glanced at the screen, and then dropped it back in. "That's the case. Though Heath should be back by the end of the summer."

"I can help out while I'm here. Volunteer. You don't have to pay me."

His father's forehead creased. "You're not certified."

"I am."

Tim Wolfe waited patiently for his son to elaborate.

"I got my certification in California. I've been working as a volunteer with a fire department out there."

His father nodded thoughtfully. "Lawyering not keeping you busy enough?"

Jack shrugged, not sure how much he wanted to confess right that minute. A minute ago, he hadn't intended to confess even this much. "I'm on call. I work around my schedule."

You're lying to your father. When he was a kid, that would have gotten him grounded for two weeks. But his mother's wishes notwithstanding, Jack preferred she not find out that he didn't finish law school before she died.

Tim fell silent again, but this time Jack didn't jump in to fill the breach. Instead, he waited for his father to process this information. Over behind the bar, Becca was smiling and chatting with Mike and one of the young waiters, a summer kid from the city. She looked relaxed and happy, two things she hadn't looked in her mother's shop last week or on the ferris wheel at the carnival. Or well, ever, come to think of it. Relaxed and happy was not the way he remembered her from high school.

She, Mike, and the waiter were all wearing matching ties, striped in navy and pale yellow. Skipjack's was a little spiffier than he remembered it, though the clientele looked the same. Resort guests, a smattering of locals, a few families with kids. He vaguely remembered his mother saying something last year about John Matthew dying. And now his son was running the place—was that it? Jack didn't know the Matthews even had any kids.

Becca caught his eye and her smile faded for an instant. Then she caught herself and smiled again, but the replacement smile was not as wide, not as genuine as the one he'd witnessed a moment earlier. Even with the cooler smile, she was pretty. Very pretty, he realized, if not conventionally so. Her nose was maybe too narrow and it was the squarish jaw that had always given her otherwise delicately-boned face a pugnacious air.

But it was her eyes that held his attention right now. Her cinnamon brows swept gracefully over her heavy-lidded grey eyes. Bedroom eyes. Something stirred in places that really should remain undisturbed. Undisturbed by Becca Trevor, at any rate.

"Your mother know this?" His father's voice was low and even.

"No."

His father's poker face was still impressive, even after all these years.

"This isn't a good time for your mother to learn you've been volunteering."

"I know that."

"I speak to the doctor every week. He said this is going to get worse before it's over." Tim Wolfe looked his son hard in the eye. "A lot worse. I don't want her hanging on because she's too worried about—"

The older man bit down on the inside of his lip and looked away, not turning back until his emotions were under control

47

again. Still, Jack could see the shine of tears over his father's hazel eyes.

"—all of us to let go." Tim nodded at the young waiter across the room. "So the answer is 'no.'"

CHAPTER 7

$\mathcal{B}$ ecca put the finishing touches on two Monster Claws
for the twin sisters sitting with their parents at table
eleven. She dropped a stemmed maraschino cherry into each
glass and then clipped a small plastic flamingo onto the rims.
Non-alcoholic drinks with silly names had been a tradition at
Skipjack's since she was a kid. The decor of the restaurant had
gone more upscale—she assumed that was the work of the new
guy running the place—and the food looked a little better, too.
But she was glad they hadn't gotten rid of the silly kids' drinks.

That thought surprised her, as she carefully set the finished
drinks onto the waiter's tray and watched as he whisked them
away. When she was in high school, the list of things she couldn't
stand about St. Caroline must have been a mile long. That list
was considerably shorter now.

What an insufferable brat I was.

She ducked beneath the bar to get a clean rag. The bar didn't
need wiping down again, but neither did she want to just stand
there and pretend not to see Jack Wolfe staring at her like he'd
been doing for the past hour. It was making her uncomfortable.
She spent a few extra minutes straightening the box of cocktail

napkins on the shelf below the bar, and counted up the remaining supply of plastic flamingo drink ornaments. Not that they were running low. Mike ran a tight ship here, a welcome change for Becca. It was hard to imagine Mike allowing one customer to harass another.

But eventually, she ran out of things to pretend to put in order beneath the bar and she had to stand back up.

"Hey sweetie."

Becca's head snapped back and she pressed her fist to her breastbone. "Mom. You startled me. What are you two doing here?" Cassidy hopped up onto the barstool next to their mother. Her sister's blonde hair was pulled back, big dark sunglasses perched on top of her head.

"We were going over a few details for the quilter's weekend with the events manager," her mother said.

"Like tiramisu or key lime pie for dessert?" Cassidy added.

"Both?"

Her mother and sister laughed. "That's what we decided on, too. When do you get off?"

"Right now." Mike appeared next to Becca. "Hi, Michelle. Cassidy."

It had turned out to be ridiculously easy to get a job at the Inn —everyone knew her parents.

"It's almost two," Mike continued. "I can hold down the fort until Rachel gets here at four." He tapped Becca lightly on the shoulder. "But I can give you all the hours you want. We've got weddings out the wazoo this summer."

"Thanks. I'll check out then." She headed back to the cash register halfway down the bar. A lot of hours would be good. She was going to work her tail off until she paid back the insurance deductible. Then she'd make a decision on what to do after, where to go. Not back to Ohio. Someplace different where she could make a fresh start, leave all the mistakes of St. Caroline and Ohio behind.

She logged herself out of the system and turned around to rejoin her sister and mother. She was dismayed to discover that, in the time it had taken her to close out her shift on the computer, Tim and Jack Wolfe had come over to the bar. Jack was talking to Cassidy but he shot a dark look over her sister's shoulder. Becca sincerely hoped she wasn't going to be stuck running into him all summer long. And the way Cassidy was furiously flirting with him, that could prove to be a real danger.

She gave Chief Wolfe a nod and a smile, then slipped around the end of the bar, careful to stay as far from Jack as she could.

"We're headed over to take a second look at the Jenks building on Azalea Street," she heard her mother tell the fire chief.

"That's a good spot," he replied. "Excellent foot traffic."

Her mother was serious about the building that was a notorious revolving door of businesses. But what choice did she have? In a town the size of St. Caroline, there was a finite supply of well-located retail space. Once you got too far past the cute touristy downtown area with its cobblestone alleys and Revolutionary War-era homes, your visibility dropped off precipitously.

"We just stopped in here to meet with Elizabeth and pick up Becca. I'm dragging her with us."

Chief Wolfe smiled. "Well, here's hoping Becca will be more enthusiastic about it than Jackie was about having lunch with me today." He tapped his son on the shoulder, and Cassidy—reluctantly, it appeared—ended the conversation.

Becca turned to her mom. "My car's parked in the lot. I can just drive home."

"I want you to come with us. I want your opinion before we sign the lease."

"I don't know anything about—"

Her mother cut off her objections. "You grew up in a quilt shop. And besides, Cass and I could use a fresh perspective. My car's in the lot too. We'll walk to Azalea Street and then we'll walk back."

Cassidy slung an arm around Becca's shoulders. "You can tell us about the quilt shops in Ohio. Maybe they have some ideas we can steal."

⁓

THE WALK to Azalea Street took less than ten minutes, and Becca wondered why so many businesses had been unable to make a go of it in the building they were about to look at. It was a great location, a block and a half off Main Street, and easily walkable from the Inn—the nicest hotel in town. The surrounding neighborhood was thick with restaurants, clothing boutiques, ice cream parlors, and art galleries. All summer long, visitors strolled the streets, reading menus, and window shopping.

Becca also wondered where Natalie was and why their mother hadn't brought her along too. She was afraid to bring it up. She'd definitely gotten the sense over the past week that Cassidy was the number two person in the shop. It had been so long since she had come home for a visit—she wasn't really sure what was going on anymore. Her mother was too Ms. Positivity to paint things in anything but the best light.

"So Becca," Cassidy began as they rounded the corner from Main to Azalea. "You've been holding out on us."

"I have?"

"Mmm-hmm. You completely failed to mention that Jack Wolfe is one fine hunk of man these days."

"I didn't realize that was news." *News to me.* "I assumed you guys see him around town when he's home."

"I don't think he comes home much," her sister said.

"He doesn't," their mother agreed. "Angie says his job in California is very demanding."

Becca didn't mention that Jack wasn't the lawyer everyone thought he was. That news was given to her in confidence, and she wouldn't betray that. Besides, she had no idea what he actually did in California for a living. Maybe whatever job he did have *was* very demanding. He hadn't confided *that* much to her. Why would he?

"Well, he's all grown up now," Cassidy said.

Becca snorted. "Says the person who is all of two years older."

"You two should probably leave Jack alone." Michelle's stride slowed as they approached the Jenks building. "I doubt he's in the right headspace for romance at the moment."

"Who said anything about romance?" Cassidy laughed. Their mother rolled her eyes.

"Romance with whom?"

Becca was surprised to see Tamara Rossi waiting by the door. Then she noticed the oversized key ring swinging from her fingers. And Tamara's rather professional outfit—a sleeveless dress, heeled pumps, and a chunky silver necklace. Tamara was the real estate agent.

"Becca, I heard a rumor that you were back in town."

Tamara took a step toward her like she was about to hug her, then stopped. Becca wasn't sure whether she should be glad for the aborted hug, or dismayed. Tamara and Becca had been good friends in middle school and high school. Maybe even closer to best friends, at least on Becca's end. But she had cut off contact with Tamara, too, when she left St. Caroline. She hadn't wanted to, but Tamara was the type of person who couldn't keep a secret to save her life. Since then, she and Becca had run into each other occasionally when Becca was back home for family events, but the friendship wasn't there anymore.

It had pained Becca to lose Tamara as a friend. Lord knew, she had few enough friends to begin with. It was a steep price to pay for protecting Jack Wolfe's future, but she'd had to pay it. And it paid off—Jack had a life in California. So he wasn't a lawyer, but he had some other type of career. Maybe he worked in advertising or computer programming. Maybe he had started some cool tech company and was now a billionaire. That would explain Cassidy's interest in him. Even as a teenager, Cassidy always had a sixth sense for which boys hanging out at the marina were the scions of wealthy summer families. No one local had ever been good enough for her to date.

"Romance with Jack Wolfe," Cassidy answered Tamara's question, putting air quotes around "romance." "Have you seen him since he's come home? We just ran into him at Skipjack's."

"Tell me about it. I heard Becca was practically the first person to see him."

Tamara winked theatrically at Becca. Becca felt her mother's hand on the small of her back, a gesture meant to calm and warn at the same time. *No worries.* Becca was already used to everyone she met bringing up the fire. *Just good-natured ribbing. And in three, two, one ...*

"I should set my house on fire so the Wolfe brothers will come rescue me."

Becca smiled at this line, even though it was probably the thirtieth time she'd heard it in the past week.

"Ladies? Shall we?" Becca's mother gestured toward the door of the Jenks building, a note of impatience creeping into her voice.

"Sorry, Michelle. Becca and I will catch up later." Tamara turned to insert the key into the door, but not before catching Becca's surprised expression.

"What?"

Becca shook her head. "It's just strange hearing you call my mother by her first name."

"Excuse me. *Mrs. Trevor.*"

Tamara pushed open the door and stepped aside to let Michelle and Cassidy enter first. She leaned into Becca's ear as she passed.

"Seriously though. Were you wearing, like, a skimpy nightie when they rescued you?"

Becca swatted at her in jest. Half in jest, anyway.

Inside, the building was quiet and dim. Becca squinted to see better, while her mother flipped a light switch in vain.

"Power's still turned off," Michelle said.

Becca looked around the large room. An empty pastry case stood at one end. A few small tables and chairs were scattered about. Becca wondered why the previous business owners hadn't taken those with them. Dust motes floated in the sunlight coming through the large front window. It looked abandoned, and sad. She had a hard time visualizing Quilt Therapy in here, the shelves of bright fabrics, the boisterous energy of the staff and customers. The old location had been small, but it was happy. Becca didn't get a good vibe with this place.

"What was in here last?" she turned to Tamara. "A bakery?"

"Cupcake shop."

"You're kidding. How could that go out of business?"

"Divorce."

She took a deep breath of dusty air. "This building really is cursed."

"I don't think your parents are going to get divorced," Tamara replied.

"No, we're not," Michelle said from across the room, where she had pulled out a tape measure. Next to her, Cassidy was tapping measurements into a tablet.

"So what's wrong with this place then?" Becca asked Tamara, suddenly suspicious of her old friend's motives. Sure, steer the desperate business owner into the building that puts every business under. In the middle of the summer, her mother didn't have much choice about where she relocated Quilt Therapy. Not if she wanted to reopen immediately. A wave of protectiveness welled up in Becca.

Tamara shrugged. "Nothing is wrong with it." Her voice was defensive. "The cupcake shop was doing fine until the owners' marriage fell apart. It would still be here if not for that, and I'd be showing you guys locations outside town instead."

"Becca!" Cassidy was beckoning to her. "Come with us. You need to see the space upstairs."

Becca followed her mother and sister up the staircase to the second floor.

"What do you think?" Her sister swept her arm in a flourish at the spacious room before them.

Becca's eyes nearly bugged out at the size of the room—and the sunlight flooding in through the windows. "This would be perfect for classes."

"I know, right?" her sister agreed.

Becca walked over to the long window-lined wall. "We could put a cutting counter along here. In the old room, people had to wait in line to cut fabric for their projects." She turned back to the interior of the room. "And we could fit probably three times as many tables in here."

Her mother glanced away from her conversation with Tamara and caught Becca's eye. She smiled.

"I mean, *you* could fit more tables," Becca corrected herself.

For a minute there, she was back in high school. Growing up, each of the Trevor girls had played different roles in the quilt shop. Cassidy was a marketer at heart, with a sixth sense for how to display new products and lay out the store. Natalie was the fabric whisperer, always able to pinpoint just the right color or print for a customer's project. Becca had felt most at home in Quilt Therapy's small classroom, sitting down with women twice her age and showing them how to line up their points or sew on a binding or explain the pros and cons of different types of batting.

But she wasn't in high school anymore, and Cassidy and Natalie were the ones who had stuck around to help their mother with the shop. Becca was just passing through for the summer, the only one who didn't have her life on track.

"Hey Becca? We're heading back down." Her mother stood at the head of the staircase with Cassidy and Tamara.

Becca hurried across the room to join them. But just before taking the first step down, she turned back to the room— picturing it filled with women (and a few brave men) sitting at sewing machines, learning to transform fabric and thread into something greater than the sum of its parts. Maybe this would be the right location for Quilt Therapy, after all. Maybe the building was waiting for the right business to come along.

CHAPTER 8

The sounds of the party beginning below drifted up to Becca's room. She had worked the lunch shift at Skip-jack's, then spent the afternoon washing and ironing the yards and yards of fabric women had been dropping off at the house all week. When her mother put out a request for donations to make a new fire quilt, Quilt Therapy's customers came through with flying colors. Now she was sorting the lengths of fabric by color and print size, her fingers itching to get started.

But today was the day of her parents' anniversary party and, from the sounds of it, people were arriving. Eighties music was playing from the speakers on the deck, and the aroma of burgers and chicken on the grill made her stomach growl.

"Hey there."

She turned to see Charlotte standing in the doorway, wearing a cute green and yellow print dress and flip flops. Charlotte walked into the room and flipped through the stacks of fabric.

"I'll help you with this. You don't have to do it all yourself." Charlotte touched Becca's arm. "I know how much you love this kind of piecing."

"Thanks. Even if you could do, oh say, four or five hundred

triangles that would help." The two sisters laughed. "I'm guessing you were sent to retrieve me?"

"Something like that."

Becca looked down at the shorts and sleeveless shirt she wore. "I'll be down as soon as I change."

"You look fine."

"Next to you? Please." Becca pulled a skirt, still on its hanger, from the shallow closet. "I got paid yesterday so I bought an outfit." And put the rest of her paycheck right into the bank, into the insurance deductible fund. "Natalie's been loaning me shorts and shirts, but her dressier clothes really aren't my style lol."

"They're not anyone's style." Charlotte headed for the hallway. "I'll see you downstairs then."

Becca quickly changed into her new skirt—solid black, for versatility—and a new pale green blouse. She pulled her hair from its ponytail and shook it out. Her reddish hair looked nice against green. Then she reconsidered and pulled it back again. It was hot outside where the party was being held and there was no need for her to look attractive for anyone in St. Caroline. But reasonably pulled together? Yes, it might be nice for people to see her as slightly more mature than she used to be.

Downstairs on the deck, she grabbed a can of ginger ale from a cooler and looked around. Cassidy's rolling laugh caught her attention. Her sister was standing close to Jack Wolfe and laughing right along with her. Images of Cassidy and Jack together ran through her mind, the way a dying person sees flashbacks to their life. Cassidy and Jack married. Cassidy and Jack with kids. Cassidy and Jack at family occasions. How awkward would that be? All of a sudden, she felt certain that Cassidy and Jack would end up dating that summer. Jack had been gone from St. Caroline long enough that her sister probably no longer considered him to be a local. Not to mention, on the walk back from looking at the Jenks Building with Tamara,

Cassidy hadn't been able to shut up about how great he looked now.

"Hi there, Becca."

Jack's brother, Matt, had snuck up on her. Although who could tell with Cassidy? If she didn't consider Matt Wolfe handsome enough to bother with—and he'd been here in town the whole time—maybe her sister really was impossibly picky. By any standards, Matt was an excellent example of the male form. Muscular and fit thanks to a childhood of sports and a job that required stamina and strength. His dark hair looked about a week past time for a trim, but a man like Matt could get away with that. It made him look like he was a man who didn't need to care quite so much about the way he looked. Becca doubted he did. In high school, he'd had all the prettiest girls practically on a string behind him. Why would things be any different now?

"Hi."

"You look nice."

Becca felt her face flame as he gave her the once-over. "Thanks."

"Better than the other week." He winked at her.

She laughed weakly. Did he really just wink at her? Was he making fun of her?

"Yeah. Thanks for rescuing me."

"It's just part of the job, rescuing pretty women from burning buildings."

"Umm, yeah." Becca had never been any good at flirting and Matt's high voltage smile was making it even harder to speak coherently. "How's your mom feeling today?"

"Good. She's around here somewhere."

Becca nodded, trying to clear the fog swirling in her brain. He had very pretty eyes, green one minute and gold the next. "If she gets tired, she can lie down inside. Just let me know."

"Thanks. I'll do that. How long are you in town for?"

He wanted to continue this conversation? "My parents want

me to stay for the summer." She grimaced. "The least I can do is help get the shop open again."

"Dad said you signed a lease on the old Jenks building. That's a good spot."

"Here's hoping quilts are more popular than cupcakes." She rolled her eyes and lifted her soda can in a mock toast. He tapped it with his beer bottle.

Then it hit her. *Of course.* Why hadn't she seen it coming? Matt was coming on to her because he thought she'd be an easy lay. Jack probably told him about the graduation party. *Yeah sure, Becca Trevor, she'll sleep with anyone.* Which wasn't true. Had never been true, but it was what everyone believed. Her heart sunk. As a teenager, it hadn't occurred to her that her parents were familiar with her reputation. But of course, they must be. Michelle and Dan Trevor were smart people. Knew everyone in St. Caroline, too. Of course, they knew their adopted daughter was rumored to be the town bicycle. *Everyone's had a ride.*

JACK LEANED down to kiss his mother's papery cheek. "What do you need?" he asked, his voice laced with concern. She had texted him, requesting that he come over to where she sat on a blanket in the shade of a giant maple tree. "Are you getting tired?"

"I'm fine, Jackie."

"Do you want to go inside where it's cooler?"

"No. I'm inside all the time. Plus, I don't want to miss the party."

His heart felt like someone had just turned it inside out. She was going to miss a lot of parties.

"I want you to go rescue Becca from your brother's clutches."

She nodded in the direction of the deck, where Matt was blatantly putting the moves on Becca. Jack had taken note of it earlier and ignored the hum of annoyance in his chest. Matt and

Becca were not his responsibility. Still, the two of them together was a bad idea—not least of which was because their parents were friends. The Trevors might not take kindly to Matt wooing and then dumping their daughter.

"Tell her I'd like to speak with her."

"You're not angry about the fire quilt, are you?"

His mother rolled her eyes. "I'm not angry about anything these days, sweetheart."

"Cassidy said she's making a new one."

"Michelle mentioned that, as well. No, I want to talk to her about something else."

He waited for his mother to elaborate, but she simply waved her hand at him.

"Go, before your brother wears out his welcome."

Jack trudged toward the deck. Wearing out his welcome wasn't usually an issue for his brother when it came to members of the opposite sex. He clapped his hand harder than necessary across Matt's shoulder blades.

"Hi Becca. My mom wants to speak to you." He ignored the irritation on Matt's face.

"About what?" Matt demanded, clearly not willing to cede the floor just yet.

Jack just shrugged. "She didn't say."

Becca looked relieved as she hurried off.

"Thanks." Matt moved out from beneath the weight of his younger brother's hand.

"Hey, don't blame me. Mom wants to see her."

"I was making progress, man."

"Just don't. You'll create bad blood between mom and dad and the Trevors."

"Maybe they want to marry her off. You don't know."

Jack resisted the urge to shove his brother off the deck. It was too low to the ground to cause him any bodily harm, anyway. "Somehow I don't see you as the person they'd be looking for.

You wouldn't know an honorable intention if it bit you in the ass."

Matt fixed a look of mock injury on his face. "Fine. The Trevors have plenty of other daughters." His brother shoved his empty beer bottle into Jack's hand. "Find the recycling."

He watched as his brother strolled over to a large metal bin filled with ice and beer. He plucked out two bottles and went in search of his next prey. *Whatever.* Jack felt way more comfortable with Matt hitting on Cassidy. Becca had already been done wrong by one Wolfe brother. Whatever she'd done in Ohio to send her fleeing home couldn't be bad enough to warrant a second.

CHAPTER 9

*B*ecca hung back at the edge of the maple tree's canopy to wait for the women sitting next to Angela Wolfe to finish their conversation with her. She tried not to eavesdrop but Ann Jeter's voice was too loud to ignore. They were discussing the baby that Oliver, the oldest Wolfe son, and his wife were expecting. It was a girl, apparently.

"Well, that'll be nice," Ann said. "Two boys and now a girl."

"We need some girls in this family," Angela laughed weakly. "I had all boys and it looked like Oliver was headed the same way."

Becca wanted to slink away, unnoticed. The baby she gave birth to had been a girl. Angela already had a granddaughter, one she would never know thanks to Becca. She started to back away but her movement caught Angela's eye.

"Becca. There you are. Can you ladies excuse us?" She fluttered her arm at Becca, then patted a spot on the blanket next to her. "Do you need a chair? I can get Oliver to bring over a chair."

"No. I'm fine." Becca sat down. "If you need to go inside …" She let her voice trail off. She didn't need to say that to Angela Wolfe, who was close enough to the Trevor family to go in and out of their home at will.

"I have a favor to ask of you, Becca."

"Me?"

"It's always been my intent to make a wedding quilt for each of my sons. I made one for Oliver. I've finished Mattie's, not that he'll ever settle down." She laughed weakly. "But I don't have Jack's done. I have it pieced, but my hands are too weak to do the quilting on it." She flexed her thin fingers. "I'd like you to finish it. You're the finest hand quilter in town. I trust you with it."

Angela wanted her to finish Jack's wedding quilt? Jack, of all people! This was so many shades of messed up, Becca felt a little faint. But what choice did she have? Angela was her mother's friend. Her mother's *dying* friend. If she said no … she took a deep breath.

"I'll pay you for your time, of course," Angela went on. "And there's no particular hurry to finish it, dear. It doesn't need to be done before I am. And heaven knows, Jack shows about as much inclination to settle down as Matt does." Angela's laugh was soft, but wistful.

"I can stop by your house to pick it up. I'd be happy to finish it for you," Becca heard herself agreeing.

JACK CONGRATULATED himself on smoothly foisting Cassidy Trevor off onto his brother. Her intentions had been clear, but Jack wasn't interested in dating anyone this summer. What was the point? He had no career at the moment, no prospects. He wasn't the great catch everyone in St. Caroline thought he was. Nor was Cassidy really his type. He didn't go in for the all-American healthy athletic type. He liked women with more unusual faces. Long limbs, delicate frames. Women who looked like maybe they could be dancers.

Women like Becca Trevor.

Amazing how smoothly his brain foisted that thought off on

him. He ignored it. His life was so not together at the moment, and it was clear that Becca needed a man who had his shit together. At least Matt had that going for him.

At the moment, she was playing frisbee at the edge of the lawn with Oliver's boys. Mason and Cam were seven and five, respectively, and accordingly not the world's best frisbee players. Becca was patient with them, though, chasing down wild tosses with a smile on her face. He tried not to stare at the toned legs beneath her stretchy black skirt. Or the way said skirt kept riding up her thighs as she jogged back and forth.

Those thighs had once been wrapped around his waist.

It was an oddly vague memory. One that felt as though it had happened in some other life. With some other woman. To a man other than Jack.

He tried to remember what she had been wearing that night at the party. Probably something black, ripped and torn. That was his general recollection of her, as much as he had paid any attention to her at all.

At the moment, he couldn't tear his attention away. Oliver called the boys over for a break, and Jack watched her chest rise and fall beneath her green blouse as she caught her breath after all that running. Her hair had settled back onto her shoulders, the strands glowing copper in the late afternoon sun. If she had allowed herself to look like this seven years ago, that night at the party would never have happened. She would have been so far out of Jack's league, even Ian Evers wouldn't have bothered suggesting it.

She turned, a frisbee in each hand, and their eyes met. With a sharp flick of the wrist, she sent one of the plastic disks winging his way. His long arm shot out and snatched it from the air, then headed her way.

She held out the other frisbee. "These belong to your nephews."

"Thanks for entertaining them."

"My pleasure. They're cute kids."

"Yeah, they are."

She started walking in the direction of the house and he fell into step beside her.

"What did my mother want to talk to you about?" He glanced over to see an odd look flash across her face. "You don't have to tell me. None of my business, really."

Her laugh was as delicate as the rest of her.

"She wants me to finish your wedding quilt."

"She wants … what? You don't have to do that, Becca."

She crossed the deck and opened the back door to the Trevor house. He followed, uninvited.

"I don't mind."

There was no way that could possibly be true. She stopped in the middle of the kitchen and looked around, as if she'd forgotten what she came in for. He glanced around the room with its white cabinets and cheery yellow curtains, his eyes searching for some clue as to what it was.

"Can I help you carry something out?" he asked.

She glanced past him, at the party going on in the back yard. "I don't know why I came in here."

"To get away from me?"

"No—of course not." Her hands fluttered nervously in front of her chest. "I don't need to …" She took a few steps back until she was leaning against the countertop.

"You don't have to finish my quilt. I'll talk to mom about it."

"It's fine. I can do it. No problem." She crossed her arms over her chest, then uncrossed them.

Clearly, he was making her nervous. He didn't want that. He should leave. Go back outside. What had happened between them was a long time ago. If anyone felt awkward about that evening, it should be him. His fumbling efforts to kiss her came to mind. He'd had no idea what he was doing back then.

Without thinking about it, he found himself closing the

distance between himself and Becca. He reached out and cupped her cheeks in his palms. Her skin was beautiful this close, smooth and radiant, and it took all his willpower not to just stand there and stroke it with his thumbs. Before he could think better of it, he leaned down and brushed his lips against hers. When she didn't shove him away or knee him in the groin, he deepened the kiss and after a moment she began to kiss him back. Hesitantly, softly. But definitely kissing him back.

The sound of voices growing louder and closer penetrated the buzzing sound in his brain. He reluctantly broke the kiss.

"I owed you that," he whispered, then turned and walked back out to the party.

CHAPTER 10

*B*ecca was up early the next morning. She made a pot of coffee and took a cup back upstairs to her bedroom. Her parents wouldn't be awake for another hour, she guessed. Or not out of bed, at any rate. Michelle and Dan Trevor had a close and loving marriage, even after all these years. Becca doubted that kind of relationship was in her future. Even if she happened to meet a good guy, she'd screw things up somehow. She always did.

Besides, she had a *reputation* here in St. Caroline. Case in point: Jack Wolfe kissing her at the party last night. She took a sip of hot coffee to wash away the memory. He was home for the summer and figured she'd be an easy lay. Right? Like the last time. Cassidy, on the other hand, would require far more effort. Dates, dinners out, movies, hand holding. Cassidy's younger sister?

Eh, not so much.

She set her mug down on the folding table her father had helped her move from the garage. It was covered now with plastic cutting mats and stacks of pre-washed and ironed fabrics. From them, well over a thousand triangles had to be cut to make

JULIA GABRIEL

a replacement for the fire quilt. She needed to get started on it. Even more so since she had agreed to finish Jack's wedding quilt.

She flipped through the pile of plastic quilt templates her mother had deposited on the table until she found the one she needed, an equilateral triangle. She unfolded a length of fabric and laid the triangle on top. She hadn't minded Jack's kiss, and that bothered her. It was … nice. Nice enough that she was disappointed when two of her mother's friends came in for more chips and salsa, putting an end to the kiss. But she didn't want to like Jack Wolfe's kisses. No good could come of that.

In fact, she needed to just stay as far away from him as possible. For the entire summer. That shouldn't be so hard. Between the three quilts she had to work on—the fire quilt, his wedding quilt and a replacement for the anniversary quilt she lost in the eviction—she had plenty to keep her busy. Plus, working at the restaurant and Quilt Therapy. It wasn't as though Jack would be venturing into the quilt shop. Avoiding him would be easy.

She picked up one of her mother's rotary cutters and, one by one, began cutting the pieces for the quilt. As she worked her way through the stack of donated fabric, a sense of calm took hold. Quilting made sense to her, in a way nothing else ever had. And she could fix mistakes. Seams crooked? Points cut off? No worries. She could take out the stitches and do it again.

There was no do-over with Jack. If she could go back and rip out the stitches of that one day, she would. In a heartbeat. But life didn't work that way. Instead she had tried to fix things as best she could by leaving town and having the baby elsewhere. She bore the consequences of their mutual lapse in judgment by herself, to save her parents the embarrassment and to save Jack's future.

Hours passed and Becca stacked up triangles upon triangles. She was flying through the fabric, losing track of time as she went. It had always been easy for her to lose herself in fabric and

70

thread. A knock on the door jolted her out of her zen-like state. She turned to see her mother in the doorway.

"What time is it?" she asked.

"Ten-thirty."

"Seriously?" She glanced down at the now cold cup of coffee on the table. She shook her head. "I lost track of time."

Her mother gave her a knowing smile.

"Shoot," Becca added. "You probably need help cleaning up downstairs, don't you?"

"I could use a hand. But I have another favor to ask first."

"Okay." Becca set down the orange rotary cutter she was holding, and flexed her fingers, stiff from hours of cutting. "Whatever you need."

"I just got a call from the woman who was going to teach the hand quilting seminar at our weekend retreat. She has to cancel. I was hoping you could fill in for her."

"Of course I can do that," Becca heard herself saying. "I'd love to teach the seminar for you." She really would, too. She wasn't simply saying that to appease her mother. Becca loved to teach quilting. It was her one area of expertise. She hadn't been a particularly good student in school, wasn't a good athlete like Lauren and Natalie had been, didn't have a head for business the way Cassidy did. Charlotte was all of those things, plus drop dead gorgeous.

But Becca quilted better than any of them. Tiny, even stitches flowed from her fingers. And she had the patience to show others how to do it. It was her one superpower.

"Truth be told," her mother said, "you're both a better quilter and teacher than she is."

"Thanks, mom. Mrs. Wolfe asked me to finish her wedding quilt for Jack."

"She did?"

"You didn't know?"

Her mother shook her head, then sat down on the bed. "You don't have to do that, you know."

"It's okay. I'm going to be here all summer. I'll have time. If you and Dad want me here all summer."

Her mother patted the bed next to her. Becca joined her.

"We want you as long as you want to stay. You know that. I also know that you're not telling me everything that happened in Ohio, and that's okay too."

Becca sighed. "I have told you pretty much what happened. I got fired, got evicted. Brandon got arrested."

"Have you heard from him?"

"I blocked his number." After several angry texts about her not bailing him out of jail.

"Good. What's your schedule like today? Are you on at the Inn?"

Becca nodded. "Dinner shift, so I'm all yours until then."

"Well, Cass and I are spending the day at the shop. Angie is sending Jack over to help put up some shelving. I want to at least have fabric for sale during the retreat, even if the shop isn't fully open yet."

"Was that Cassidy's idea?" Becca rolled her eyes.

Her mother shrugged. "I don't think Cass is really Jack's type. And he has a life in California to return to, eventually. "

Becca watched as her mother fought to contain her emotions. She was so used to seeing her mother be strong, it hurt to watch her confronting something that being strong couldn't help. Michelle Trevor was the rock of the Trevor family. All those times Becca had gotten into trouble when she was young—her mother was the one who never let her disappointment show.

She reached out and touched her mother's hand.

"I'm good, Becs. It's just hard sometimes."

Becca leaned over and gave her mother a quick hug. "I'll help daddy clean up the yard before I go to work. So you can focus on getting the shop open again."

Ordinarily, Becca would prefer helping out at Quilt Therapy over putting the backyard into order after a party. If Jack was going to be at the shop, though, she'd rather stay home. If he wanted to dally with a Trevor sister this summer, it would have to be with Cassidy. Becca had a future to figure out. That was her priority—and she couldn't afford to screw that up again.

~

JACK TUCKED INTO HIS OMELET, while across the table his mother barely touched hers. He pushed a plate toward her.

"Toast?"

She smiled, but left the plate alone. "I'm not hungry. I'm sorry, honey."

Jack had driven to his parents' house early to fix breakfast for his mom.

"Food tends to upset my stomach," she added.

Jack was a tightly squeezed ball of fury these days. Why his mother? *Why dammit?* In the back of his mind, he knew that swearing at God probably wasn't going to help his case. But Jack found it hard to care about God much anymore, even as he found himself talking to God more and more. *She's a good person!* If his mother had hurt even a single person, Jack had never heard of it. He seriously doubted anyone else had, either. *She doesn't deserve this. My father doesn't deserve this.* A case could be made that Jack had done things to deserve this fate. Matt too, in all likelihood. Oliver? Who knew? Ollie played things close to the vest.

Make it be all just a mistake. It's a stomach ulcer!

His mother's sleek silver laptop sat open on the table. She'd been up for hours, he assumed. Oliver mentioned that she slept only a few hours a night anymore. Jack didn't have the nerve to ask why that was. The pain was getting to be too much? She didn't want to spend the time she had left unconscious? He stared

73

at the laptop and took a large gulp of hot coffee, daring it to burn his throat.

"What are you working on?" he asked.

"Typing up all of my recipes for your father. I can send them to you, too, if you want them."

He nodded numbly. Her recipes. It never would have occurred to him to ask for something like that. But it made sense. It was a good idea. He'd be able to cook the family recipes for his children someday. Since their grandmother wouldn't be around. *She'll have grandchildren she'll never meet!*

He stood up so quickly, the chair tottered on its back legs. He rushed to the coffee maker to splash more hot brew into his nearly full mug, splashing his hand in the process. *Have someone come up with a cure for this! Right now!* He sucked the coffee off his burned skin, then held the pot aloft.

"More for you?" he asked.

"No thanks. I've had too much already this morning. It'll make me jittery if I have any more."

He set the pot back onto the heating unit and carried his mug over to the table.

Deargodletherhaveanotheryearplease.

"How's your job, sweetie?" She cut off a small piece of the omelet with her fork, but didn't lift the utensil to her mouth.

Four months! At the outside! What do you mean, four months!

"It's going good. Busy, you know." He let his words disappear into another hot gulp of caffeine. No way could he tell her the truth. *See the position you've put me in!* Better for her to live out her life believing he was the lawyer she'd always wanted him to be. *Give us another year!* He needed to change the subject. *Then I could tell her the truth!*

"Why did you ask Becca Trevor to finish my wedding quilt?"

Six months! Come on, dammit!

She flexed the bony fingers of her free hand. The movement was slow; Jack could feel the pain in his own fingers.

"I don't have the dexterity to quilt anymore. I'm sorry, Jack."

"You don't have to apologize. I just meant, why her?"

She looked at him quizzically. "She's the finest hand quilter I've ever met." She slid her hand across the table to weakly cover his. "Only the best for my baby."

"Mom, don't make me cry."

There has to be some other chemotherapy that will work! We aren't quitters! Wolves. Are. Not. Quitters! Dammit!

"It seems like an imposition on her." He pinned his emotions to the mat. "I can pay someone to finish it at some point. It's not like I'm getting married anytime soon."

"You never know."

Not while working as a security guard in California, he thought. He was sharing an apartment with three other guys and still barely making ends meet. Not to mention, the whole apartment sharing setup was a serious obstacle to romance.

My mother won't be at my wedding, you know? Have you thought of that? She'll never meet my bride, never hold my children? Dammit, it's not FAIR and you know it!

"It's between the two of you now," she added. "If you want someone else to finish it, that's fine with me. Or if you want to pay her. You're adults. You can sort it out."

CHAPTER 11

*J*ack parked his car at the firehouse and set off on a hard, punishing run—ignoring the heavy lump of breakfast in his belly. The Sunday morning streets of St. Caroline were empty, but despite the early hour the air was humid and close. Every breath seemed to catch in his lungs as his feet pounded the sidewalk. In the distance, the bells of the Episcopal Church pealed, as they had for three hundred years.

Jack wasn't sure he believed in God anymore. Not a benevolent one, anyway.

He ran down Main Street, where the stores and restaurants were still closed with the exception of Two Beans, the coffee shop. A few people milled around on the sidewalk outside chatting. A friend of his father waved to him. Jack waved back, not breaking his stride. Two blocks on, Main Street returned to a residential thoroughfare with small but neat homes and immaculately kept front lawns. Like his parents' home. His mother had always kept flowers planted in the beds flanking the front door and more in the stone vases on the stoop.

He kept running until he reached the narrow gravel path that led to Secret Beach. Secret Beach wasn't much of a secret though its complete lack of parking and facilities discouraged summer visitors from bothering with it. Jack hoped he'd find a cool breeze blowing in off the bay. The gravel path widened to a narrow sandy shoreline. He glanced left and right, relieved to see that the beach was empty. He collapsed onto a patch of warm sand and took a deep breath of sea-laced air.

There was no breeze. The water of the bay was calm, and Jack sat and stared across it. A fishing boat motored past, working even on a day of rest. Fish didn't rest, he supposed. Minutes later, a couple in matching kayaks glided by, their paddles soundless as they sliced through the nearly still water. He hadn't been out in a kayak in years. He suddenly missed it, another thing that had fallen by the wayside in law school. Maybe Oliver still had his veritable fleet of boats. Jack could borrow one and paddle out into the bay, let the gentle rocking of the waves soothe the pity party that was constantly raging inside these days.

He was twenty-five and way too old to be bawling over losing his mother. But hell, even Matt had a moment that morning when Jack told him he was going over to the house to make her breakfast. His brother was on shift at the fire department today, and for a moment Jack had seen a look of wistfulness and envy on Matt's face.

Breakfast with his mother had been nice. Pleasant. If he ignored the way her clothes hung off her emaciated body— and the sunny scarf covering the stubble on her scalp—he could almost pretend that things were normal. He'd told her that he wasn't gay, contrary to Matt's suggestion. He just didn't have a girlfriend at the moment. As he watched the kayakers disappear around a bend in the shoreline, it occurred to him that maybe his mother had hoped he was gay—it might make it less likely that she'd miss out on grandchildren. Jack definitely wanted children. Someday.

Or maybe not.

He wouldn't wish this pain, the sheer agony of losing your mother, on anyone else.

He didn't tell her about law school, though. He was torn. On the one hand, he didn't want his mother to die being lied to. He hadn't been raised to lie. None of the Wolfe boys were. On the other hand, he wasn't sure he wanted her to go knowing that her youngest son wasn't who he said he was.

It's not the crime, it's the cover-up.

That certainly applied here. Learning that he had dropped out of law school probably would have been less upsetting to her than learning now that he'd spent the past year lying to everyone. He brushed the sand off his calves, then pushed his exhausted legs into an upright position to begin the run back. At the fire station he waved to Matt and the other guys on his way in. After a shower and a change of clothes, he knocked on his father's open office door.

"Come on in, Jack." His father looked away from his computer. "Have a good visit with mom?"

"Yeah." Jack sat in one of the visitor's chairs. "I told her I'm not gay."

Tim Wolfe held up his hands. "I'm sorry, Jack. You've never brought any girls home to meet your mother."

"And Matt does?"

"He's brought a few. Granted, none of them ever seem to stick but …"

"Well, I date some. But I'm not really in a position to get serious with anyone."

"Understood. Getting your career established first is not a bad plan."

"Yeah. About that …" He took a deep breath, then took the plunge. "I didn't finish law school."

"Come again?"

"I dropped out of law school last year."

His father leaned way back in his chair and templed his

fingers. "So what have you been doing in California? Besides volunteering with a fire department? We all believed you worked for some hotshot technology firm."

"I do. I'm a security guard there."

He could see his father processing this information, reassessing him. "Okay. But you have a history degree. Summa cum laude. From Cornell. I was at your graduation so I know that for a fact. It's not like you don't have other options."

Jack scrubbed his face with his hands. "I don't know what to do, dad. I spent so long planning to be a lawyer and then ... I just hated it so much. I thought I'd work the security job for awhile and figure out what I really wanted to do."

"And you haven't come up with an answer."

"Except ..." He glanced back toward the main bay of the fire station.

His father regarded him carefully. "After ..." There was no need to finish that thought. "You can do what you want. I'll give you a recommendation if you need one. I might even be persuaded to make a few calls to other fire departments on your behalf. But I'm not hiring you on here. I'm not springing that on your mother at this point."

"I understand that, dad."

"Nor am I telling her about law school. You'll have to tell her that yourself."

"Do you think I should?"

Tim Wolfe shrugged. "Honestly, Jackie, I don't know whether you should or not. Your mother would love you even if you were digging ditches for a living. But I'm trying to make things as easy as possible for her right now."

"I don't want to make things difficult, either. Whatever you want me to do, I'll do."

"Well then, if you're going to be around all summer and you don't have law cases to work on in your spare time, I'm going to put you to work."

~

BECCA LIFTED up her end of the water-filled cooler and helped her father carry it over to her mother's rose bushes.

"All right. On three. One, two …" Dan Trevor counted. On "three," they tipped the cooler over and poured the water into the flower bed. They carried it back to the deck and repeated the process with the other two coolers.

"Thank you for helping out, sweetheart." Dan gave his daughter a tight squeeze around the shoulders. "What are your plans for the rest of the day?"

"I work the dinner shift. Before then, I need to swing by Mrs. Wolfe's house and pick up the quilt she wants me to finish for her." *And hope Jack isn't there.*

"What kind of quilt is it?"

"A wedding quilt. It's for Jack."

"Didn't realize Jack was getting married."

"He seemed unaware of that, too." Then she laughed softly. "He's not. I mean, not that I know of." He could very well have a girlfriend out there in California. Had Cassidy thought of that? "Mrs. Wolfe has it pieced but she's not going to be able to finish it."

"That's nice of you to agree to do that. You've managed to put a lot on your plate since you've come home."

Becca shrugged. "Good to keep busy, right?"

"Depends on what the 'busy' is."

He held open the door to the kitchen and she walked through. "I'm used to being busy." As if to prove her point, she immediately opened the dishwasher and began unloading it.

"Maybe you should take some time this summer and not be busy. Think about where your life should go from here."

She paused, a fistful of utensils in her hand.

Her father continued. "We paid for your sisters to go to college. We'll pay for you, too."

"Kinda' late for that. Plus, I've already cost you ten thousand dollars."

"It's never too late to get your degree. We still have your 529 education account. It's had a few extra years to grow, so there's plenty of money in it."

She sorted the utensils into the drawer. Forks, spoons, knives. "I don't know what I'd study." Charlotte and Cassidy had both studied business at Talbot College. Lauren had gone to New York to study acting, then moved to Los Angeles with her boyfriend. "My grades in high school weren't that impressive. As you know."

"Anyone can take courses at the community college. You could transfer to a four-year school afterward."

Certainly, she had pondered the course her life might have taken had she gone to college like her sisters. Pondered it quite a few times, in fact. Along with a whole host of other "what ifs." What if she hadn't gotten pregnant? What if she hadn't gotten mixed up with Brandon? Or Jace before him? Or Wayne before that? What if her mother hadn't died and she'd been raised in Ohio? What if, what if, what if.

Her father's light touch on her arm halted her busyness in the kitchen. "Take some time this summer to think about it, Becs. Please? Your mom and I are very happy to have you home this summer. We both miss you, but she feels like she failed you somehow."

"I failed myself."

"Failure isn't forever. You're young, Becca. Young enough to start over. I see a lot of your old classmates in my practice. They're married with kids. Some are divorced with kids. They can't reset their lives at this point, not easily anyhow. But you can." He cupped her cheeks in his palms. "You did not cause the fire at Quilt Therapy. You absolutely did not. But even if you had, the best way to repay us would be to spend the summer here and let us help you reset your life."

~

IT WAS ALMOST noon when Becca pulled her car up to the curb in front of Mr. and Mrs. Wolfe's house. The house was a sunny yellow Colonial with a pretty white front porch. She pushed open the gate to the white picket fence that enclosed the front yard with its profusion of colorful flowers. She climbed the steps to the porch and let herself into the front parlor. Mrs. Wolfe had told her that the front door would be unlocked.

"Mrs. Wolfe?" she called out.

"I'm in the back. In the sunroom."

Becca headed through the house toward the sound of Mrs. Wolfe's voice. The Wolfes' house was older, built probably in the nineteenth century. The wide plank pine floors creaked beneath her feet with each step. The house was small, as houses tended to be two hundred years ago, and it was hard to picture three rambunctious boys playing in here. Becca imagined that the noise level had been pretty high when Jack, Matt, and Oliver were young.

The back of the house opened up into a sunroom and it was there, sitting in the sunshine streaming through the wall of windows, that she found Angie Wolfe. Despite the heat of the day, her mother's friend was curled up under a blanket on the loveseat.

"Hello, Becca. Don't you look lovely?"

Becca tugged at the hem of her navy blouse. "I borrowed it from mom."

"Ah, the perks of having a family of girls. A shared wardrobe. I always envied your mom, getting to dress up so many little girls. We'd go shopping together sometimes and she was picking out dresses and cute hairbands while I was stuck with jeans and tee shirts." Mrs. Wolfe slid the blanket over to one side and patted the space next to her on the loveseat. "So make sure you have lots of girls. More fun to shop for."

Becca sat down, awkwardly. *Add that to my list of crimes.* Not only had she deprived Jack's mother of a grandchild, but she had deprived a dying woman of the pleasure of shopping for a grand*daughter*. Her father had said failure wasn't forever, but in this case it was. Jack's mother was going to die before any of her sons had more children. She could have spent the past six years with her granddaughter, if Becca hadn't made the choice to let another couple adopt her. Of course, she wouldn't be sitting here with Mrs. Wolfe right now if she had. No doubt she would have despised Becca for trapping her youngest son in an early marriage.

Sometimes you just can't win. If she had learned anything about life, that was it. Growing up, her parents had talked to her and her sisters about good choices and bad choices. For Becca though, it often seemed like bad choices were the only options available.

Mrs. Wolfe leaned slowly over the far arm of the loveseat and lifted up a large shopping bag. Becca hurried to help her.

"So this is the quilt," Mrs. Wolfe said. "It's totally pieced, but that's it. There's a queen-size bat in the bag and fabric for the backing and binding."

Becca carefully lifted the quilt top from the bag and opened it partway on her lap. It was a double wedding ring pattern, pieced in white on white. She took a deep breath, but not quietly enough to avoid Mrs. Wolfe's notice.

"Now you see why I need an expert quilter," the other woman said.

Becca did indeed see why. A one-color quilt? No hiding uneven stitches in the print of a fabric on this one. She ran her finger along a seam. She could do it though. If there was one thing Becca Trevor was, it was an expert hand quilter. It was the one thing she was good at it. The only thing.

"But none of that fourteen stitches per inch business," Mrs. Wolfe continued. "I know you're capable of it, but this quilt doesn't require that." Mrs. Wolfe's sudden grin made her look younger, healthier. Just for a moment.

"So twelve per inch would be sufficient?" Becca grinned back, one quilter to another. Even twelve stitches per inch was pretty darn impressive. Professional quality, for sure.

"Jack won't know the difference," his mother added.

"Yeah, I doubt he'll get out a ruler and start counting."

"I'm pretty sure he doesn't even know that quilters count stitches."

Becca folded up the quilt and put it back in the bag. *Focus on the here and now.* There was nothing she could do about the past, or the granddaughter she had deprived Angela Wolfe of. But she could finish this quilt for her, give her that closure. She'll miss Jack's wedding someday to a lovely, smart, competent woman. But she'll be there in spirit through the wedding quilt. Becca could give her that.

"How's the fire quilt coming along?" Jack's mother asked.

"Good. The piecing will go quickly."

"I never had the attention span for that kind of pattern, just one shape over and over."

Becca knew Mrs. Wolfe was just being nice, saying that. The woman had been a history professor at Talbot College, for pete's sake. It took quite an attention span to go through that much schooling. No wonder Jack was so smart.

"So are you planning to stay in St. Caroline?"

Becca wasn't surprised by the question. She was getting used to hearing it. Everyone she ran into wanted to know.

"Probably not," she answered. "Though dad wants me to think about going to college. The community college," she clarified.

"You don't sound so keen on that idea."

Becca shrugged. "I don't know what I would major in, and it's been a long time since I was in school."

"What has always stuck in my mind about you, Becca— besides your fierce independence—is how patient a teacher you were at Quilt Therapy. You had the patience of Job as a teenager. So teaching might be something for you to explore."

Becca shook her head incredulously. "There are a lot of teachers in St. Caroline who would probably shudder at the thought of me teaching. Being fiercely independent didn't exactly put me on the honor roll."

"Some of us take longer to come into ourselves. I always thought it was kind of silly expecting teenagers to know what they want to do with the rest of their lives." A car door slammed outside. "I think Jack must be here. He was bringing me lunch from the Purple Pickle."

Becca gathered up the quilt and her purse, then stood to leave.

"Oh, you don't have to rush off," Mrs. Wolfe said. "I didn't mean that."

"I need to get back home and work on the fire quilt some more before my shift at Skipjack's." *And the less I see of your son, the better.* That kiss he had deposited on her in the kitchen had felt way too good.

Outside, she found Jack hunched over next to her car, peering into the back seat. *Great.* Not hard to figure out what he was remembering. Yup. Some failures are forever. She couldn't stay in St. Caroline. Spend the rest of her life facing the Wolfe family, always wondering when Jack was going to spill the beans? She certainly couldn't date or marry someone who lived in St. Caroline because sooner or later they would see the evidence of her pregnancy on her body. She would spend the summer here, pay her parents back the insurance deductible, and figure out what to do next. Maybe that would be college, just not one nearby. Her parents would have to accept that she didn't want to live out her life here.

She descended the steps from the porch and hurried to her car. Jack straightened up, noticed the large bag nestled in her arms, and attempted to open the car door he had just been peering through. The locked door didn't budge.

"You don't have to lock your car in St. Caroline," he said.

"Force of habit," she replied. She held out the quilt. "Hold this for me while I get my key out."

He reached beneath the bag to take it from her arms. She felt his knuckles brush against her breast, and her traitorous nipples perked up. From the look on Jack's face, he knew what he had touched, too. She took a hasty step back and buried her attention in her purse, rummaging until she found the key ring. She unlocked the door and he leaned into the back seat, carefully setting down the bag of fabric—right where the biggest mistake of her life had taken place. Of course, that's what he had been thinking about. Jack may have been raised by parents who were pillars of the community, but he was still a man. A very attractive man. She cut that thought off right at the pass.

"Thanks. That's your wedding quilt in there. I'll try to have it finished before—" She almost said "before your mom passes." She might not be able to promise that though. Angie Wolfe wasn't looking good. "Before your wedding," she finished instead.

CHAPTER 12

*J*ack leaned down to set a red plastic firefighter's helmet atop a toddler's blonde head.

"What do you say, Alex?" the boy's mother prompted. "What do you say to …" The woman's voice trailed away.

"Max the Fire Dog," Jack supplied.

"Wasn't it nice of Max to give you a helmet?"

Alex patted the plastic helmet on his head. Nonetheless, the glance he directed up at Max the Fire Dog was dubious at best. Which was perfectly understandable—it wasn't every day that one saw a six-foot-five-inch dalmatian walking down the street.

"Thank you," Alex mumbled and grabbed onto his mother's hand, holding it tight.

Jack ambled away. When he was young Alex's age, he probably already knew his way around the St. Caroline fire station like a pro. In fact, his earliest memories all centered on the firehouse. His mother's hopes to keep him out of the family business were doomed from the start.

Not that his father wasn't trying to honor her wishes. When he told Jack he was going to put him to work, walking around downtown in the Max the Fire Dog costume wasn't what Jack had in mind. Especially not in ninety-degree heat. He could feel the sweat trickling down the backs of his thighs. Living in northern California, Jack had almost forgotten how hot summers were on the east coast.

He was remembering now.

July was peak tourist season in St. Caroline, and the chamber of commerce had decided to stage a street fair this year. Main Street was closed off to traffic so local businesses and restaurants could set up tables and booths. Jack strolled down the middle of the street, looking for children to give out plastic helmets to. He waved at the two teenaged girls manning a table for Two Beans Coffee. Their iced coffee samples were proving popular. No way for Jack to drink one, not without taking off the costume head.

There was a man Jack didn't recognize sitting by an artist's easel, sketching anyone willing to sit down for a spell. Jack was willing. He spent half an hour sitting with children on his knee while the man drew their portraits. The kids walked away smiling, wearing a red plastic helmet, and clutching a picture of themselves with Max the Fire Dog. Jack had done his share of community involvement activities with the department in California. He had risked life and limb at busy intersections, collecting money in his boot, and corralled a frenzied mob of hot chocolate-fueled kids waiting for the Christmas train to arrive. He liked it, even. He'd rather not do it while wearing a head-to-toe dog costume in ninety-degree heat, that's all.

When he stood finally, he held out his hand—er, paw—to shake the artist's hand. "Jack Wolfe. With the fire department."

The man gave Jack a leisurely once-over. "I surmised."

Up close, Jack saw that the man was younger than he'd initially thought. Mid-thirties, he guessed, with dark hair and piercing blue eyes. He wore a loose linen shirt, untucked over khaki shorts.

"Elliott Parker," the man introduced himself.

"Nice to meet you—wait, did you say Elliott Parker?"

The man nodded, smiling. "Surprised a dalmatian knows who I am."

"I dated a woman who was a curator at the San Francisco Museum of Modern Art. For a few months." Elliott Parker was an artist popular with the tech crowd in Silicon Valley. According to Jack's ex-girlfriend, Parker's work fetched five and sometimes even six figures.

"Ahh. You're a cultured dalmatian, then."

"You have a house around here?"

"I do, yes."

"Nice of you to do this." Jack gestured toward the easel. "Those kids don't know what they're walking away with here. A signed portrait by Elliott Parker. They could pay for their college tuition with that."

Elliott shrugged. "Part of it, maybe. Books. Or beer money."

Jack spent a few more minutes shooting the breeze with the artist about sailing and the state of the blue crab population in the Chesapeake, then headed back down Main Street in search of more kids to distribute plastic helmets to. Matt had practically rolled on the floor, laughing his ass off, when Jack told him how he'd be spending the day.

He passed the small canvas tent for Evers Landscaping & Design, but kept his distance. He knew he couldn't keep avoiding Ian Evers in a town the size of St. Caroline, but his old friend was a reminder of what had happened at the graduation party with Becca Trevor. He didn't want to be reminded of his bad behavior all the time. It was bad enough that Becca herself was a living, breathing reminder.

Even worse that he couldn't stop thinking about her.

He had apologized. She had accepted his apology, as far as he could tell. So what was his brain's problem? Why did images of her face pop up at the oddest times? Why could he still see, clear as day, the way her hair had floated in the air between them on the ferris wheel?

Because it's not your brain doing the thinking, buddy.

He stopped to kneel down and talk to another youngster. Another helmet. A brief chat about fire safety. Another mumbled "thank you." He was supposed to stay at the street fair until he ran out of helmets. *Or until I pass out from the heat.* When he reached the northern end of Main Street, he ducked around the corner and stripped off the head of the costume. He gulped in huge breaths of air, which were only marginally cooler than the air inside the costume. At least they were fresher. Even here in the heart of town, one could smell the bay. Hear the hooting of seagulls. Savor the relative absence of manmade sounds. The peacefulness of it was soothing to his soul, and his soul needed soothing right now. His mother was dying.

And his heart was breaking over it.

He leaned over and rested his palms on his knees. It hurt. It actually, physically hurt. He'd never had his heart broken before, not by a woman, not by disappointment. Not by anything. Until now. And damn if it didn't hurt so much he could barely breathe.

He straightened and put the costume head back on, picked up his shrinking stack of plastic helmets. *Stay busy.* Not that it made his heart hurt any less, but it was a distraction for awhile. Since he came home, his time had been split between spending as much time as possible with his mother and trying to stay busy and distracted.

Thoughts of Becca Trevor were an effective distraction.

He passed out the rest of the plastic helmets and made lots of honorary firefighters. His heart wasn't in it anymore, though. Despite the heat, he was glad to be hidden inside Max the Fire Dog where no one could see the forces ripping his heart into a million pieces. Distraction only went so far.

He handed out the last helmet across the street from the Purple Pickle Deli. He was about to turn and head for the lot where he had left his car when he spotted Becca and Cassidy Trevor. He watched as they climbed the short stoop up into the deli, their legs long and shapely in shorts and sandals. Jack was a leg man, always had been, and he was suddenly feeling more charitable toward the costume he was wearing. The cover was coming in handy at the moment.

Becca had nice legs. Even to a connoisseur of legs, hers were damn near perfect. Not as tanned as her sister's, but Jack didn't mind that. He wasn't a fan of tan lines, particularly. He preferred one continuous expanse of perfect, unblemished skin that he could trace with his fingers from the gentle curve of a calf up to a sleek thigh and then on over the point of a hipbone and a—by then—quivering stomach.

He shouldn't be noticing her legs. What he should be doing was marching over there and telling her not to bother with his wedding quilt. It wasn't as though he'd be getting married any time soon. He couldn't bring another person into his uncertain future. That was why the museum curator had dumped him. He was "unfocused." "Wandering through life."

Looking back now, he could see that he had been something of a project for her. She'd even gone so far as to get him an interview at the company her brother worked for. And Jack went. Put on a suit, rehearsed his interview answers, did everything you're supposed to do to land a nice, steady job. Halfway through he had realized it wasn't just the practice of law he couldn't stand. It was the thought of sitting in an office all day long, barely moving, in a building where the windows didn't even open.

His attention snapped back to the present at the sight of Ian climbing the steps into the Purple Pickle, right behind Becca and Cassidy. Cassidy turned her head back to look at Ian, laughing at whatever he had said to them. Jack had no idea how many people might know that he and Becca had hooked up once. She said she hadn't told anyone, and he had no reason not to believe her. He had no reason *to* believe her, either. Jack certainly hadn't told anyone, but Ian was there that night. He had watched Jack follow Becca to her car. For certain, Ian Evers knew—and had probably told others. He wasn't exactly the sort of person you trusted with the key to your safe deposit box.

Did it even matter at this point? It was seven years ago, and it wasn't like Jack had taken her virginity. His, yeah, but not hers. His parents would certainly be upset to learn of it, given that the Trevors were close friends of theirs, but again it all happened seven years ago. He and Becca were adults now. So they had hooked up once. No harm, no foul.

BECCA SET down the large plastic bag and fished in her purse for the slip of paper on which she had written the shop's new security code. It was late and she had worked a double shift at Skipjack's. And that was after helping her mom, Cassidy, and Natalie at the shop in the morning and early afternoon. But she also needed to get the fire quilt done. She'd spent every spare minute over the past week piecing the top. Seam after seam, row after row. Sew. Press. Repeat.

The finished top and the fabric for the backing were in the bag. A shipment of bats, the inner material of a quilt, had come in yesterday. She bought one, a low-loft cotton that would quilt easily and show off the stitches. It was inside the shop, waiting.

Her fingers finally found the slip of paper and she punched in the six-digit number. Inside, she felt along the wall for the light switch and closed her eyes reflexively at the sudden burst of light. She closed and relocked the door behind her. It was after ten o'clock at night and she was exhausted. Cassidy had made an excellent suggestion that morning, though, as they set up the new quilting frame. Put the fire quilt on the frame and let customers come in and work on it. Becca balked at the idea, at first—the shop's customers had already quilted the first fire quilt, the one that was lost in the fire. Then Cassidy pointed out the obvious.

"My phone's been ringing off the hook with people wanting to know when the shop will reopen. They're used to hanging out here, seeing friends, talking. The shop's not fully stocked yet, but put up a quilt and they'll be here in a heartbeat."

Her sister was right. Quilt Therapy had always been more than just a store. It was just as much a social club. As much as she hated to ask other people to finish what should be her responsibility, it would be better for the store if she did. She owed her mom and sisters whatever was best for them.

She carried the bag over to the brand new wooden quilting frame. It was big enough for eight people to work on a quilt at a time, three on each side, one on each end. In the old shop, the frame had been tucked away next to a wall. Here, her mother wanted it right in front of the big window so passersby could stop and watch the quilting. Natalie had declared that she would only quilt in the dark from now on, rather than have people watching her "like an animal in a zoo." But Nat was famously shy.

Becca ignored the stiffness in her fingers as she spread the layers of the fire quilt across the frame and attached them to the rails. It had been a few years since she had used a quilting frame like this. She couldn't afford one, for starters. Even if she could, Brandon would never have let her set one up in the apartment. She was never going out with a man again who didn't respect her need to quilt.

She got the top, batting, and backing fabric onto the frame with no problems. She had grown up in Quilt Therapy. She could do this stuff in her sleep. She stepped back to admire the sight of the quilt on the frame, ready for the shop's customers to start work on tomorrow. Her gaze skimmed across the pyramids of fabric—nearly two thousand in all—and over to the shop's front window.

A face stared in at her from the darkness. She yelped and jumped back, before she recognized who it was. Jack Wolfe.

Immediately his features rearranged themselves into an apologetic expression. He held up his hands, then pointed to the door. She let him in.

"Sorry. Didn't mean to scare you."

She shot him a look of pure skepticism.

"I was driving past and I saw the lights on. Thought I'd stop in and see how the shelves are working out. And then ..." He gestured toward the quilt. "It was fascinating, watching you put it on there. You've obviously done it plenty of times." He walked over to the frame. "So this is the Thousand Pyramids quilt?"

She was surprised he remembered the name of the pattern. "Yeah, but closer to two thousand pyramids."

Now it was his turn to shoot her an incredulous look. "You cut and sewed together almost two thousand pieces?"

She nodded. "It goes pretty fast, actually, once you get in a groove."

"The zen of quilting?"

"Exactly."

"So you're going to quilt it here in the shop?"

She nodded. "Cassidy suggested I let customers help. That way it'll get done quicker and I can get it to your dad. Then I can start work on your quilt."

"Yeah, about that ... you don't have to do that, Becca."

"Your mom asked me to."

"I know she did. She's trying to tie up loose ends, but it's going to be years before I get married."

Becca shrugged, thinking of how agog every woman in St. Caroline under the age of thirty was over Jack. "You never know."

He rolled his eyes, a move that had always annoyed her when Brandon did it. Which he did often. But it was considerably cuter on Jack. She didn't allow herself to ponder that idea.

"I'm in no position to get married anytime soon," he said.

"Who knows? I mean, just because you're not a lawyer—"

"I'm a security guard."

"Well … nothing wrong with working with your hands."

He laughed. "I don't work with my hands. I sit on my ass all night long watching the security camera feeds."

"But you have a girlfriend, right?" Cassidy was dying to know the scoop on Jack's relationship status. "That could get serious."

"Nope. No girlfriend. I have a low-paying job. I share an apartment with three other guys." He laughed again. "I'm not exactly a catch out there, not compared to all the software engineers and tech boy wonders." He ran a finger across the quilt. "So seriously, Becca. You don't have to finish that quilt. I'm sure you have better things to do."

She watched as he stroked his finger back and forth on the quilt, on the fabric she had spent hours sewing together. It almost felt as though he were touching her. Stroking her shoulder. Tracing circles on the palm of her hand. She probably did have better things to do but right that minute, she couldn't think of anything she'd rather be doing than watching Jack Wolfe.

The room seemed lighter since Jack arrived, which made no sense since there was also a somberness about him. Dark shadows stained the skin beneath his eyes. He looked tired. Gorgeous, but tired.

"Can I ask you something?" he lifted his hand from the quilt.

"Sure. If I can ask you something."

A look of surprise flashed across his face. "You go first, then."

"Was that really you in the dog costume today?"

A pale pink flush crept over his skin, from his ears to his cheeks. "Yes. My father's put me to work."

She gave him a smile. "Ian said it was you, but I wasn't sure whether to believe him or not." She stepped around the quilt frame. "I don't mean to imply that he's a liar," she backtracked. "I know he's a friend of yours."

Jack shrugged again. "We've lost touch."

"Me too. I mean, with the people I used to know. So what was your question?"

"Speaking of stuffed animals ... why do you have that sock monkey in your car?"

That was it? That was the big question?

"I've had it since I was a baby. Sentimental value, I guess."

$\mathcal{B}$ecca pulled a chair up next to the fiftyish woman squinting through her glasses at the tiny needle she was trying to rock back and forth through her practice fabric. Outside the Chesapeake Inn's glass-walled reception room, sunlight bounced off the whitecaps of the bay. It was a gorgeous summer day, but roughly a hundred and twenty-five women had holed themselves up inside for Quilt Therapy's first-ever quilter's retreat weekend. As promised, Becca was teaching the hand quilting workshop.

"I had no idea they even made needles this small," the woman sighed and set down her fabric. Becca and Natalie had spent yesterday basting together eighteen-by-eighteen-inch squares of fabric and polyester batting for the attendees to practice on.

"They do take some getting used to." She picked up the woman's practice "quilt" and glanced at her name tag. "What do you do, Sylvia?" She pulled out the needle and slowly showed her how to move the needle through the fabric.

"I'm a child psychologist."

"Private practice?" Becca demonstrated the stitches again, then handed it back to Sylvia.

"Used to. Now I work for a school system outside Washington."

"I had a few run-ins with the school psychologist when I was a kid." Becca watched as Sylvia took a few slow, awkward stitches.

"I find that hard to believe."

Becca chuckled. "You can pretty much stop anyone on the street here, and they'll corroborate my story. But look. You're getting the hang of it."

Sylvia's needle was moving more smoothly now. Becca had just needed to get her to stop overthinking the motion by talking to her about something else. Focus without thinking, that was Becca's secret to hand quilting.

She left Sylvia to practice on her own. She made the rounds of the room, patiently demonstrating the technique over and over. Before she knew it, forty-five minutes had flown by. She was surprised when Cassidy poked her head into the room to announce that lunch was being served in the ballroom in ten minutes.

"If you're doing the color theory workshop after lunch, you can leave your things in this room," she announced.

Sylvia fell into step beside her on the short walk to the ballroom. "Are you teaching the color theory session?"

"No. I'm doing an improvisational piecing class. Then I have to go to work. I work at the restaurant here."

Becca got into the lunch buffet line behind her mother.

"How did your workshop go, sweetie?" Michelle asked.

"Good."

"Your daughter is a natural teacher," Sylvia said.

Michelle smiled at her. "She is, that's true. And a naturally gifted quilter."

"It must run in the family."

Becca slipped around in front of her mother to begin scooping salad onto her plate.

"It does, though Becca is the most talented of my daughters."

Becca rolled her eyes at the sandwich platters. She speared two slices of bread with a fork, then added mayonnaise and turkey. At the end of the line, her mother peeled off to go mingle with other attendees. Becca scanned the room, searching the tables for her sisters. They weren't supposed to eat together. Their mother wanted all of them mingling and making everyone feel welcome. If this initial retreat went well, she wanted to hold more.

Becca wasn't sure who would manage that. Cassidy was terrific at marketing, but not detail-oriented enough to coordinate all the moving parts of an event. Lauren was the fabric buyer for the store. She had her hands full staying on top of changing trends and keeping the right mix of bolts, fat quarters, and jelly rolls in the shop. Plus, she spent a lot of time advising customers on fabric selection. Charlotte helped here, there, and everywhere but she was looking for a job in Washington, DC.

Their mother did everything else.

"Mind if I sit with you?" Sylvia appeared at Becca's elbow, a full plate in her hands. "How about that table over there? They still have a few seats open."

Becca followed Sylvia to the table and, after introductions were made all around, fell back into conversation with her. Sylvia, it turned out, was going to become a grandmother in a few months and wanted to make a baby quilt for her new granddaughter. She pulled out her phone to show Becca a picture of the quilt top. It was an Ohio Star in cheery pink, yellow, and lavender. It would look right at home in a girl's nursery. For a split second, Becca thought of the white-on-white quilt Jack's mom had pieced for him. Then she pushed the thought away.

"It's lovely," she said as Sylvia zoomed in on the photo. "I'm sure your granddaughter will cherish it."

Sylvia put her phone away. "I'm not sure she'll ever get it, actually."

"Why not?"

Sylvia looked down at the half-eaten food on her plate. "I'm estranged from my son. His father and I had a, well, rather ugly divorce. I wasn't even invited to his wedding."

"I'm sorry."

"I know they're expecting because I internet-stalk him. Yes, yes. I know it's wrong, but he's my only child. You can't just turn off a mother's love that way."

JACK WAS SITTING at the bar in Skipjack's when the Inn's fire alarm went off. Everything in St. Caroline was conspiring to remind him of what he wanted and couldn't have. A job as a firefighter. Not a job playing Max the Fire Dog.

"Huh. Wonder if that's real," Mike said as the restaurant's customers looked around for guidance on what to do. Should they leave? Wait and see?

"Well, the fire department will be notified automatically," Jack offered. He still knew which businesses in St. Caroline were linked to the station that way—which put him ahead of any new recruit walking in off the street. "I'll go see if I can find out what's up." He hopped off the bar stool and headed for the doorway that led to the main part of the Inn.

In the lobby, guests were beginning to mill about but no one seemed overly concerned. Not even the front desk staff. He headed down the hallway on the other side of the lobby. The pool and exercise room were down that way, then the Inn's conference and events center. At the door to the locker room, he paused. Locker rooms were notorious for "spontaneously" igniting. A contraband cigarette in the trash or a short in the sauna wiring. He flattened his palm against the door and pushed it open. He inhaled. There was no smell of smoke immediately apparent, so he let the door close behind him.

He walked through the rows of gleaming wood lockers. He had never been inside the Inn's locker room, nor in any locker room quite this nice. *How the other half lives.* Stacks of fluffy white towels worthy of a luxury hotel popped up around every corner. Well, the Chesapeake Inn was a luxury hotel, so that made sense. This was the side of St. Caroline Jack and his brothers never saw … unless there was a fire. Which he was beginning to sense there wasn't here. He had a sixth sense about fire.

A scuffling sound came from the back of the locker room. Jack strode through to find a shirtless young boy, maybe five or six years old, standing below the red fire alarm. The white handle was pulled and there was a distinctly guilty look on the boy's face. Chlorine-scented water dripped from the boy's navy blue swim trunks.

"Did you pull that?" Jack's voice was stern. The boy's eyes widened in fright. Jack immediately felt bad. At his height, he cut an imposing figure, even to many adults. He forgot that sometimes.

He kneeled down, putting himself at the boy's height. "Did you see a fire?"

The boy hesitated, then shook his head.

"Well, that's good. We wouldn't want to see this nice place burn down, would we?"

The youngster shook his head again.

"But that alarm is for emergencies only. All the fire trucks are on the way."

The boy's face lit up … along with the light bulb in Jack's brain. Fire trucks.

"You wanted to see the fire trucks, didn't you?"

Just then, the locker room's back door swung open and a man rushed in, followed by another boy.

"Landon!" The man nearly slipped on the wet floor, in his rush to get to the boy Jack was talking to. "You can't wander off like that! We've been looking everywhere for you. There might be a fire."

"There's no fire," Jack said.

The man looked Jack over, then looked at his son. The situation dawned on him. "Landon, seriously? You pulled the alarm?"

"Sorry, daddy."

His older brother looked at the red alarm on the wall, then seemed to take in the distance between it and the top of Landon's head. "How did you reach that?"

Jack had been wondering the same thing.

"I jumped." Landon gave a little demonstration. His father caught him mid-air.

"He has a thing for fire engines," the man said to Jack.

"So do I." Jack smiled. He pulled out his phone to send a quick text to his own father, letting him know there was no fire.

"I am so sorry," the other man said. "My wife's at the quilting retreat and I'm trying to keep the boys entertained, but ..."

"Why don't you bring them by the station later this afternoon? My father is the chief. I'll give them a tour."

Relief and gratitude rolled off the man in waves. Jack patted Landon's wet head as the boys and their father headed for the door to the pool. "But no more pulling fire alarms, okay?"

Jack reset the alarm, then backtracked through the locker room and out to the lobby. His brothers were there, suited up, and Jack was hit by a pang of longing so fierce he could almost taste it.

"There's no fire," he told them. "Just a little boy who pulled the alarm."

"Well, we have to follow procedure and clear the building anyway. Can't just take a civilian's say so," Matt snarked.

Jack ignored it.

"At least Becca Trevor doesn't need rescuing today. She's already outside." Matt jerked his head toward the front lobby door. "You can go see for yourself, if you don't believe me."

"Let it go, Mattie," Oliver warned.

"Maybe I will," Jack said. He was pretty sure Becca didn't want to see him again, but at least she was polite about it. She was raised by a pediatrician, after all. She was probably saying "please" and "thank you" before Jack was able to walk.

He waded into the crowd of women milling about on the Inn's spacious front lawn, but it didn't take long for him to spot her. She was standing by herself beneath the giant white oak, her head bent to her phone. He took in her sleeveless dress and flat sandals. Her hair was pulled back into a high ponytail. He was struck again by how very pretty she was.

As he headed toward the tree, another thought occurred to him. Had his father told Matt and Oliver about the fire department in California? He'd said he wasn't going to tell their mother, but nothing was said about his brothers. Maybe that was behind his brother's pissiness back there—that Jack wasn't actually a "civilian." He was a certified firefighter and perfectly qualified to correct his brothers' procedural understanding.

Behind him, one of the engines rumbled to life as it headed down the Inn's long driveway. He could ask his father later, but decided against it. If a secret was to be kept from his mother, telling Matt and Oliver wasn't the way to go. The Wolfe brothers had always been close, but as kids they'd never been above ratting each other out.

BECCA STOOD beneath the old white oak tree, her index finger hovering over the social media icon on her phone. She tried not to check much anymore. Who knows, maybe Shari had unfriended her by now. Maybe she no longer wanted Becca to know what was going on with Jacqueline Michelle.

Jacqueline Michelle.

Shari had let Becca name the baby. She had insisted on it.

Jacqueline Michelle. That's how Becca thought of her in her mind. The formality of it had always enforced a certain distance that Becca needed. Made it easier to think of her as someone else's daughter. Which she was, of course. She was Shari Weber's daughter.

Her finger tapped the screen of her phone, but too lightly to activate the icon. Once upon a time, she had checked Shari's page often. After awhile, seeing the photos became too hard. The milestones started piling up. First birthday. First word. First steps. It was too much for her. She didn't need confirmation that Shari was a wonderful mother. She was. Becca had known from the very start that she would be.

She did the right thing. Over and over, she reminded herself of this. Jacqueline Michelle had a great life with Shari. Shari could afford to give her things Becca would never be able to. *I'd be a terrible mother anyway. I'm not exactly a good role model.* Every time she was faced with a right choice and a wrong choice, Becca always chose wrong. Except for Jacqueline. The wrong choice had resulted in her birth, but letting Shari be her mother was absolutely the right choice.

Absolutely.

And yes, it had been wrong to hide her pregnancy from Jack, but sometimes you had to go with the lesser of two evils. Her deception there had given both Jack and Jacqueline Michelle better lives. If she and Jack had been pressured into getting married, they'd be divorced by now. They'd hate each other's guts. It would have ruined their parents' friendship. No question about that. She wasn't the kind of woman a man like Jack fell in love with—not to mention legally bind his life to. It wasn't something she held against him. No one in their right mind would throw in their lot with her.

But Sylvia's lunchtime confession that she internet-stalked her son had cracked open that door again. Her finger tapped the screen harder this time and the app opened. It didn't take long to find a post from Shari. Becca had opened this account just for her. Or for Jacqueline Michelle, to be more precise. She had few "friends" on it otherwise. Unlike Cassidy and Charlotte, who somehow had thousands of "friends" all over the world.

She tapped a photo and a little girl's figure zoomed to fill the screen. She was seven now. She'd start second grade in the fall. *Time flies.* All parents say that, right? She was surprised to see how big Jacqueline Michelle was these days. Becca wasn't known for self discipline but in this she was—she refrained from torturing herself by looking for photos of the baby she'd given up.

Jacqueline Michelle stood tall next to a pink bicycle, her long blonde hair streaming past her shoulders. She was tanned and slender. Obviously healthy. Athletic. Her eyes were lit with intelligence.

She had "golden child" stamped all over her.

Jacqueline Michelle looked like Jack. No escaping that reality. Becca hadn't seen her in person since the day she was born. But year after year, she bore an increasing resemblance to her father.

She scrolled through Shari's pictures. Nearly all of them were of Jacqueline Michelle. Her last day of first grade, her smile as wide as the ocean as she got off the yellow school bus. Swimming in a community pool somewhere, blue goggles and pink swimsuit. There was a short video of her riding a sparkly carousel horse in an amusement park, her blonde braids bouncing off her shoulders each time the horse rose and fell.

"Hey there."

Jack's deep voice startled her and the phone bounced from her hands as she tried to close the app before he could see. She watched as the phone flipped into the air. Luckily, Jack caught it before it hit the ground—and unluckily, because to her complete horror he caught the phone right side up and glanced at the screen before handing it back to her. Becca thought she was going to faint.

"Cute kid there," he said, smiling.

Really, fainting was probably the best option right now.

"Are you okay?" He reached his arm to steady her.

She shoved the phone into her purse. "Yeah. Sure … the heat, you know."

"Yeah, I forgot how hot it gets back east."

"It's not hot in California?"

"Not in the San Francisco area. Not melt-your-hair hot anyway."

"Oh. I've never been."

"You should go. Beautiful city."

"Maybe I will someday." Behind Jack, the firefighters were returning to the remaining trucks. "I think the fire's out."

"Ah, no fire. Just a bored little boy in the locker room. He pulled the alarm."

The Inn's guests and the quilting retreat attendees were slowly beginning to file back into the building. "Your ride's leaving, I guess." She nodded toward the fire engines.

"Oh, I didn't come with them. I just happened to be at the bar when the alarm went off. I spent the morning with mom, and then she got tired so … I'm sorry. I don't know why I'm telling you all that."

He shoved his hands hard into his pockets, which only served to draw Becca's eyes downward. Between the dark grey shorts and the low hiking shoes were two expanses of finely-muscled calf, tanned skin beneath a light veil of golden hair. She'd already noticed the finely-muscled chest that filled out his Cornell tee shirt. Hard not to notice—Jack was so tall it put his chest right at her eye level.

"I thought you were working for your dad." She changed the subject for him.

He made a sound that was half snort and half laugh. "He's not putting me on a crew. He's sending me out to talk to camps and the nursing home about fire safety. Stuff like that." He laughed again. "I guess I should have come here in costume today. I could have entertained bored kids."

He looked at her with a gaze that was far too serious, far too thoughtful. Her heart hiccupped into her throat. She hoped against hope that he wouldn't ask about the picture of the girl on her phone.

"You helping your mom today?" He nodded toward the Inn. The lawn was empty now, except for Jack, Becca, and a lone Inn employee on a smoke break.

"I'm teaching a few classes. Guess I should get back in there." She took a step toward the Inn and he fell into step beside her.

"I should too. I need to settle my tab with Mike." He chuckled, his mood a little lighter now. "I ran off to see where the fire was."

Becca gave a tiny laugh, too. "They know where to find you, I'm sure."

Inside the building, she expected him to peel off and go his own way. Skipjack's was to the left of the lobby. The conference center was to the right. Instead, he veered right and walked down the hallway with her.

"What kind of class are you teaching?" he asked.

"Improvisational piecing."

"And that's French for what?"

He elbowed her gently right as Cassidy stepped out of a classroom up ahead. Her sister's eyes widened, then one eyebrow lifted ever so slightly.

"Making it up as you go," she answered his question.

"I've never been any good at that." His voice was low as Cassidy approached, his words meant just for Becca.

"I've never been good at planning ahead," she hurried to reply. Her sister was gaining on them.

"Rescuing my sister from another burning building?" Cassidy said.

"Saving you all from the machinations of a bored little boy is more like it."

His smile was amused and seemingly genuine, Becca thought. For an instant, Jack Wolfe felt like … a friend. Then Cassidy rushed her right past that thought.

"Mom texted me. Wanted me to go find you."

"I'm delivering her now," Jack said.

Becca caught the look on Cassidy's face. She shot back her own look. *Don't get any ideas.*

"Ladies. I'll see you around." Jack took a step back, pivoted, and headed down the hallway toward the lobby and Skipjack's.

Becca noted the appreciative look on her sister's face as Cassidy watched Jack leave.

"Sure you weren't the one who pulled the fire alarm?" she asked, nudging Cassidy back into the moment.

"No, but it'll probably be me the next time." Cassidy laughed. "Although you seem to be the Wolfe family's top priority when it comes to rescues."

Becca rolled her eyes and headed into her classroom. Fifteen minutes later, she had everyone slicing through their fabric with rotary cutters and was walking around the room, offering help and demonstrations as needed. As she gazed across the twenty heads bowed to their work, she had the sensation of being watched herself. She looked toward the open door of the classroom, and saw Jack leaning against the opposite wall of the hallway. She gave him a little wave with her fingers, unsure what he was doing there, and he gave her a little smile back.

Maybe if that night at the graduation party had never happened, she and Jack could be friends. He seemed to be the outsider in his family, as she was in hers. They had that in common. And he seemed to be pretty laid back, which might make him more willing to overlook her checkered past and just accept her for who she was right now. She was still basically a screwup and totally directionless in life, but less aggressively so than when she was younger.

If only that night hadn't happened.

But it had.

CHAPTER 14

*J*ack deposited a red plastic helmet on Landon's head, then one on his brother. Madsen, his name was. He doubted those were family names. *Lucky kids.* Landon and Madsen sounded like monikers straight off one of the "most popular baby names" lists that sparked arguments between Oliver and his <u>wife</u>. Oliver and Serena practically split up every time they needed to name a kid—and Serena was pregnant again. A girl this time. Jack knew better than to ask what names they were considering. Girls' names were uncharted territory for his brother and sister-in-law.

Not that Jack had given it much thought on his end, but he definitely wasn't giving his children family names. He was his uncle's namesake, an honor that rested heavily on his shoulders. Jack hadn't started life with a blank slate, free to write out his own destiny. Instead, his life was meant to make his uncle's death —his mother's shattering grief over losing her brother, his father's stoic loss of his best friend—worth it somehow. And Jack was failing miserably at it, because the thing he wanted most was to follow in his uncle's footsteps.

What better way to honor his uncle's legacy than to do what he had been so proud to do?

Unfortunately, his mother didn't see it that way. Jack suspected that his father would be fine with all three of his sons working as firefighters, but making his wife happy was more important to him.

"Thanks." Landon and Madsen's father gave Jack a firm handshake. "The boys had a great time."

"No problem. I had a great time showing them around."

Those weren't just empty words for Jack. He remembered his own fascination with all things firefighting when he was Landon and Madsen's age. Even at twenty-five, he still loved it. Landon and Madsen practically jumped out of their skin when he asked if they wanted to sit in the driver's seat of the ladder truck. They had tested some of the cots in the bunk room, sampled the doughnuts in the kitchen, turned up their noses at Jack's joking offer of some coffee, and proved themselves nimbler on the slide than most of the station crew.

When they left—with directions to the Ice Creamery on Main Street—Jack headed for his father's office. Tim Wolfe was sitting at the desk beneath the portraits of past fire chiefs. There were a lot of them. St. Caroline was an old, old town. He tapped on the door jamb. His father looked up and waved him in. It took an instant for the strained expression on Tim Wolfe's face to relax into a smile for his youngest son.

"Come on in. Your fan club is gone?"

Jack glanced at the official-looking letter his father had been reading. "What's that?"

His father's sigh was heavy. "The superintendent of the Naval Academy is building a house down by Oyster Point. The governor is concerned that we don't have the manpower to handle all these new high profile homes. And we don't. But every time the town council turns down a building request, the people run to the governor's office and he pressures the town until they give in."

"So put me on a crew."

"I can't, son. You know that."

"Come on, dad—"

His father shook his head and for the first time, Jack was struck by the evidence of his father aging. Tim Wolfe was fifty-five, the same age as his high school sweetheart, Angie Wolfe. He'd spent his entire adult life in a stressful job. Lost his best friend and fellow firefighter on a call when they were twenty-eight. Watched his two older sons put themselves in danger all the time. And now he was losing the love of his life. So Jack didn't press the issue. His future wasn't here in St. Caroline anyway. He'd known that since about the age of ten. It was great that Matt and Oliver had stayed in town, but Jack just didn't see it for himself.

"Did you know that Elliott Parker has a house around here somewhere?" he asked.

"Who's Elliott Parker?"

"An artist. Big out in California."

"Never heard of him."

"He was at the street fair, drawing pencil portraits."

"That was nice of him."

The conversation faltered. Truth was, Matt and Oliver were closer to their father than Jack was. Jack's stronger bond was with his mother. He was going to feel even less like home in St. Caroline when she was gone.

"Yeah. Well, anything else you need me to do before I head home?" he offered.

"Yes. There is one thing. Your mother would like you to invite Becca Trevor to the hospital gala."

Jack frowned. "Why?" Although the thought of a date with Becca wasn't an entirely unpleasant one, he didn't think she'd feel the same way. She couldn't get away from him quick enough at the Inn earlier.

"Because Michelle is her friend and Michelle is worried about Becca not getting out enough since she came home. Apparently all she does is work and stay in her room, quilting."

"What if she doesn't want to go with me?"

"Well, if she says 'no,' then she says 'no.' It's either you or Mattie."

"I'll do it."

JACK HELD OPEN the door to Two Beans and let Becca enter first. A shiver convulsed her body at the sudden change in temperature. Outside, it was—to put it in technical terms—stinking hot. Inside the coffee shop, both the air and the vibe were chill. Amazing how people could sit around pouring caffeine into their bodies and yet be totally relaxed.

Not that a cup of coffee was going to relax Becca. Not if that cup were consumed sitting across from Jack. He had spent the last hour of her shift at Skipjack's nursing a beer at the bar. It took him awhile to get around to asking her if she wanted to go have a coffee when her shift ended. So here they were.

But her feelings were torn. On the one hand, there was a high probability that having coffee with Jack would be a pleasant—if not totally relaxing—way to spend the next hour. A very pleasant way. Jack was easy to talk to, and easy on the eyes. Her eyes couldn't stay away from his tanned calves.

And unlike most—no, make that all—of the guys she had dated in the past, Jack was a decent sort. On the other hand, they had a history. Baggage. The last thing she needed was for that baggage to pop open and spill its contents all over the ground.

She followed him through the front part of the shop, where the counter, espresso machines, and pastry case were. Jack walked straight through to the newer addition on the back. When she was a kid, Two Beans had been just a standard mom-and-pop coffee shop inside yet another of the historic storefronts lining Main Street. While she was in Ohio, it had acquired new owners and a much hipper look. She vaguely recalled her father mentioning the hoops the current owners had to jump through to renovate the interior.

"What can I get you?" he asked, pulling out a chair for her.

She sat. "Do they still have that iced Vietnamese coffee?"

"They do. Had some a couple days ago."

"One of those would be good."

"Coming right up."

She looked around the newer section of the shop, tilting her head back to gaze up at the light streaming in through a giant skylight. The walls were exposed brick, and scattered around the room were leather sofas and armchairs. She was seated at one of the wooden tables lining the back wall.

Minutes later, Jack returned with two iced Vietnamese coffees and a plate of miniature caramel scones.

"I know it's kind of late in the day for scones, but ..."

"It's never too late for scones."

His smile could have powered every shop on Main Street. "That's my philosophy, too."

She took a sip of the cold, sweet drink. "You like these too?"

"Yeah. Drink them a lot in San Francisco."

She took another sip, savoring the chill that spread down her throat and into her chest. "You were smarter than I was."

"How so?"

"You moved to San Francisco. I moved to Columbus."

"I've heard good things about Columbus."

She shrugged. "It's a nice little city. But I imagine San Francisco is more exciting."

"If you have money, it is. If you're a security guard and a volunteer firefighter, not as much."

"You're a volunteer out there?"

A pained look crossed his face. "My mother doesn't know about that. Just my dad."

"Don't worry. I won't say anything to my mom. I'm not as close to her as my sisters are." She picked up a scone and bit into it. Jack did the same. After a minute, she spoke again. "So I take it you didn't invite me here to tell me you're a firefighter like the rest of your family."

He gave her a rueful smile. "No. I wanted to ask you to go to the Champagne and Chocolate gala with me. At the hospital."

She studied him for a moment. "Our parents put you up to this, didn't they?"

He made no reply.

"I'll take that as a 'yes.'"

"Yes, my parents asked me to invite you."

"Why me? Why not one of my sisters?"

"You're the workaholic in the family, apparently. Your mom is worried that you spend all your time working."

"Oh."

"So you could ask someone else, I guess. It doesn't have to be me. Although if you turn me down, Matt is their second choice, it sounds like." He popped another miniature scone into his mouth. "Of course, you might prefer Matt."

She didn't, actually. "I hadn't really anticipated needing a social life this summer."

"Me either." A few moments of silence passed. "Mike says you're a great bartender. He's thrilled to have you working for him."

Becca shrugged, thankful for the change of subject. Her mother had chosen the absolute worst person to invite her on a date. Her mother didn't know that, of course, but still. "I was tending bar in Ohio. It's what I know how to do."

"And quilt."

"Pour drinks and quilt. Those are my two top talents."

"So how did you get fired in Ohio? Mike can't say enough good about you."

She bit back a sigh. Changed subject, but only marginally better than the first. "There was a female patron being harassed by some jerk and I tried to intervene. Unfortunately, the jerk was the owner's brother."

"That sucks."

"Yeah, no good deed goes unpunished."

"I know this is kind of awkward. My parents don't know about ... I haven't told anyone."

"Mine don't know either. They have no idea that I'm the last person you'd ever want to ask out."

"I wouldn't say that." His eyes held hers. "You're very attractive, Becca."

As was he—even with his hair and tee shirt still damp with sweat from the humidity outside. Somehow in the past seven years, he had turned into the best-looking guy in their graduating class. She imagined trying to explain to her parents—not to mention her sisters—why she turned down Jack's invitation. On the surface, there was no good reason to say 'no.' Below the surface, there was every reason.

"Why did you kiss me at my parents' party?"

He set down his glass of iced coffee, nearly empty now. "I shouldn't have done that. I apologize. Ego, I guess." He was struggling with finding the right words, but to his credit he didn't glance away from her. He kept his eyes on hers. "At the party, in your car ... that was my first time, you know."

"I know."

"Well, I'm sure it was obvious. I didn't even know how to properly kiss a girl. At your parents' house ... I don't know what came over me."

"You wanted to show me that you know how to kiss now?"

"Something like that, I guess."

"I sort of assume you know a little more these days." There

was one scone left, and Becca nudged the plate in Jack's direction. "You have the wrong idea about me."

"I do?"

"Yes. I know everyone always thought I was the town bicycle and all. But I wasn't. Even though, well, I guess I was with you. But that's not me, and it's even less me now. So if you're looking for someone to hook up with this summer, it won't be me. If we go to the gala together, that doesn't mean that I'll—"

"And I don't expect you to. That's not why I invited you."

"You invited me because your parents browbeat you into it."

"I invited you because my mother wants me to, and I'm trying to make these last months happy for her. But she'll probably be just as happy if Matt takes you."

"Matt wouldn't be interested in me."

"If it breathes and has a vagina, Matt is interested."

Becca felt her face grow hot.

"Maybe we can both agree that what happened at that party was uncharacteristic for both of us. I was a teenaged boy too under the influence of beer and friends to care that I was being offered a pity fuck."

"It wasn't—"

He held up his hand to stop her words. "I know it was, Becca, and that's okay. I was probably the last virgin standing in our class. And I'm guessing you had some peer pressure on your end, as well."

Beer and peer pressure. Tamara Rossi. "I'm sorry," she said. "You deserved better for your first time."

It was Becca who looked away first. She couldn't hold his stare. He was circling the truth of her: she didn't deserve better.

He held his hand out across the small table. "Why don't we agree to start over with each other? It was one time and I'm sure I wasn't that memorable, to begin with. Let's just say it never happened."

That was easy for him to decide. Just say the words and

JULIA GABRIEL

"poof!" Regrettable pity fuck gone. It was considerably less easy for her. Damn impossible, to be exact. She'd had his baby without telling him. It had been the best option. The only option if his life was going to proceed along the path it was supposed to. The only option for Jacqueline Michelle to have a better life than two teenagers could have provided for her.

The deceit of it would always eat at her. She knew that, and it was no less than she deserved. *No good deed goes unpunished.* For Jack Wolfe's sake, she had spent the past seven years pretending it never happened. She put her hand in his and let him shake it. And for his sake, she would continue pretending.

CHAPTER 15

*B*ecca let the door of the dress shop close quietly behind her, shutting out the heat and noise of the outlet center's vast parking lot. Inside, the array of dresses on display was nearly as vast, and she stopped to take a deep breath and corral her bearings. She'd never shopped for a formal dress before. Not even for the prom. Her then-boyfriend had dumped her two months before and took a college girl he met at a party in Annapolis. *Whatever.* Becca had still gone to several of the after-prom parties. The parties were the fun part, anyway—not trying to slow dance in an uncomfortable dress and heels, worrying about your fancy updo coming undone.

She was skipping the fancy updo part for the hospital gala, but there was no getting around the uncomfortable dress and heels part. So here she was. She had the day off from Skipjack's because she was working a wedding at the Inn tomorrow, and of course her mother had given her time off from Quilt Therapy to shop. This was her mother's brainchild, after all.

She waded into the sea of silk and polyester, discreetly flipping over price tags as she went. There had to be a sale rack at the back of the store, she told herself. She had agreed to go with

Jack, but she wasn't willing to break the bank doing it. She was going to buy something marked down, regardless of how it looked. She just needed to look presentable and not embarrass her parents. She wasn't trying to look pretty for Jack Wolfe. That was dead last on the list of dress criteria. In fact, she needed a dress that would thoroughly repel Jack without embarrassing her parents.

Sure, he had said he didn't expect a repeat of the graduation party but she had known enough men by now. Even the nice ones still tended to think with a certain part of their anatomy. She didn't want Jack, in a moment of weakness or temporary insanity, to even try—because Jack Wolfe was way too attractive these days. She wasn't sure she could trust herself enough to say "no."

She flipped through the sales rack. Nothing strapless. Nothing low cut. Nothing skintight. It didn't take long to scan every dress on the rack. Strapless, low cut, skintight—that ruled out ninety percent of the dresses. She headed for a section of the store where the options looked less "formal gown" and more "afternoon wedding." She was surprised to find her sister, Charlotte, lurking among the displays.

"Hey. What are you doing here?"

"I have an interview in DC next week. I'm looking for a suit."

It was hard for Becca to picture her youngest sister working in an office in the city. Looking at her now, in her shorts and tank top, sneakers and ponytail, Charlotte could pass for a high school kid still.

"Not many suits in here. Sure mom didn't sent you to help me, the fashion-challenged daughter?"

Charlotte looked sheepish. "It might have been six of one, half dozen of the other. You're not mad, are you?"

Becca squeezed her younger sister's shoulder. "I probably need the help anyway."

"No offense, Becs, but you do."

"So what kind of dress did mom tell you to look for? This gala thing sounds like an old person's party."

"It is. That's why the rest of us aren't going." Charlotte laughed. "Mom said to steer you toward a floor-length dress."

"You're kidding. It's that formal? What do the men wear?"

"It's black tie optional. Dad usually wears a tux."

An image of Jack in a sharp black tuxedo popped into her head, sending an unexpected rush of heat through her body. And that was saying something, given that it was ninety degrees outside to begin with.

Charlotte reached into the front pocket of her shorts and pulled something out. "Mom, gave me her credit card."

"No no. I'm paying for it. I can't repay the insurance deductible if I'm taking money from them at the same time."

"They're not going to take your money, Becca." Charlotte began pushing aside dresses.

"I'll leave it in an envelope on the table on my way out of town."

"You're not staying? Mom could use you at the shop. She's already had, like, four requests for you to do another hand quilting workshop."

"I don't think Cass is happy about me muscling in on Quilt Therapy."

"Cass is never happy. And I think she's more jealous that Jack Wolfe comes home and you're the one he's interested in."

"I'm pretty sure he's being blackmailed into this. Or paid off, one of the two."

Charlotte shrugged. "All the same, there's a new guy in town and he goes for you while Cassidy is still a virgin at twenty-seven."

"She is? You're kidding."

"Nope. She's too picky." Charlotte pulled a long emerald green dress from the rack and held it up to herself for Becca's inspection. "She won't date any of the local guys and it's unrealistic to expect to land some rich summer guy. Especially when she won't sleep with them. That's what they want—a summer lay." Charlotte made the silky green fabric shimmy. "What do you think?"

"The color's right for my hair." The dress shimmied again. "But, the top …" Becca waved her hands in front of her chest. The bodice of the dress looked small before flaring out to a fuller skirt. "Too form-fitting, I think."

Charlotte frowned down at the dress in her hands. "What? You have the perfect figure for this."

How to explain her criteria to her sister? *I need the dress to be appropriate, but ugly.*

"I don't want it to be too sexy. It's the hospital. And mom and dad will be there."

Charlotte rolled her eyes as she put the dress back on the rack. "You're going to make Jack look like he's there with his grandmother."

Exactly. Becca flipped through dresses on the next rack over. "Jack's local, anyway. Why would Cassidy care?"

"He's also a lawyer. So he's a local guy made good."

Not exactly. But his secret was safe with her. *People in glass houses and all that.*

"What about you?" She lifted up a long halter dress in a watery blue and white print. It felt like silk. She liked the style, though it was still too sexy to meet her criteria.

"What about me?"

Becca put the blue dress back. "Are you still a virgin?"

Charlotte blushed. "Um, no. I had a couple boyfriends in college."

"What happened?"

"One ran its course. The other went back home for the summer and he's starting medical school in the fall in Boston." Charlotte had a wistful look on her face.

"You still like him."

She nodded. "Yeah. But we're young. And he has to go to the

medical school that matched up with him. It's not like he can just decide to go somewhere closer." She came around to Becca's side and pulled out the blue dress. "I like this one. You should try it on."

"Do you think it's formal enough?"

"Try it on and we can text a picture to mom to see what she thinks."

Becca grabbed a few other dresses and headed for the changing rooms, Charlotte in tow. She pulled her tee shirt dress over her head and dropped the blue and white halter dress on. She adjusted the tie at the back of the neck before slowly spinning around for Charlotte.

"What do you think?"

"I love it, Becs. Let me take a picture for mom." She sent a quick text. Seconds later, Charlotte's phone rang. "Uh oh. She's calling on video chat." Charlotte tapped to answer.

"Let me see in real time," their mother's voice spilled from the phone.

Charlotte pointed it at Becca.

"Hi mom."

"That's beautiful, sweetheart. Fits you well."

Becca ran her hands down the dress, smoothing the skirt. "But is it formal enough?"

"For someone your age? Yes. You'll look darling next to Jack."

That wasn't the look Becca wanted to go for. "I have a few other options, too."

"Try those on and let me see."

Charlotte chatted with their mother about her upcoming trip to Washington as Becca put on dress number two. It was a high-necked style in bubblegum pink. Guaranteed to repel any man. It was such an unattractive color that Becca half-marveled that someone somewhere had actually approved its manufacture. Predictably, it got thumbs down from both Charlotte and their mother. Dresses three and four received the same reception.

"The blue and white one, sweetie," her mother reiterated. "You look so pretty in that one. Try it on again."

Becca swapped out dresses and stood before the full-length mirror. It *was* pretty. It skimmed over her slender waist and the skirt moved almost like water itself. She turned to look at the back, peering over her shoulder. If she and Jack danced at the gala, his hands would have to touch her bare skin.

Suddenly she wanted Jack's hands on her bare skin ...

"You're young. You don't even have to worry about a bra," her mother added.

... her breasts pressed into Jack's chest as they danced to some eighties song their parents liked. Air Supply or Journey.

Her mom had a sad, faraway look on her face.

"What's the matter, mom?"

Michelle forced her mouth into something resembling a smile. "I wish my sister could be here to see what a beautiful young woman you grew up to be."

Her sister. Becca's biological mother.

"She would be proud of you, sweetie."

Becca looked at herself again in the mirror. The dress *did* look good on her, and she liked dressing up these days. She wasn't the Becca Trevor everyone used to know, the angry teenager trying to keep all comers at bay with attitude, dyed black hair, and ripped clothing. She might not be all American pretty like her sister or mother, but she didn't feel the need any longer to make a statement about it. She was twenty-five years old and had been supporting herself since she was eighteen. Why should she spend her hard-earned money on an ugly dress?

Jack had asked her to the gala. He was just going to have to deal with her the way she looked now, the person she was now. A person who made a mistake seven years ago hooking up with him but who wasn't going to repeat that mistake.

She moved a few inches to the side so her mom could see her reflection in the mirror. "What kind of shoes do you think?"

~

"Don't let them keep me here."

Jack looked up at the sound of his mother's voice. Her eyes, closed a moment ago, were now open and filled with fear. An I.V. line snaked down to her arm.

"They might want to, just for the night, for observation. You were dehydrated."

"Please, Jackie. I want to be at home."

Hospital sounds leaked in from the hallway. Scratchy announcements over the intercom. Shoes squeaking against the waxed floor. The creak of cart wheels.

"Dad's on the way. He left the meeting in Annapolis right away."

It had become Jack's routine to stop by the house first thing in the morning to see his mother. Mornings were when she had the most energy. But today, he had found her disoriented and weak. He called his dad from the car, on the way to the hospital.

He felt his phone buzz against his thigh, and he pulled it from the pocket of his shorts. "He just crossed the Bay Bridge."

That news didn't seem to relax her any. Then it hit him. She wasn't worried about spending the night here. *Don't make me die in a hospital.* That's what she was terrified of. She wanted to be at home when it happened.

He moved to the hard vinyl-covered chair next to the bed, and took her hand in his. The bones beneath her cool skin felt as frail as a bird's. The noxious brew of anger and desperation that was always swirling in his chest threatened to boil over again. *Why? Why dammit?* The other constant in his life these days—his running argument with God.

To his right, the door opened and a nurse entered the room. "How are you feeling, Mrs. Wolfe?" The nurse strode over to the bed, pressed her fingers to his mother's wrist. She glanced up at Jack. "Mr. Wolfe, can you wait outside, please?"

He leaned down and kissed his mother on the forehead. Even as he did it, he realized how backward it was—him kissing his mother like she was a child. The desperate anger was like knives trying to squeeze through his veins. The pain of this was everywhere, with no relief. Not even for a moment.

"We'll take you home, I promise," he said before leaving her alone with the nurse.

He took the elevator down to the lobby, then headed outside for some fresh air. He stood beneath the canopy sheltering the hospital's entrance. On the other side of the door, an exhausted-looking man stood smoking a cigarette. Jack had never been tempted to smoke but now he wished there was something like that he could turn to relieve the stress. He leaned back against the hospital's brick exterior and closed his eyes. He couldn't believe this was happening. Nor could Matt. According to his brother, their mother had felt "out of sorts" for months before finally going to see a doctor. By then the cancer had spread and there wasn't much to be done about. Chemo to give her a few extra months, but that was it.

Months! And then there would be years ahead without her.

"Hey there."

He recognized that voice, and it wasn't God's. God had been remarkably silent in response to Jack's entreaties. He opened his eyes to see Becca standing there, her cinnamon hair pulled back into a neat, tight ponytail. Maybe God wasn't all bad—if he had to talk to another human being right now, Becca Trevor would be the human he'd choose. He'd ponder the why of that later. Right now, he was just unaccountably pleased to see her.

"I'm afraid to ask why you're here," she added, shifting the weight of the large bundle she was cradling in her arms. A quilt, he realized. The fire quilt.

"Mom was admitted. Dehydration, that's all. They've got her on an I.V."

"Is there anything I can do?"

Wave a magic wand. Just stand here and stare at me like that.

He shook his head. "I'm waiting for dad to show up. A nurse kicked me out of the room." He forced a smile.

"Speaking of your dad." She jiggled the quilt in her arms. "He asked me to drop this off here at the hospital. The fire department's donating it to the silent auction at the gala."

Jack reached out and lifted the quilt from her arms. "Where do you need to take it? I'll carry it for you." As he pulled the quilt into his chest, he realized how ridiculous that offer was. The quilt wasn't heavy at all. Becca could easily carry it all over the hospital without any help. He couldn't hand it back to her now though. He was committed to a course of action.

Becca fished a slip of paper from the back pocket of her shorts. That gave him an excuse to check out her legs. Right? What if she dropped that tiny piece of paper on the ground? Picking it up for her would be the gentlemanly thing to do, so he needed to watch and see whether she dropped it or not. Yeah, it would be easier for her to pick it up, given that he now held an armful of fabric. If she dropped it, that was. Which it didn't appear as though she was going to. Her slender fingers unfolded the paper to reveal a room number.

Dear lord. She has nice legs. His memory of that night at the graduation party held no visuals on her legs. Between the alcohol and the lust-fueled anticipation, he hadn't noticed those. His loss, evidently. Actually—thanks to both of those things—he didn't remember a whole lot from those fifteen minutes in her car. That damned sock monkey, which in his memory was pretty creepy. Did he even kiss her first? Foreplay didn't figure prominently in his memories, either.

Hands down, you were the worst sex she ever had. No way that wasn't true.

"Room 177," she read the number off the piece of paper, then pushed it back into her pocket.

That drew his attention back to a certain part of her anatomy he'd love to see. They hadn't seen much of each other's bodies that night. They'd undressed only as much as was necessary to get the job done.

That's what it was, wasn't it? Those fifteen minutes in her car had been a task—the task of dispensing with his virginity. Maybe he was overthinking the whole thing. It wasn't like he was the only man she'd ever been with. In all likelihood, she never even thought about that night. They were two kids who, under the influence, had hooked up—and if they had to do it again, they probably wouldn't.

Except you probably would.

In the distance, thunder rumbled. They both glanced up at the clouds.

"We should get this inside," he said.

Jack carried the quilt to room 177, the office of the hospital's vice president of development, and handed it over. Carmen Schwartz was effusive in her praise of the quilt. Jack might as well have been invisible. It occurred to him to quietly slip away and leave the two women alone, but his feet weren't that eager to move.

Carmen unfolded the quilt partway and ran her finger over the lines of tiny stitching. "This is beautiful, Becca. How on earth did you guys get it done this quickly?"

"Mom kept the shop open late a few nights because there were so many people who wanted to work on it." Becca laughed lightly. "With two dozen quilters, it goes pretty fast."

"Well, I'm sorry I couldn't get over there to help. As soon as the gala is over, I've got a few UFOs to get back to."

"I've got a couple of those myself," Becca replied.

"Are you coming to the gala?"

Becca nodded. Jack took a step back toward the doorway. Maybe he really should leave. But *damn.* Those legs. And ankles, too. He'd never really appreciated the loveliness of a woman's ankles before. But the way the tiny leather straps of her sandals wrapped around the base of her calves ...

"Are you bringing a date?" His attention snapped upward at the sound of Carmen's words.

"Yes." He and Becca answered the question simultaneously, and Carmen Schwartz seemed almost surprised to see him still there. He trained his eyes on her—her business attire, navy slacks and beige jacket—in the hope that they hadn't noticed him ogling Becca's gams.

"Jack and I are going."

"Well ... that's great." Carmen was still looking at him, a look of faint disdain on her face, like she was trying to decide whether or not Jack was really good enough for Becca. "Tell your father I said 'thank you' for donating this quilt to us. That was very generous of the fire department."

"I will. He's on his way here."

"Oh?"

"My mother is upstairs." He cocked his head back toward the hallway. "She was admitted a little while ago."

"Oh Jack, I'm sorry to hear that. How is she?"

"She was dehydrated, that's all. It sounds like she'll be back home tomorrow."

A loud crack of thunder sounded outside and Becca's eyes widened in alarm.

"You should get going," Carmen said. "So you're not driving in the storm."

Jack silently concurred. With the flat terrain of the eastern shore and the proximity of the bay, storms here could be sudden and vicious.

As they hurried down the hall, he had to ask, "What's a UFO? I'm assuming you two aren't working on alien spacecraft."

"It's an unfinished object, an unfinished quilt. Like your wedding quilt."

"Ah. You don't have to—"

She waved her hand in a dismissive gesture. "We already discussed this, and it's between me and your mother."

By the time they reached the lobby, rain was coming down in sheets outside.

"Yuck," Becca sighed.

"Give me your key. I'll go get your car."

She looked at him like he was crazy. "You'll get soaked."

"So would you." *And don't even think about her little yellow tee shirt soaked through with rain. You're a dog.*

Lightning lit up the sky outside.

"Let me be a gentleman here, okay?"

She handed over the key.

"Where's your car, roughly?" he asked.

"Toward the back."

He took off running. Fortunately, the hospital's front parking area was not as large as the lot behind. That would lessen his chances of getting struck by lightning. Still, he was soaked through to the skin by the time he reached the right row. He narrowed his eyes at the sock monkey as he unlocked her little white car.

"Ouch." He rubbed his kneecap where he had just jammed it into the steering column and slapped his hand along the side of the seat, trying to find the lever that would allow Jack to actually fit into this tuna can of a car. He groaned in relief as the seat finally pushed back. This was why he drove an SUV. Not because he ever went off road or even needed the four-wheel drive in the Bay Area's mild weather, but because it more comfortably accommodated his six-foot-five frame.

He inserted the key into the ignition and backed the car out of the parking space. By the time he circumnavigated the lot, his father had arrived and was standing with Becca beneath the canopy sheltering the hospital's entrance. He pulled right up to them, put the car into park, and was about to open the door when Becca opened the passenger's side and climbed in. Immediately, she realized her mistake and laughed.

God, he loved that sound. Not that he was telling that to God. He and God were not on speaking terms at the moment. Her laugh made him think of the early morning cooing and chirping of birds. Not that she sounded like a bird, but that was the way it made him feel—that feeling of a new day, peaceful and calm, before any shit could hit any fans.

He opened the door on his side and unfolded his body from the car. They passed each other at the trunk, and Becca slipped into the driver's seat while Jack took the passenger side. Immediately, he realized his mistake. But he didn't care. He even forgot about his father standing on the sidewalk mere feet away.

Because the loveliest girl he could imagine was looking right at him, searching his face for ... what? Truth be told, Jack's experience with women couldn't be classified as expert level. In bed, yeah, he thought he was pretty hot stuff by now. But the mysteries of a woman's mind? Totally clueless. Whatever was going on behind Becca's calm grey eyes right then, he couldn't begin to fathom. He just knew that he liked having those eyes trained on him.

"Your dad's here," she said at last. "Do you need a ride home?"

He blinked. "No, um. Thanks though. I've got to go back up ..." He made an upward movement with his hand, barely missing the low ceiling of her car.

He felt like he should kiss her before he got out of the car. Rationally, he knew that was not the proscribed action for this moment. Or this situation. But the moment felt like the end of a date, somehow, and his hands itched to reach over and cup her face, draw her toward him, pull her soft lips onto his. The air was charged, and not from the storm that was still raging outside.

"So, Saturday?" she asked.

Her gentle question nudged him back to reality, and more realistic expectations. "Right. Saturday. What time should I pick you up?" They were definitely going in his SUV. More room for him. And he was not taking that damned monkey along. He fought the urge to glance at it. Bad enough that his peripheral vision allowed him to see its grubby stuffed paws clinging to the posts of the headrest.

"When does it start?"

"Cocktail hour is six to seven, according to the web site," he answered.

"Five-thirty then?"

"Five-thirty it is."

He felt his head start to incline toward her before he caught himself. Right, no kissing. He unfolded himself from her car and watched as she pulled away from the curb, resisting the urge to flip his middle finger at the monkey. He shouldn't feel such animosity toward a ratty old stuffed animal, but he'd taken intro psych in college. He was transferring his guilt over what happened in the back seat of her car to the monkey. Something like that.

"Nice of you to get Becca's car for her."

Jack turned toward his father. *Good thing you didn't kiss her.* He'd completely forgotten about his father's presence.

"Yeah well, I wasn't raised by wolves, you know."

His father stretched his arm around Jack's shoulders and squeezed him hard into his side. They walked wordlessly toward the hospital's automatic doors. *You're acting like you're being raised by wolves.* How many times had he and his brothers heard those words from his mother when they were growing up? Admonishment and joke at the same time.

As the hospital doors parted before them, Tim Wolfe spoke. "We're going to be so screwed without her, Jackie."

Jack reached his own arm around his father and squeezed him back, just as hard. *Screwed! Do you hear that? If you don't care about me, care about my dad. He doesn't deserve to spend the rest of his life without the only woman he's ever loved. Only woman!*

"I know. Totally screwed."

Upstairs, Angie Wolfe was alone again in the room. His father leaned over and kissed her forehead. Her eyes fluttered open and she immediately reached for his hand.

"Sorry it took me awhile to get here," Tim said. "Accident on the bridge and then I had to wait while Jackie here played valet downstairs."

"Oh? How so?" His mother's eyes were soft as she glanced toward Jack, the fear he had seen in them earlier now gone. Of course. His father was here now. The man who had pledged to care for her until death do them part. *A man who honored those vows for thirty-five years, and this is what he gets?*

"Jack went and fetched Becca Trevor's car for her so she wouldn't get soaked."

Jack lifted the hem of his wet shirt.

"Well, my boys weren't raised by wolves." His mother managed a weak smile.

A choking sound came from his father's chest, before he covered it with a forced cough.

"I *was* raised by wolves," Jack said. That had always been his and his brothers' standard rejoinder. *We are raised by wolves!* Followed by the laughter of kids who thought themselves clever … kids who knew even back then that they were thoroughly, unconditionally loved. Of the three Wolfe boys—Oliver, Matt, and Jack—only Mattie had inflicted a rough adolescence on their parents. Oliver had been the stereotypical oldest child, responsible to a fault. Jack, as the youngest, had been "pampered and privileged" (in his brothers' words), with no reason to rebel.

"She still has that sock monkey in her car," Tim redirected the conversation.

"Oh, she still has that old thing?" His mother's loving gaze returned to her husband.

"What's the story with that?" Jack asked. When he asked Becca directly, she had said simply "sentimental value." That seemed true of most stuffed animals, but he hadn't pressed for a fuller answer. For a wild child, she was pretty reserved. Not that she seemed to be all that wild anymore.

His mother lifted her stubbled head from the pillow. "When Michelle and Dan brought her home from Ohio, she wouldn't let go of that stuffed animal for a week."

CHAPTER 16

"*W*here's Jack?" Becca's mother joined her in the Grand Ballroom of the Kings Landing Country Club. All around them, the hospital's annual fundraising gala was in full swing. "It looked like you two were having a good time at dinner."

Becca nodded. Her worries about not having anything to talk about with Jack had not come to fruition. Jack turned out to be surprisingly easy to talk to, one of those people who seemed to know at least a little bit about everything. And he'd been happy to tell Becca all about San Francisco, a city she dearly wanted to visit someday.

"The food was good, too," she said. She wanted to bypass questions about Jack or the ridiculous notion that this was in any way a real date. Something she hadn't been able to get through Cassidy and Charlotte's thick heads. Her parents and Jack's had conspired to fix them up, that's all. The evening was half over. They'd made it through the cocktail hour and dinner. A band was setting up at the end of the ballroom. She wasn't sure whether Jack would want to dance with her or not. On the one hand, the last time she had slow-danced with someone was in high school and that would not have been in heels. Sneakers, probably. The odds of tripping over her own feet tonight were pretty high.

On the other hand ... Jack was looking especially fine in his tuxedo. He cleaned up nicely. Becca bit back a smile at that thought, then remembered her mother's original question. She glanced across the ballroom.

"I think he got waylaid by those men over there."

Her mother followed her gaze to where Jack was standing in a circle of older men. "Maybe he's being pressed for legal advice. I lost your father to a couple who wanted to talk to him about vaccination schedules." She reached out and adjusted the halter strap of Becca's dress, the pretty blue and white one. "Let's go peruse the auctions. Your daddy has his eye on a salmon fishing trip for six to Alaska."

"What are you bidding on?" Becca asked, as she and her mother left the ballroom for the smaller adjacent room where the auction tables were set up. Becca had no plans to bid on anything. Working as many shifts at Skipjack's as she could was putting money in her bank account to repay her parents for the insurance deductible. She had splurged on a dress for the gala, but it could be dry cleaned and taken to a consignment shop next week. Otherwise, she was spending as little as she could.

"A Broadway weekend in New York. But I'm not going crazy with the bidding in order to win."

The auction room was crowded with guests looking for something to do between dinner and dancing. The gala was Talbot Hospital's main fundraising event, and popular with well-heeled St. Carolinians, as well as some of the summer residents. Becca hadn't been to the country club since the time she was invited to a pool party there in elementary school.

"How much were the tickets for this?" she asked.

"Mmm, your father picked them up this year."

"How much were they last year?"

"Does it matter, Becs? I'm sure Jack can afford it."

No, he probably can't. She knew how much security guards made. Brandon had been one for awhile. For twelve days, to be exact, before he got fired.

"You and dad paid for mine, didn't you?"

Her mother's sigh was audible. "Yes, we did. You need to learn to let people do nice things for you, Becca."

"Thank you. I'm glad you didn't make Jack pay for it."

"Jack could have said no if he wanted to."

Becca knew that wasn't true, not really. Jack would do anything for his mom right now. She remembered how strained his face had looked when they ran into each other at the hospital last weekend.

They approached the first table, but Becca's eyes were drawn to the far end of the room. The fire quilt, all one thousand seven hundred and fifty triangles of it, hung on the wall. She nudged her mom.

"Did you know they were going to hang it?"

Her mother looked up. "Yes. Cassidy and Natalie came over to advise them on it."

"Why doesn't anyone ever tell me anything?" she said with a gentle laugh.

"We wanted it to be a surprise. Looks gorgeous up there."

They moved closer to the quilt. It was amazing—put a quilt up on a wall and it looked like art. And yet, it was the best thing to sleep under. Becca could never sleep well in a hotel with their heavy, scratchy comforters. Even down duvets made her feel like her body was swimming in fluff. But a quilt with a thin, low-loft batting was soft and supple. It conformed to the body like a lover's embrace in the middle of the night. Or what she thought that would feel like, anyway.

She cocked her head and studied the quilt. "I think I'd piece it differently if I could do it again."

"How so? I think it looks fine."

Becca pointed to the left side of the quilt. "The balance

between the light and dark fabrics is off over there. And see the
—" She squinted and counted off rows. "—ninth row from the
bottom? There's a stretch there where the fabrics all have really
small, dense patterns. I would break that up with some solids or
larger prints." She sighed. "I was in a rush to get it done."

Michelle shook her head, then hugged Becca into her side.
"No one else would even notice. Come on. Let's go see what the
bidding on it looks like."

Someone could have knocked Becca over with a feather when
she read down the list of bids. "It's up to twenty-four hundred
dollars," she said quietly. At the carnival, the fire department was
lucky if the fire quilt brought in five hundred dollars.

Her mother patted her on the back. "And the night's not over
yet."

JACK WATCHED Becca and her mom disappear into the auction
room, desperately wanting to join them—if for no other reason
than to extricate himself from his current company. The CEO of
the hospital had pulled him into the circle of older businessmen
to talk about tech stocks and the technology company Jack
worked for.

As a security guard—which, of course, the men didn't know.
Jack wondered how the CEO even knew what he was supposedly
doing. He doubted his parents were in that social circle. Maybe
the man's house had caught on fire? Whatever the case, Jack
needed to get away before his lie was caught out.

Liar liar pants on fire.

Some fires couldn't be extinguished before they burned down
everything you held dear. Like his parents' respect.

So far, he had held his own in the conversation. It wasn't as
though he knew absolutely nothing about the company he
worked for. He kept up with the business press, but he certainly

didn't know as much as a person working in the legal department would.

"So should I invest in Bumbershoot or not?" a balding, heavyset man asked. He owned a chain of restaurants in the mid-Atlantic and a summer home in St. Caroline.

Another man laughed and slapped Jack square between the shoulders. "You can't ask a lawyer that. He'll qualify his answer with ten pages of legalese."

The men's raucous laughter rolled over Jack. Pictures flipped past in his mind ... the men smoking cigars outside later that night, playing golf here at the country club tomorrow afternoon, their wives putting their dry-cleaned tuxedos away for the next philanthropic event on the calendar. That was the future Jack had bailed on, the life he hadn't been able to picture himself living. He didn't care about the stock market or IPOs or whatever the next hot business idea was. If you were a good student, you were expected to want that kind of life. Sure, Jack was smart ... and smart enough to know he'd be miserable sitting behind a desk all day.

Becca and her mother returning from the auction room caught his eye. He hadn't intended to leave her this long, but the conversation with these men had gone on and on. He wondered how high the bidding on her quilt was now. It was impressive, at least to his untrained eye. He admired people who could create things like that with their hands.

The CEO noticed Jack's diverted attention. "Looks like we've kept you from your lovely date." He reached out his hand and pumped Jack's in a firm handshake.

Jack was relieved to get away before the men figured out he really wasn't a lawyer. Crossing the room, he caught Becca's eye just as the band struck a few warm-up notes. The thought of her in his arms as they danced set every nerve ending in his body aswoon. She looked beautiful tonight, and he told her as much when he picked her up at the Trevors' house. Her dress had swished around her legs as she walked to his car, each step revealing a shapely calf. And those white-strapped heels gave her hips a sway that he'd barely been able to pull his eyes up from. He was lucky he hadn't fallen off the curb of the sidewalk.

The band launched into a slow song and couples began filling the parquet dance floor. He watched as Dan Trevor whisked his wife away from Becca's side. In high school, his perception of her had been that of a wild child. How bad could Becca have been back then, really? With Dan and Michelle Trevor for parents? Her father was a pediatrician, for heaven's sake.

When he reached her, he held out his arm. "Dance?" he asked, not one hundred percent sure she'd really accept.

But she did, allowing Jack to lead her into the middle of the dance floor. He was careful to stay away from her parents, guessing she'd feel more comfortable that way—and he wouldn't have to worry so much about holding her too tight.

Because thoughts of holding her tight were just about the only thoughts his brain was juggling right now.

He pulled her into his arms. The top of her head barely came up to the base of his throat, even in her heels. That inch between her cheek and his pectoral muscles would be so easy to close. Her flower-scented hair was pulled up into some kind of swirly style, sexy and pretty all at the same time. He let his hand settle on her lower back, on the fabric of her dress—thin, silky fabric that let the warmth of her skin seep into his palm. She felt so right, so *true*, in his arms. He'd been too much of a nervous virgin to notice that seven years ago. *Not a virgin anymore.* And, surprisingly, not feeling that nervous either. As they moved to the music —some sappy eighties song his parents liked—he imagined himself peeling her dress off in a darkened room. He'd stand there for a moment and admire her body in lingerie. Although given that her back was completely exposed—the dress simply didn't exist between the tie at her neck and her waist—his imagination was leading him to believe that there was no bra in this scenario.

He needed to stop thinking about this, or else he was going to end up walking off the dance floor with a hard-on. Right past her parents.

Just as he was about to loosen his arms an inch, their feet collided and Becca stumbled. Automatically, he tightened his grip to keep her from falling.

"Sorry," she said, her voice sounding a little breathless. "I haven't done this since high school."

When he felt her balance steady, he relaxed his arms around her. "The last time I did this was in college. In the basement of a fraternity house at a party." He got the two of them back into rhythm. "It's hard to dance when your shoes are sticking to all the old beer that's been spilled on the floor."

Her body jiggled with laughter, a movement that sent his mind right back into the gutter.

"You were in a fraternity?"

"Yeah. I did eventually outgrow my nerdiness." The song they were dancing to ended and another began. He didn't recognize the new song, but who cared about music anyway? There was a pleasant enough humming coursing through his veins right now. "Well okay, so I pledged the nerdy fraternity." Her body jiggled with laughter again, the exact effect he'd been going for.

"You're a good dancer."

Her compliment warmed his chest. He wanted to be a good dancer with her, wanted to be a good … *this is not a real date.* Their parents had set this up. But he was too old to let his parents determine whether something was a real date or not.

He was starting to want real.

CHAPTER 17

"*A*re you hungry?"

Becca tilted her head back to look up at Jack. Right on cue, her stomach rumbled. She was thankful the music drowned out the sound.

"Yeah, kind of," she answered. "Dinner was good but ..."

"A little too fancy for my taste," Jack finished her sentence. She gave him a smile.

"When this song is over, why don't we go get something to eat?" he added.

"Oh you don't have to do that. You can just take me home." She glanced around the dance floor. "Or I could go home with my parents. That's probably easiest."

"I would never take a date home hungry."

"Yeah well, you weren't raised by wolves, right?"

Immediately, she wished she could swallow the words back. She tilted her head down, but not before seeing his adam's apple bob as he swallowed hard.

"I'm sorry. I wasn't thinking." *You're never thinking when you need to be.* That was the joke his mom was fond of making; Becca had heard of it from her own mother. *Way to go. Remind him that his mother is dying. Real swift, Becca.* "You can just take me home." She leaned out of his arms, but he pulled her back in and bent his head to her ear.

"I think we've fulfilled our filial duty here. Unless you're really digging this music."

He was trying to make her laugh, and there was something incredibly sexy about it. Brandon had never tried to make her laugh. On the contrary, she'd always been worried that she would laugh at the wrong thing around him. It was nearly impossible to predict what would piss him off. She didn't miss him.

And what else was sexy? The feel of Jack's body against hers. Hard, strong, made for rescuing people. And his sun kissed hair in a room full of grey. His breath on the lobe of her ear, sending unvoiced whispers down her spine.

But Jack Wolfe was way out of her league. She didn't miss Brandon, but those were the kind of guys that were attainable for her. Jack might poke fun at the "nerdy fraternity" he'd belonged to, but at least he'd gone to college and gotten into law school. Becca was lucky she had enough days in attendance after suspensions to graduate from St. Caroline High.

She felt his lips brush her ear again.

"Becca, I asked you to this event because our parents wanted me to. But I'm asking you to go get something to eat with me because *I* want to." His hand slid from her lower back, over her hip—for a mere instant—and to her hand, which he clasped. "How does Nick's sound?"

The sensation of his fingers threading through hers made the whisperings in her body grow louder. "Nick's Burger Barn? Sounds like there could be a milkshake in it for me."

"There is. Any flavor you want."

The song they had mostly stopped dancing to a few minutes ago finally ended—and not a moment too soon. Because that was quite possibly the sexiest thing anyone had ever said to her. And

JULIA GABRIEL

if she didn't put some space between their bodies soon, her dress was going to melt right off.

They said their goodbyes to her parents and Jack had the valet bring his dark green SUV around. He helped her up into the passenger seat. He pulled out the seatbelt for her, closed the door. He walked around to his side of the car, started the ignition, fiddled with the air conditioning vents on her side to get them just so. All the things her dad still did for her mother.

Nick's Burger Barn was busy, as it always was on a Saturday night—even in the off-season. With good reason, too. Nick's made the best burgers, fries and shakes in the area. Nick was a transplant to St. Caroline, formerly a high-powered executive who'd gotten tired of the rat race in Washington, DC, and chucked it all to open a restaurant. The Burger Barn was housed in an actual barn that Nick had found in Vermont, then had disassembled and trucked to Maryland. It was quaint, but noisy.

Jack and Becca stuck out like sore thumbs in their formal attire, even though Jack had left his tuxedo jacket and bowtie in the car. There was still a chasm between their outfits and the shorts, tee shirts, sundresses, and flip flops everyone else wore. Although Becca imagined that, with Jack's height, he stuck out everywhere.

"Let's get it to go," Jack suggested.

"Good idea."

While they waited for their order to come out, Becca took in the restaurant. The Burger Barn was new since she'd moved away. Her sisters had brought her here once, on one of Becca's rare visits home from Ohio. In many ways, St. Caroline was the same town she remembered from childhood. There were things that remained unchanged even from hundreds of years ago. People still made a living from fishing. City folks still came here to escape the summer heat.

But things were different, too. The college was growing so

there were more young people around. On more than one occasion, Becca had found herself driving down a back road, surprised to see a new mansion there. The town felt personally different, as well, less claustrophobic than when she was a teenager. As she mulled over that thought, a familiar figure stood up from one of the long picnic tables in the back of the restaurant. Ian Evers. There were still some aspects of the town that made her feel hemmed in, and one of them was walking straight toward her.

She plastered a smile on her face as Ian approached, and wished hard for the kitchen to hurry up. Ian winked at her, then slapped Jack on the back.

"Getting a bite to eat after the prom?"

She saw the annoyed look in Jack's eyes, but it disappeared before he was fully turned around and facing Ian. She wondered, not for the first time, why Jack and Ian had ever been friends. Ian was smart, to be sure, and he and Jack had been in lots of classes together. Calculus. Physics. The college prep classes. But Ian had always been a little obnoxious.

Ian glanced over at her again. "At least he upgraded from the dog costume to a penguin one, eh?"

Even though there were a couple of inches between their bodies, she felt Jack stiffen. "I thought he was rather cute as a dog." She shot Jack a reassuring smile.

"Number eighty-seven!" one of the counter staff called out.

"That's us," Becca said. *Saved by the bell.* She walked back to the counter to retrieve their food. She held up the white paper bag when she returned. "It was nice running into you again, Ian," she said and took a few steps toward the door. Jack shook Ian's hand and joined her.

"He knows, doesn't he?" she said in a low voice as Jack pushed open the door to the parking lot.

It wasn't until they were back in the car that Jack answered. "Yes, he knows. I'm sorry."

"He seems a little antagonistic toward you. Or maybe it's me." Becca settled the paper bag onto her lap.

"Here. Let me take that. You'll get grease on your dress." Jack's long arms easily set the bag onto the back seat—but not before his fingertips accidentally brushed her silk-covered knee. "I'm sure it's me, though I confess to not knowing why. Ian and I haven't seen each other in years."

"Is he married?"

Jack shrugged as he pressed the ignition button. "Not that I know of." He shifted the car into drive. "How about we go to Secret Beach and eat?"

"Secret Beach is fine."

They were quiet on the drive back through town. She wracked her brain for something, anything, to talk to Jack about. But her mind kept circling back to Ian. Of course, he knew what happened at the party. He'd probably told other people, too. Though if he had, then her parents would surely have heard and there was no way her mother wouldn't broach that subject.

"Becca?"

Jack's voice cut into her worrying. She hadn't noticed that he had parked the car and killed the engine.

"Sorry. I was … thinking."

"Thinking or overthinking?" He popped his seatbelt open, then turned back toward her. "I don't care if Ian has told people. I'm not embarrassed that I hooked up with you. Embarrassed that I didn't know what I was doing and therefore couldn't make it any good for you …"

She waved his concern away and he caught her hand midair.

"Just don't tell Ian how awful I was, okay?" he added.

When she lifted her gaze from their joined hands to his face, she saw the boyish mischief in his eyes. "Okay then, for the record," she smiled, "you were amazing. A true studmuffin—"

"Maybe not a studmuffin?"

She laughed. "A lady doesn't kiss and tell then. How's that?"

His lips halted her laughter. Immediately she knew this wasn't a kiss like the one in her mother's kitchen. This was a serious kiss, a confident kiss … a premeditated kiss. An oh-god-this-feels-so-good-don't-let-it-ever-stop kiss.

He pulled back just far enough to murmur, "I don't think there was any kissing to tell about, was there?"

"If you had kissed me like that, I'm sure I would remember."

She felt his lips curve against hers in a smile.

"I'm sure I didn't have that kind of kiss in me back then." His lips brushed hers again and made it official: every bone in her body now had the consistency of jelly. He sat back and, by the tiny flare of his nostrils, she could tell he was doing exactly what she was. Trying to get air into lungs.

"We should probably eat," he said, glancing at the Burger Barn bag in the back seat.

"Before it gets cold," she agreed—though Jack could probably reheat the fries just by looking at them.

They walked down the narrow gravel path in companionable silence, kicking off their shoes when they reached the sandy beach. She spread the blanket Jack kept in his car for emergencies —he was the son of a firefighter, after all—on the sand and they sat down. The breeze blowing in off the water was too mild to cool either the air around them or the heat his kiss had stoked in her body.

He opened the bag and they began to eat, the food not as cold as Becca expected. As hungry as she was, almost anything would have tasted good at that moment. The beach was empty, save for another couple sitting closer to the water—too engrossed in each other to notice Jack and Becca. She had come here with a boy or two in high school. When the beach was empty, people often did a little skinny dipping and the St. Caroline police tended to look the other way. Literally and figuratively.

"You're different than I thought you were in high school," she said, between sips of chocolate milkshake.

"Oh yeah? How's that?"

She considered her words for a moment. "I always thought you had a giant stick up your ass."

He clapped a hand over his mouth so he didn't spit his own milkshake all over the sand. When he stopped laughing, he said, "I did have a giant stick up my ass back then. You're absolutely right." He grew serious again. "Though I'm thinking that you maybe weren't quite the way I thought you were."

"What way was that?" Though Becca was all too aware of what people thought of her back then.

"Tough little girl, mad at the world."

Her laugh was soft, but laced with sadness too. "I really was that way back then. But I've grown up since. I mean, I'm still a whirling dervish of disaster, but at least now I'm not trying to be." She sipped at her milkshake. "It just seems to be my biggest natural talent."

"Being the opposite isn't always all it's cracked up to be."

"Why did you drop out of law school?"

"Didn't want to be a lawyer. That's a fairly common revelation among law students, actually."

"So what *do* you want to be?"

"What I want to be and what I'm allowed to be are two different things."

"You seem like the kind of person who could be anything you wanted. You're smart."

"I want to be a firefighter, but it would break my mother's heart."

"Because of your uncle."

He nodded. "I was volunteering with a fire department in California, but what I really want is a full-time position."

"Your father won't hire you?"

"Not for anything more than running around in a dalmatian costume."

"Well, I don't know what to do with my life either. I'm here for the summer until I pay back my parents' insurance deductible. After that, I don't know. The only two things I'm good at are tending bar and quilting."

She balled up the foil wrapper her burger came in, and Jack lifted it from her fingers. He dropped it into the paper bag, then lay back on the blanket. Becca joined him.

"The stars are out tonight," she said.

She felt the weight of his hand cover hers on the blanket.

"We were stupid kids," he said.

"We were."

"Can we pretend that never happened?" His fingers closed a little tighter around hers.

Becca thought of the scars on her stomach, and the little girl in Ohio. *Not really, no.*

"And then what?" she asked. She watched a spot of light move across the black ink of the sky. A plane headed off to somewhere. She swallowed a yawn. It was late, and this was turning into a serious conversation. One she was too tired to have.

"And then we're friends. So I don't have to spend all summer hanging out with my brother or Ian."

"Well. I wouldn't wish that on anyone." She closed her eyes for a moment. Agree to be friends with Jack? Sure, why not? She doubted his interest in being friends with her would last the entire summer anyway.

JACK LOOKED down at Becca's closed eyes and peaceful face. Had she just fallen asleep? He watched for another moment. Yup. She had. Her tiredness had been evident on her face when he picked her up earlier that evening. It sounded like she was burning the candle at both ends.

In sleep, though, her face was relaxed and smooth. Her fancy hairdo had started coming undone in the night breeze. Truth be told, he had never particularly liked waking up next to a woman. It made him claustrophobic, the weight of all the possible expectations that morning could bring—beyond just pancakes and coffee. But the idea of waking up next to Becca Trevor held a surprising appeal, and not just because she was so damn beautiful right now.

How had everyone not noticed how gorgeous she was before? How had it escaped his notice? That silky, cinnamon-colored hair ... her creamy skin, not a line or blemish in sight ... the long, graceful neck ... she wasn't just pretty for a town the size of St. Caroline. Becca would turn heads in San Francisco, for sure.

Jack had dated pretty girls before, even let some of them spend the night. But it wasn't just Becca's general loveliness that was slaying him tonight. When they were dancing ... it felt so completely, utterly right to have her in his arms.

He looked up and down the beach. The other couple was gone now, and it was just him and Becca. Alone. He stared out over the dark water of the bay. So much had happened in his life in the past seven years. And there was so much that hadn't happened. He was a different person, undeniably, but maybe not necessarily a better one. The more time he spent around Becca, the clearer it became that she had grown into a better person. Certainly, she was one of those people who could get more done in a week than most people accomplished in a month. She played a pretty good game of frisbee, too. He smiled into the darkness at the memory of her playing with Oliver's boys in her parents' backyard.

There was a centeredness about her. His own life was anything but centered these days. In fact, it felt as though everything was coming apart at the seams. His mom's cancer, his lack of direction, his inability to find something—anything—he wanted to do other than be a firefighter.

He lay back down on the blanket and rolled onto his side to watch her sleep. Did he remember thinking she was pretty that night at the party? He peered deep into the recesses of his brain, looking for such a memory. To be honest, his memories of that night weren't that sharp—and getting fuzzier the more time he spent around her. Maybe they were never that sharp to begin with. It wasn't like he had spent a lot of time thinking about it—or Becca—in the intervening years. Really, the clearest memory he had was of that damn sock monkey staring at him with those unseeing, plastic eyes.

He brushed the back of his hand against her smooth cheek, then looked down at her body stretched out beside him. The fabric of her dress was so pliable it outlined every line and curve of her figure. The gentle swell of her breasts, the flat plane of her stomach, the points of her hipbones. Maybe it was just as well that he couldn't recall any of that. She was damned hard to resist as it was.

He touched her cheek again and she stirred. "Hey sleepyhead," he said softly. "I think I should take you home."

CHAPTER 18

*B*ecca dropped red and white swizzle sticks into the tall glasses of bright blue liquid and slid the tray across the bar to the waitress. She ducked beneath the bar to open another box of swizzle sticks. The Yankee Doodle kids drink Mike had concocted was popular today. That Skipjack's was so busy on the Fourth of July surprised her. She remembered going to picnics and swimming as a child on the fourth, not eating out at a fancy resort. But she was glad for the hours.

When she stood up, swizzle sticks in hand, Jack was sitting there. She'd neither seen nor heard from him since the night of the hospital gala. The night she fell asleep on him at the beach. *Exciting date I am.*

"Hey there," he said. "Can I get one of those?"

She held out a swizzle stick. "Just this or do you want a drink to go with it?" He smiled and her heart stuttered a beat.

"I want one of those things you're giving all the kids."

"A Yankee Doodle?"

He nodded.

"There's no alcohol in it."

"I should hope not."

"Do you want me to put some in it? It would probably be good with a little rum."

"No, I want what the kids are getting."

She gave him a puzzled look, but set about making the drink for him. "What are you up to today?" She tried to keep her voice casual, as though she hadn't spent even one minute since Saturday night thinking about him. Or that kiss in his car. A kiss he had repeated when he took her home and walked her right up to the door of her parents' house.

No, she'd spent way more than one minute thinking about that. Hours, maybe. That tuxedo … how incredibly sexy his undone, bowtie-less shirt had looked at the Burger Bar … the way the breeze on the beach had toyed with the ends of his hair. Not that he didn't look pretty damn hot right now, wearing just a red polo shirt. He had a chest made for shirts, she thought.

"Besides chatting up pretty bartenders?" he answered.

She dropped a maraschino cherry into the tall glass, where it sunk for an instant and then bobbed back up to the surface. She set the drink down on a napkin in front of him. "Besides that."

"I'm taking Oliver's boys out on his boat to watch the fireworks from the bay. Serena's too queasy to go, and Oliver doesn't want to leave her home alone."

"That'll be fun. You'll get to see the Annapolis fireworks, too, if you're on the water."

Jack took a sip of his Yankee Doodle. His eyes widened. "Damn, that's sweet."

Becca laughed. "Hey, it's Mike's recipe."

"You should stick a toothbrush in here instead of a swizzle stick."

She plucked a suggestion card from the stack beneath the bar, and slapped it on the bar in front of him.

"Got a pen?"

She rolled her eyes but pulled her pen from the pocket of her skirt. He uncapped it and began to write.

"Give ... your ... bartender ... the night ... off," he recited as he wrote. He slid the card back to Becca, then held out the pen.

She stared at the card, not sure what to make of it.

"Actually, I came here looking for a pretty bartender to go see the fireworks with me."

Becca made a show of looking down toward the far end of the bar. "Mike'll be back from his break in a few minutes. You can ask him then. He's pretty handsome. But married, so that could be a problem."

"You've been talking to Mattie, eh?"

"No, why?"

"Apparently he told my parents that I was gay."

"Are you?"

He rolled his eyes. "I see my kiss goodnight did not communicate what I had hoped. Well, if you're not interested in helping to definitively establish my sexual orientation, maybe you can come along to help ensure that I return with both of my nephews intact."

"That's quite the sales pitch there." She topped off his Yankee Doodle.

"There might be fried chicken involved. And ice cream afterward. And if the sky stays clear, we might even get to see a little of the Baltimore show, too."

Becca pretended to consider his offer. Out of the corner of her eye, she saw the waitress approaching the bar with more drink orders. She had to make up her mind fast—though, really, what was there to decide? Did she want to see Jack again? Her better judgment cautioned that it wasn't the smartest idea.

But then again, she'd never been a person swayed by better judgment—or the smarter of two ideas.

"Well, when you throw all that in, how can a girl say no?"

∽

THE SUN SLIPPED below the horizon and the night air was alive with anticipation of that first sizzle and crack ... the flare of light you almost miss because your attention wandered for a moment ... then the sudden bloom of sparkling light overhead. Five-year-old Cam, wearing a bright orange PFD, was sprawled on a bunched-up blanket on the deck, sound asleep, lulled into dreamland by the gentle rocking of his father's boat. His older brother, Mason, was regaling Jack with his surprising knowledge of pyrotechnics.

"I hope they start with chrysanthemums," he said. "Those are my favorite. Then I like to see beehives to mix it up."

Becca smiled to herself as she gathered up the remains of their dinner—the promised fried chicken, Serena's quite excellent macaroni salad, an astounding number of juice boxes.

"The grand finale is usually peonies and comets launched one right after the other." Mason continued to describe his ideal fireworks show.

"What are the kind that do ..." Becca made an upward fluttering motion with her hands and fingers. "That go off in all different directions?"

Mason's face grew thoughtful for a moment. "I think you're talking about crosettes. They split up when they get to the top."

Mason was a smart kid. Articulate, too. Becca remembered Jack being like that when they were in elementary school. He was the kid who always had his hand up to answer a teacher's question, the kid who knew more about any given topic than was included in the lesson.

"How do you know all this?" Jack shot Becca a comically worried look.

"I saw a show on TV." The pride in Mason's voice was unmistakable.

"Well, it's not safe to play with fireworks. You know that, right?"

Mason nodded, casually brushing off his uncle's concern. "Dad won't even let us have sparklers."

"I think your dad is probably an expert about those kinds of things," Becca chimed in. She carried their dinner trash below deck. When she returned, Mason was still schooling Jack about fireworks.

"Sometimes they use forty-thousand shells in one show." Mason nodded his head and lifted his eyebrows to emphasize just how impressive that fact was. Becca didn't know Oliver all that well but Mason clearly had a lot of his uncle in him, too.

Becca leaned down into Jack's ear as she passed behind. "Kind of fitting that there's a budding firebug in your family," she whispered. She gracefully sidestepped the elbow Jack playfully poked back at her.

Just then, a high-pitched whistle split the night as the first shell took flight. Jack grabbed Mason as he leapt into the air in excitement. Cam woke up with a startled shriek, scrabbling to his feet in panic.

"BOOM!" Mason shouted in perfect synchrony with the firework's report. His brother wailed with fright.

"Mason, stay here," Jack said, then strode over to where Cam was pressing himself back into the boat's bench seat. "Hey dude, are you okay?"

"He's afraid of fireworks," Mason called over his shoulder. "BOOM!"

Becca heard Jack's muttered "Thanks for letting me know," barely audible beneath the noise of the fireworks bursting overhead. Jack perched his nephew on his knee and tried to talk him through it, but there was no consoling Cam. The boy kept his face hidden in Jack's red polo shirt, his small hands clenched into white-knuckled fists. Each wail and shriek was louder than the last. Jack looked up helplessly at Becca.

It had been obvious all evening that Mason and Cam were about as different as two people who shared common genetic material—and parents—could be. Becca imagined Mrs. Wolfe looking at Jack and Matt and thinking the exact same thing.

She sat down on the bench and lifted Cam onto her knee. "Hey there, Cam. You don't like fireworks?"

He shook his tear-streaked face.

"You know what? I don't really like them much myself. They're awful noisy, aren't they?"

Cam nodded again.

"I was thinking about going down below. Do you want to come with me?" She leaned into his ear and whispered. "I saw some brownies down there. I don't think Mason knows about them, so don't say anything."

When she leaned back, the terror in Cam's eyes had been replaced by a spark of conspiratorial interest. He looked over at his brother, who was engrossed in the fireworks and couldn't care less about what was happening behind him. Then Cam slid off Becca's knee. She stood and took his small hand in hers, then led him toward the short but steep set of stairs.

"Let me go first," she said and turned around to climb down the stairs backward, which was safer. When she was halfway down the short flight, she reached up for Cam. He turned around also and she grabbed him by the waist. She glanced over the edge of the deck, which was now at eye level, to look at Jack.

"Thank you," he mouthed, then went to join his other nephew.

"BOOM!" came Mason's voice, again.

Boom indeed.

MASON'S HEAD was heavy on Jack's shoulder as he carried him into Oliver's house. With his foot, he held the door open for Becca who was carrying a sleeping Cam. He wished he'd known that she didn't like fireworks; he wouldn't have invited her. He could have invited her on a real date instead, and not wasted whatever goodwill he had with her. It surprised him that Becca was afraid of fireworks as a kid. She didn't strike him as a person who was afraid of much.

Oliver was waiting inside and Jack handed off Mason to him. "Thanks for the heads-up about Cam," he said. He kept his voice low so he wouldn't wake Mason.

His brother grimaced. "I thought Serena would have told you."

Jack shook his head.

"Sorry about that."

"No worries," came Becca's quiet voice beside him. He turned and relieved her of Cam. He followed Oliver up the stairs to the boys' room. A few minutes later, they were back out in Jack's SUV.

"I think you're headed the wrong way," she said as he made a left turn at the next cross street.

"I promised you ice cream."

"Yeah, that was a little optimistic. Expecting the boys to last that long."

"I never expected they would." He looked over at Becca, but her expression was neutral, her face turned straight ahead. In addition to being surprised that she didn't like fireworks, he was surprised at how carefully she protected her thoughts.

He drove them to Kings Creamery, which sold homemade ice cream on the front side of the white clapboard building and operated a putt-putt golf course on the back. Even now, at ten-thirty, the putt-putt course was busy and the line for ice cream long.

"I haven't been here in years," Jack mused as he scanned the chalkboard list of the day's flavors. At his height, he could easily see over the entire line of people. Overhead, the white ceiling fans hummed and pushed around the warm air inside. A lock of hair had escaped Becca's ponytail. He lightly tucked it back behind her ear.

"Thanks." She turned and smiled at him.

The line inched forward and Jack thought about the fact that he was as close to Becca right now as he'd been since they danced at the hospital gala. Her red, white, and blue tie-dyed tank top left her shoulders bare and the nape of her neck exposed beneath her ponytail. He closed his eyes against the sight. The desire to kiss that nape, inhale the scent of her skin, wrap his arms around her was almost more than he could resist. He'd never been the sort of guy to fall hard and fast for a woman. But he was falling hard and fast for Becca Trevor. It made no sense. None whatsoever. He wasn't in town for good. And despite their agreement to behave as though the graduation party never happened, it had. He had acted abominably that night, and any self-respecting woman would hold it against him.

Resistance was futile, however. His hands settled on her bare shoulders and he leaned down until his head was next to hers. "So what are you thinking?"

"Mmm, black raspberry, maybe?" She made no attempt to shrug off his hands. "But the cookies and cream here is always good, too."

"We could get one of each and share." She smelled like sunscreen and salt, smelled like a beautiful summer day spent on the water. He wanted to return to the marina, take Oliver's boat back out on the water, and make love to her on the deck beneath the stars.

"We could," she said.

For a split second he thought she was replying to his thought of making love to her. But no, she was referring to the ice cream. Of course. Because after they had agreed that the graduation party never happened, they had also agreed to be friends. *Friends. You idiot.* His brother, Matt, would never make that kind of bone-headed mistake.

"Let's do it then," he said as they stepped up to the head of the line.

"One large black raspberry and one large cookies and cream," Becca ordered.

"Cup or cone?" the girl working behind the counter asked.

Becca looked toward Jack. "Cup or cone?"

"Whichever you want." He was surprised, though, when she turned back to the counter and asked for cones. Not that he minded sharing a cone with her. He was certainly not overly squeamish that way. But it was ... *intimate.*

And he wanted intimate.

She pulled out her wallet to pay.

"No, no. Let me get it."

She handed a twenty to the girl behind the register. "You bought dinner." When the first girl held their filled cones over the counter, Becca nodded toward Jack. He took one cone in each hand as she slipped her change back into her purse. Outside, the tables on the small porch were full so they headed for a spot on the lawn beneath a large old maple tree. He let Becca sit first, then handed her the black raspberry cone and sat down right next to her. He stretched his legs out alongside hers.

They spent several minutes trading cones back and forth, and watching people come and go. The lights illuminating the putt-putt course gave the area a weird daytime feel despite the late hour. He heard Becca take the first bite into one of the cones.

"How are things coming along with Quilt Therapy?" he asked. Jack had never worked retail, nor anyone in his family, but even he knew that reopening a store in the middle of the busiest season was a tough task.

She licked ice cream from her lower lip. Just the sight of that one small action fired every neuron in Jack's brain. They were all screaming *kiss kiss kiss!* With the boys around, he hadn't been able to kiss Becca on the boat. Mason and Cam were sound asleep at home now, though. And damn but he wanted to kiss her.

"We're doing a soft open on Friday," she answered his question, a question he'd practically forgotten he asked. "The grand re-opening is Saturday. Things aren't entirely ready, but mom and Cassidy don't want to wait too long. July and August are the big months for summer customers." She held up crossed fingers. "I guess we'll see how it goes."

They traded cones again.

"How's your mom?" Her question was quiet, wary— the way everyone was around him these days. Unsure of whether they should really bring this up, but not wanting to pretend like they didn't see the elephant in the middle of the room. Actually, it was more like a bomb than an elephant—ticking louder and louder with each passing day. Jack could barely take his eyes off it.

He shrugged in answer to her question. "She's getting weaker. I can see it."

"I'm sorry." A drop of melted ice cream fell onto Becca's knee. She ignored it. "How are you guys holding up?"

He stared at the grass, the thousands of blades of grass that lay between his crossed legs and hers. It seemed so simple, grass. It grew easily. Came up every summer. It would sprout up again next summer, and the summer after that. And every summer for the rest of his life.

But this was the last summer his mother would be here. He fought the urge to curse at God again.

He took a deep breath, held it in his lungs before letting it out again. Not that it really helped. "We're okay, I guess. Or not okay, but there's nothing to be done about it."

"I'm sorry, Jack."

Her hand lighted on his bare knee. Just that single touch— soft, gentle, warm—quieted the storming neurons in his brain.

"I can't imagine what you're going through," she added.

He covered her hand with his, and in that moment he felt safe. Like nothing that lay ahead would destroy him.

Then a different thought occurred to him. Maybe Becca was God's way of distracting him this summer. Maybe she was the answer to all his requests for help. *That's using her, dammit.* He felt

Becca lean into him and dear lord, it felt so good—even as his brain protested the wisdom of his next move. But he was power-less to stop his hand from lifting off hers, powerless to keep his arm from encircling her shoulders and pulling her close against his ribs. *Don't make me fall for her and then rip it all away! Aren't you torturing me enough already? I'm going to be struck down by lightning for arguing with you, aren't I? Or hit by a bus. A church bus, right? You know what? Do it. Take me instead. Leave my mom.*

He felt her small body relax into him, then the gentle pulsing of her breathing as she inhaled and exhaled beneath his arm. "I can't imagine it myself."

CHAPTER 19

$\mathcal{B}$ecca leaned against one of the long cutting tables and watched as Quilt Therapy filled with customers—some new, many old. The day of Quilt Therapy's grand re-opening was here, and already the shop was a beehive of activity. Charlotte stood on the sidewalk outside, handing out free fat quarter bundles of fabric to anyone who walked up to the shop. Becca spent four hours yesterday helping Charlotte cut and tie the bundles.

Behind Becca, the shelves Jack helped put up were filled end to end with hundreds of bolts of fabric. Solids and prints. Reproduction fabrics and more contemporary designs. Natalie had arranged everything by fabric line and color. With the shop open again, she was back in her element and doing what she did best: helping customers find the right fabrics for their quilting projects.

On the other side of the large front room stood the new quilting frame. Stretched across the frame was a simple strip quilt awaiting the needles and hands of the shop's volunteers. Natalie and Cassidy had pieced the top. There hadn't been time to piece a more complex top, but Michelle thought it more

163

important to have something—anything—on the frame for the re-opening.

Becca pushed herself away from the cutting table, ready to head upstairs to the shop's new classroom. On her way to the staircase, she peered into the back room, where the notions and thread were displayed. Her mother was waxing poetic about the virtues of some new English quilting needles they were stocking for the first time.

"Best I've ever used," she said over and over to each person who stopped. Becca had given them a try, too. Her mother was absolutely right. They were heavenly needles.

At the top of the stairs, she felt her phone vibrate in her pocket. She pulled it out to see a Facebook notification on the screen. It was a friend request from Sylvia, the child psychologist whom she'd met at the quilter's retreat. The one with the estranged son and granddaughter she was making a baby quilt for. Becca tapped her finger on "confirm request" and started to slip the phone back into her phone. Then she stopped and pulled it back out. As she headed into the shop's classroom, she scrolled through her newsfeed, looking for posts she shouldn't be looking for ... posts she'd been looking for way too often lately. This was why she had made a point of staying off social media as much as she could—she knew once she let her guard down, she wouldn't be able to stop.

It didn't take long to come to one of Shari's posts. "Birthday party for Sophia at the waterpark!" In the photo, a gaggle of girls lounged around a pool on giant round floats. Becca zoomed in on the picture with her fingers. Jacqueline Michelle was in the center of the group, wearing a navy one-piece swimsuit, her hair in a long wet braid, squinting and grinning happily at the camera. The picture took Becca back almost twenty years, to pool outings with her sisters—long, lazy afternoons that ended with them all tanned and waterlogged.

Her thumb hovered over her phone. She didn't "like" Shari's

photos, as a matter of course. It had been Shari's idea for them to be "friends" online, but it made Becca uncomfortable to be a visible presence. It was an open adoption but she felt she owed it to Shari to leave her alone.

Her thumb tapped the screen. *You and 16 other people liked this.*

She slipped the phone back into the pocket of her Bermuda shorts before anyone else came upstairs. She was supposed to run demonstrations on hand quilting and improvisational piecing in the classroom today. Everything was set up and ready to go—sample squares of fabric and batting for people to practice hand quilting, and large cutting boards for the improv piecing.

Her phone buzzed in her pocket again. She pulled it out, her eyes widening at the name on the screen. *No no no.* She couldn't accept a friend request from Jack. She couldn't risk him seeing a photo of Jacqueline Michelle. There was very little physical resemblance between Becca and their daughter; no one would guess the relationship. But Jack ... that was a different matter. He and Jacqueline Michelle shared hair color and height. Maybe he wouldn't notice. But maybe he would.

Back into her pocket the phone went, and just in time as footsteps and excited chatter sounded on the stairs. A moment later, Cassidy appeared with four of the shop's long-time customers, women Becca had known since she was knee high to a grasshopper.

"There she is!" one of the women cried out, holding her arms out for a hug.

"See, I told you she was back in town," Cassidy said.

Becca allowed each woman to hug her, in turn.

"So grown up!"

"Love this hair color." Tug on Becca's ponytail.

"Oh look at this stitching, will you? This is insane."

One of the women picked up a sample Becca had created for her hand quilting demo.

"Are you home for good?"

Becca was brought up short by that question, though it was one she should have expected. "For awhile, maybe," she waffled.

"She's thinking about taking some classes at the college in the fall," Cassidy interjected. "Right?"

Becca shrugged. "Maybe. If I get in." Truth be told, the thought of staying in St. Caroline beyond the summer felt sort of … lonely. The off-season had always felt that way to her when she was younger. With the summer people gone, the town felt smaller and even quieter. And whom did she know here other than her parents and sisters? Tamara Rossi. Jack. And Jack was leaving town soon, too.

Suddenly, the thought of being in St. Caroline without Jack felt very lonely.

"You'll get in," one of the women said. "You're a smart girl, Becca. Now show us this improvisational piecing. Your mother said we'll all be making art quilts by the end of the summer."

Becca spent the rest of the day conducting demonstrations in the classroom. Charlotte brought her a chicken salad sandwich and bottle of iced tea just after one o'clock, but the sandwich went untouched. She never even got hungry.

"Having fun?" Her mother appeared at her side.

Becca nodded. She *was* having fun, actually. More fun than she could remember having in years. Life with Brandon hadn't exactly been a barrel of monkeys. But today, she could practically feel herself glowing. Teaching was giving her some kind of endorphin rush, and it felt good. No, better than good. Downright amazing.

A fortyish woman sidled up to the table to check out the quilts spread out as examples on the table. They were all art quilts—not traditional patterns like Ohio Star or 54-40 or Fight —but freeform landscapes and outright abstract designs. They were smaller, too, made to be hung on a wall, not draped over a bed. These were the kind of quilts Becca most loved to create. No points to match up or seams to align. Both her mother and

Natalie were all about the precision. Becca was about going with the flow, enjoying the journey as much as the destination.

The woman studied the quilts carefully. Becca couldn't tell whether she approved or disapproved. Some people just didn't like art quilts. She tried sizing up the woman, to steel herself for a negative reaction. In her expensive clothes, she was clearly a summer or weekend resident. Becca knew fabric and could spot high-end from a mile away. The woman wore a sleeveless silk blouse that buttoned down the front and was tucked neatly into crisp linen shorts. Expensive linen, unlike the cheap stuff Becca was wearing. The woman's hair was a medium brown shade but expertly threaded through with gold highlights. Also not cheap.

"These are beautiful quilts," the woman said at long last.

Becca fought the urge to let out her breath in one long, theatric sigh.

"All made by my daughter here," her mother replied, holding out her hand in greeting. "I'm Michelle Trevor, owner of Quilt Therapy. This is Becca."

The woman shook Becca's hand, too. "Wendi Brown. Nice to meet both of you."

"Are you a quilter?" Michelle asked.

"Used to be. Don't have time anymore." Wendi laughed. "Doesn't stop me from buying fabric, though. I stopped in to ask if you know of anyone who does commissions?"

Michelle gave Becca a meaningful look. Quilt commissions? Becca had no idea what to even charge. But the idea was undeniably appealing. She could pay off her parents' insurance deductible much quicker.

"What kind of commissions?" she asked.

Wendi glanced down at Becca's quilts. "I'm moving my company into a new office building where we are the only tenant. I want to hang art quilts in the lobby. I've got a lot of wall space and it's a very modern interior. I was thinking quilts might warm it up."

"So you're talking large quilts." Becca extended her arms.

"Yes. Right. Colorful and abstract were my thoughts. I saw the Gee's Bend exhibit in New York a few years back."

Becca nodded. "We went up to see that too." The entire Trevor family had taken the train from Washington to New York. A family pilgrimage. The quilts were made by four generations of African-American women in the town of Gee's Bend, Alabama, and had as much in common with modern art as with quilting.

The woman unzipped her leather purse and fished out a business card. She handed it to Becca. "You're very talented. Call me if you're interested."

~

THE CANDLE'S scent assaulted Jack's nose the instant he pushed open the door to his parents' house. It was the apple pie candle. *I'm a man. I shouldn't be able to identify candles without reading the damn label.* But he could. This one had a smoky cinnamon odor that gave way to a sharper fruity tang after the second inhale.

Still, it didn't entirely mask what it was intended to. Not for Jack, anyway. Not for anyone who spent any amount of time in the house.

The smell of sickness.

He swallowed the urge to argue with God again.

A man's voice was coming from the sunroom, where his mother spent her days. She tired easily now and his father had set up the sunroom so everything she might need was within a few steps. It was shocking how quickly she was deteriorating.

Take me instead.

Yet every morning, he woke up on the sleeper sofa in Matt's cabin, his back aching from the worn-out cushions and sprung springs.

He found Dan Trevor in the sunroom with his mother. It must be the Trevors' day to feed his parents. The town seemed to have set up a schedule for dropping off meals. The woman who had fed him and his brothers for years could no longer stand long enough to cook a simple meal.

When I get to the pearly gates, I'm going to ... Who was he kidding? Threatening the Almighty wasn't going to put him within spitting distance of the pearly gates.

"Hey there, Jack." Dan held out his hand and Jack shook it. Then Jack leaned over his mom and kissed her cheek. Even her skin smelled different now. Maybe that was nature's way of preparing him for what was coming.

Nature, you hear? Atheism had been on his mind lately. *Because you don't exist. If you did, this wouldn't be happening.* He began to straighten but his mother cupped his head with her hand and weakly pulled him back down. She pressed her dry lips to his cheek. He closed his eyes. *You are not going to see me cry.*

Benevolent God, my ass.

He pulled back to stand with Dan, but the expression on his mother's face said that she had caught his distress.

"How were the fireworks out on the water?" Dan asked. "You know, I've never seen them from out there."

"They were good. It's a good place to watch them from."

"Becca must have loved that. She's like a little kid when it comes to fireworks. Adores them. Always has."

Jack thought back to the boat. Had Becca seen any of the fireworks?

"Mason said Cam got scared and stayed below deck with Becca," his mother said.

"Yeah, I'm afraid she didn't get to see much," he admitted. "I didn't realize Cam had a problem with them."

"Well, I'm sure Becca didn't mind much. She's always been good with kids. She was the shop's unofficial babysitter while the moms shopped." Dan chuckled and looked at his watch. "I've got to get back to the office."

"Thanks for dinner," Angie said.

She barely got the words out before the fire department pager on the side table squawked. The dispatcher's voice barked out an address. All three of them cocked their heads to listen.

"Isn't that—" she started to say.

"The Secretary of State's house," Dan finished her sentence. "Mona Barrett and her husband."

"Hope it's a false alarm," Jack ventured quietly.

No such luck. A minute later, another call came over the pager.

"They're calling for mutual aid," his mother said, just as quietly.

Jack's muscles sprang into high alert. St. Caroline was calling in other fire departments for help. For a high profile person's home.

"I'm heading out there," he said without thinking. Then he looked at his mother. "If you're okay, that is."

She waved him off. "Go see what's going on."

JACK COULD SEE the plumes of thick, dark smoke before he even hit the edge of town. The Barretts' house was a stately old home sitting on a lush green lawn that sloped gently down to the waterfront. The type of home you expected to belong to an important person—which Mona Barrett certainly was. Even in the universe of important people who owned property in St. Caroline, she was impressive.

The Barretts' house was built in the nineteenth century. Those older homes tended to burn more slowly than newer construction, but the amount of smoke Jack was seeing was not a good sign. He parked his car a good ways down the road to stay out of the way of the fire trucks arriving from other nearby towns. Most of those towns were as small as St. Caroline, though, and some not nearly as well off. Annapolis was bigger, but an hour away.

He walked slowly along the road, sizing up the scene as he went. One end of the house was nearly fully engulfed and he wondered what had sparked a fire that spread that quickly. The smoke got thicker as he drew closer, and small particles of debris floated in the air. He lifted up the hem of his tee shirt to cover his mouth and nose.

His leg muscles quivered in readiness. The pull of the fire was strong. He wanted to be in there with his dad and brothers. He didn't mind donning the Max the Fire Dog costume and going to the local summer camps to talk about fire safety, or helping to plan the fall fundraisers. But it was hard to stand by and watch when they so clearly needed all the help they could get.

It took hours but by four in the afternoon, the fire was out and the trucks from the other towns began to load up and leave. He watched as his father, clearly exhausted and overheated, peeled off some of his gear. The St. Caroline firefighters were a quiet bunch as they decided who would stay for awhile longer, just to make sure the fire didn't reignite. Without a word, Jack retreated to his car down the road. He was never in the mood to chat after a fire like this. He respected that the others probably weren't either.

Putting out a large fire was a humbling experience. There was so much one couldn't control, and so many things that could go wrong no matter how prepared the crews were. A change in wind direction ... unknown structural problems in a building ... plain old bad luck. And when it was over, Jack always crashed from the rush of adrenaline straight into utter exhaustion.

Back at the station, he helped the guys clean the trucks and put away equipment. His father headed straight to his office, and closed the door. Within minutes, he was on the phone, his head resting heavily in his hand.

"I don't even want to think about who's on the other end." Matt clapped Jack on the shoulder. "Thanks for the help."

"I could help more."

"So come with me to pick up the sandwiches Ollie called into the deli." Matt headed for the open bay door. Jack followed. Outside, it was hot and sticky—typical Eastern Shore summer weather—but even a slight breeze would have been welcome after the fire.

"I can help more than that," Jack said as he yanked open the passenger side door of Matt's pickup.

"Yeah, you can do my laundry for me." Matt laughed as he turned the key in the ignition.

On his phone, Jack pulled up the web page for the fire department in California, scrolling until he found the list of volunteers. When Matt pulled the truck into a parking spot in front of the deli, Jack handed over his phone. His brother's eyes widened in surprise, then settled into a gaze of respect Jack didn't often see from Matt.

"Dad know this?"

"Yes. But he won't send me on calls."

"What about mom?"

Jack shook his head. "No. I haven't told her. And dad said he won't."

"Uncle Jackie …"

"I know, all right?" Jack knew he should feel honored to be named after his uncle. His uncle had been his mother's twin, and Tim Wolfe's best friend since childhood.

His uncle was twenty-eight when he died—only three years older than Jack was now. It was completely understandable why his mother wanted one person in the family doing something other than running into burning buildings. But there was nothing else Jack wanted to do more.

He and Matt picked up the sandwiches and returned to the station. Jack leaned against a truck and ate while he watched his father through the glass window of his office door. He was still on the phone. For the first time, Jack noticed how deep the wrinkles were on his father's face. He looked older than fifty-five. His wife's illness was taking its toll. At long last, Tim Wolfe ended the call and rubbed his temples. Jack waited a moment, then knocked on the door. His father waved him in.

"That was the governor," his father said without even being asked.

Not a good sign.

"Put me on a crew," Jack said matter-of-factly.

His father shook his head.

"It makes no sense when you're calling in mutual aid and you have someone right here who can help."

"We still would have needed mutual aid today. One more person wouldn't have prevented that."

"What did the governor want?"

"He said that, with all the dignitaries who own property here, St. Caroline has to be more than just a small town fire department. I told him we only have a small town budget because dignitaries contest their property tax bills every year."

"What did he say to that?"

"What do you think he said? He's the person they call when our property assessor gives them a number they don't like."

Jack leaned over his father's desk, his weight heavy on his hands for emphasis. "Add me to the department. You don't have to pay me, even. But you're short-staffed already."

He locked eyes with his father. There were other words he wanted to say, but held back. *I'm not a kid anymore. Let me make my own decisions.* "You're putting other people at risk because you don't have enough personnel," he said quietly, continuing to hold his father's gaze. "And no one else is going to walk in off the street and be immediately trained like I am."

Finally, his father broke Jack's stare and looked over his shoulder. Jack was sure Matt and Oliver were out there, watching the standoff. Jack straightened up, sensing that he had won.

"Fine. And I will pay you." His father pushed back from his desk. "I'll tell your mother."

"No, I'll do it."

CHAPTER 20

*B*ecca's fiberglass paddle sliced into the dark water of the cypress swamp. Behind her in the tandem kayak sat Jack, his paddle doing most of the work as they glided beneath a low ceiling of leaves. This was their first real date, as in a date the two of them had agreed to and set up. No parents involved this time.

They picked up the kayak and paddles at Oliver's house, said hello to Serena and the boys, and then drove the hour and a half to Snow Hill. She had to admit, she'd been more than a little skeptical when Jack suggested kayaking in a swamp. For starters, she had never kayaked before. And, while she had heard of the bald cypress swamps in Maryland, they didn't sound like a place she'd want to spend an afternoon exploring.

She was wrong, a fact she admitted to herself within the first five minutes. The swamp was like nothing she'd ever seen before, like a place from a movie. The big, ribbed tree trunks rising from the river ... their long branches stretching like arms across the water ... the heavy green canopy of leaves that blocked nearly all the light. The swamp was dark and quiet, the only sounds those of the wind whispering through the leaves and the almost imperceptible splash of their paddles dipping in and out of the water.

Imperceptible until Becca's paddle smacked Jack's paddle with a loud crack.

"Sorry!" she yelped and a large white bird, hidden from view until that moment, spread its wings and lifted off from the shore. "I guess I lost the rhythm. I wasn't paying attention. Sorry." She glanced back over her shoulder at Jack, expecting to see a look of annoyance on his face. Instead, his face was perfectly calm and composed.

"No worries."

"I'm not that coordinated."

She felt the touch of his fingers on her shoulder blade. "You don't need to paddle at all, if you don't want to. I can do it."

She let her paddle rest across the rim of the boat's cockpit. Water dripped onto her bare thighs, prickling her skin into goose bumps.

"Thanks for bringing me here," she said quietly. She felt his fingers brush her shoulder again. It was almost magical—the swamp *and* his touch.

"This was always my zen place. In a kayak on the water."

"You never seemed like the kind of person who needed a zen place."

She felt him smoothly steer the kayak around the knobby knees of the cypress trunks that jutted up from the water.

"Everyone needs a zen place."

His voice was deep and comforting. Had she ever noticed that before? She could picture him as a lawyer, standing in a courtroom and addressing the judge and jury. People would believe everything he said.

"Quilting is my zen place. Guess that's not a place, though."

"The zen is probably more important than the location."

After a few more minutes of quiet paddling, she asked about

the fire at the Secretary of State's property. It was the talk of the town, even at Quilt Therapy. "I wasn't there. I swear."

His voice broke into an amused chuckle. "You were on Oliver's boat, too, and we weren't set ablaze by any fireworks."

"True. Maybe the presence of a firefighter cancelled me out."

"Why didn't you tell me you love fireworks? I would have gone below with Cam."

"Who told you that?" She lifted her paddle again and dipped it into the water.

"Your dad. He was dropping off a casserole at my parents' house the other day."

"Oh. Most people like fireworks, don't they? Not the end of the world if I miss one year."

"You missed the chance to see them from the water. You might not be in St. Caroline next year."

"You might not, either," she countered. *Almost certainly won't be.* "So what caused the fire at the Barretts'?" Time to change the subject. Where Jack was going to be next summer shouldn't matter to her. *Didn't* matter, she mentally corrected herself.

"A cigarette. Apparently someone tossed one into a bush next to the house."

"Hmm. Sounds like Max the Fire Dog needs to do some more educational presentations." There was a playful poke in her side.

"My father's promoted me to a paid firefighter for the summer."

"I thought your—"

"I haven't told her yet. But the department is short-staffed and he's getting a lot of grief from the governor over the Barretts' fire."

"What could your father have done differently?"

"Not much, probably. But it doesn't look good to be short-staffed. St. Caroline's in a bit of a bind. We don't really have the year-round population to justify a larger fire department, but the summer residents expect a big city level of service."

"And after the summer?"

He was quiet for a long while. Becca waited. What kind of answer did she want to hear? There was no long-term potential between them, unless they could be intimate only in the dark where he couldn't see the scars from her pregnancy. On the other hand, spending time with Jack was … easy. Brandon was so much work all the time. His moods had to be managed. It was like walking on eggshells; she never knew what was going to crack the peace.

Jack wasn't like that. Everything about him said calm, steady, levelheaded. She would miss him when he went back to California. Miss him as a friend.

But even being just friends seemed unrealistic, given the secret she was keeping from him. What kind of friendship was based on that?

"After the summer," Jack's answer interrupted her thoughts. "I don't know. I can't even imagine what it's going to be like."

He wasn't talking about his career options or staying on at the St. Caroline fire department. If they weren't squeezed into these two separate cockpits on the kayak, she would have turned around and wrapped her arms around him. He was in so much pain over his mother's illness, Becca wanted to just take it all away.

She looked back at him over her shoulder. His face was still composed, but tighter. He wasn't in his zen place anymore.

"When I think of leaving St. Caroline," he went on, "I think of going back to my normal life. But life isn't going to be normal again, no matter where I am."

Keeping one hand on her paddle, Becca reached her other hand back toward him. He took her offered hand in his and an odd sensation shot up her arm. She felt comfortable with Jack. Connected to him. Maybe it was just that she'd had his DNA in her body seven years ago, had grown his child—their child—in her womb. Maybe he was forever imprinted on her.

But that didn't explain the heated look she was seeing in his eyes right now. Or the fact that he hadn't let go of her hand.

"The minute we're out of this kayak, I am kissing the everloving hell out of you," he said, his face still composed. "Just so you know."

And he did. He expertly navigated the long boat up to the shore where his car was parked in the small lot. He climbed out, then took Becca's paddle from her, and then took her hand to help her onto shore. He leaned over to lift the boat from the water. Becca stepped back to make way for him to carry the boat over to the car. Instead, he simply set the kayak on the ground and turned to her.

"You can say 'no.'" His long fingers wrapped around her biceps and pulled her into him. She looked up into his eyes, which were no longer a milky shade of chocolate, but dark with determination and desire. She knew that if she said "no," he would respect that. His fingers would uncurl from her arms. He would step away from her. She would no longer feel the heat of his chest wrapping around her shoulders, her ribcage.

"Yes." The word came out more firmly, more confidently, than the whispered permission she had intended.

Her heart fluttered wildly as he lowered his head to hers. Someone moaned at the first touch of their lips together. "Someone" was her. That tiny sound unleashed something in both of them, and she reached her hand behind his head, threaded her fingers into his soft blonde hair. She felt a strong hand on her lower back, pressing her hips into his. The kiss deepened and it was like the ground beneath her feet opened up and she dropped into it, weightless and untethered. He kissed her and kissed her, then kissed her some more. When it was over, they clung to each other, breathless and stunned, next to the cypress swamp with its eerie, sun-dappled gloom and trees' knees. He cupped her head gently against his hard chest, and Becca knew she had just found her zen place.

~

JACK'S PAGER went off the minute his car crossed the town line. He swallowed the groan that rose up in his throat. There went his plan to take Becca out to lunch. But after demanding that his father send him out on calls, he couldn't very well be annoyed— even if the fire he really wanted to attend to right now was the one raging in his body. He doubted the feel of her lips parting beneath his was going to fade anytime soon.

He hoped not.

He listened as the dispatcher relayed the details. Bay Acres Nursing Home. He looked at Becca, sitting in the passenger seat. The Trevors' house wasn't exactly on the way to the station. She was realizing that, too.

"I can walk to the shop from the firehouse," she said.

"You sure?" Not that he had much choice. He couldn't afford to be the last one there.

"No problem. I'm sure someone at the shop will give me a ride home." She smiled broadly at him, which did absolutely nothing to put out his own personal fire.

At the station, he gave her a quick peck on the lips then ran inside to suit up and jump in the engine. Matt was waiting in the driver's seat.

"How'd the kayaking go?" Matt inquired as he pulled the engine out onto the street. "Anyone go in?"

"No. And it was fine."

"Just 'fine?' You're quite the loverboy there, bro." Matt rolled his eyes.

"If you weren't driving, I'd hit you right now."

"Just kidding, Jack. Chill. It's not like you and Becca haven't …"

Jack's head spun to look hard at his brother's profile. "Haven't what?"

"Hooked up."

Jack remained quiet, studying Matt's face. "We've only gone out a few times."

Matt chuffed out his breath, and Jack couldn't tell whether it was a laugh or a snort of derision. "You know what I'm talking about."

"Who told you that?" Jack already knew the answer to that question, or hoped he did.

"Ian. Apparently he was there?"

"Not *there* there."

"Yeah, I should hope not. I wouldn't want to watch your scrawny ass—"

Jack socked his brother in the upper arm, million dollar fire engine be damned. "Is this common knowledge around town?"

Matt shoved Jack's fist away. "I don't know, man. What does it matter? I doubt she told anyone. She moved away that summer. Maybe she was too embarrassed to stick around." He jerked out his elbow. "Don't make me pull this truck over."

Matt pulled the engine up to the Bay Acres Nursing Home, a sprawling one-story brick building. Jack and Matt were directed to help evacuate residents. It was a kitchen fire and not big enough to likely spread, but the safety of the residents was paramount. As he quickly pushed a gentleman in a wheelchair down the hall, he remembered his mom saying there was no way they could ever put her in a nursing home unless it had high speed internet and a bookmobile came by every other day. And they brought her a cappuccino from Two Beans every morning.

The crazy thing was, his father would have done all that and more. His father would have been one of those spouses who moved into the nursing home too, just to be with his wife. Jack wanted that kind of relationship. His father was right—he was different from his brothers. Mattie? It was hard to imagine him ever settling down. Oliver? He had a good, stable marriage with Serena and they were awesome parents to Mason and Cam. But if there was a spark there, Jack had never been able to see it. Oliver seemed to have been born middle-aged.

Jack wanted a woman who took his breath away, a woman he couldn't keep his hands off of, a woman he couldn't stop daydreaming about. As he went back inside to fetch another resident, he tried not to count up all the hours he'd spent daydreaming about Becca Trevor. They were the unlikeliest pair, weren't they? And yet being with her felt so right. Easy. Relaxing. Like he didn't have to impress her or worry that she was judging him.

Which maybe meant they were more friends than anything else. Except she had let him kiss the everloving hell out of her at the swamp. She had kissed him back, too.

CHAPTER 21

*B*ecca sat in the comfortable upholstered chair in her bedroom, her lap and legs completely covered by Jack's wedding quilt. A hoop stretched the section of the quilt she was working on. It was late afternoon and she was back in her zen place, her real zen place—not in Jack Wolfe's arms. That could never be it, as good as it had felt to be there that morning.

And it had felt *really* good. Scary good.

She rocked the tiny quilting needle back and forth through the quilt top, taking several small stitches and then pulling the thread through. And then repeating the motion over and over, as though she were in a trance. Quilting was her safe place, as well. She could do this. Here, lost in a quilt, she was competent. She knew what she was doing. With Jack Wolfe, she was out of her depth.

Sure, she had dated men before. Lived with Brandon for over a year. But none of them had been serious prospects for settling down—and that had been okay because she'd been too young to settle down. But Jack Wolfe …? Any woman would be lucky to settle down with him. Only she could never be that woman. She'd have to make up some story to explain away the c-section scar on her stomach. *Brandon had gotten her pregnant and then she had miscarried late in the pregnancy.* Except her parents and sisters knew she hadn't been pregnant in recent years. As far as they knew, she had never been pregnant. And a lie like that was hardly a good basis for a relationship, especially one with a man like Jack.

A good man.

"Hey there."

She yelped and felt a sharp prick in her finger. She jerked it away from the quilt so she wouldn't bleed on the white fabric. Then she looked up. The good man himself was standing in her doorway, looking good enough to eat. His blonde hair was damp ... his shoulders broad beneath his green polo golf shirt ... his hips narrow beneath the leather braided belt looped through his shorts.

"You look nice," she said.

"I'd say the same for you but, honestly, I can't tell whether you even have anything on under all that."

If the innuendo in his words hadn't fired the deep blush soaking her cheeks, the unmistakable innuendo in his smile would have. She secured the quilting needle in the fabric then lifted the quilt from her body to reveal the rolled up denim shorts she was wearing and now-wrinkled linen blouse.

"Darn," he said. Then he laughed. "If you blush any more, your face is going to burst into flames."

"I think there's a fire extinguisher in the kitchen." But something in his eyes said he wasn't interested in extinguishing what he was starting. "To what do I owe the pleasure of your visit? And do my parents know you're here? Or did you sneak in the back?"

"Your mother told me I could come up."

He took a step into the room and sat on the edge of her bed. And didn't that fire up all sorts of ideas? Becca tried not to go there.

"I didn't get to buy you lunch," he went on. "So I'm here to offer dinner. Something nicer than the Burger Barn."

She looked down at her shorts and wrinkled shirt. "I'm not dressed for anything nicer than the Burger Barn."

"So put on a cute dress and meet me downstairs."

Her mouth fell open. This was a new side of Jack Wolfe—one she kind of liked. Flirty. Unexpected.

Five minutes later, Becca did meet him downstairs in a button-down linen dress and strappy sandals, her hair pulled up into a loose chignon. Jack was discussing major league baseball standings with her dad, but he looked over as soon as she appeared.

"Is Skipjack's okay?" he asked. "Just kidding. I got us a table at the Blue Crab."

"Have her back by ten, son," her father said. Her mother elbowed him in the ribs, and he winked at Becca. "Just kidding." He made a shooing motion at Becca and Jack. "Just have her home by tomorrow evening."

"Hmm, you have quite a generous curfew," Jack murmured as they walked down the driveway to his car.

"Don't get any ideas."

"Too late for that." He opened the passenger side door for her. "Way too late."

"Inside or out?" the hostess at the Blue Crab Bistro asked.

Becca looked at Jack. "Do you have a preference?" He shook his head. "Outside then," Becca replied.

They followed the waitress through the crowded restaurant and out into the back courtyard. Becca tried her best to ignore the little voice in her head. *You chose outside because it's more romantic.* But it was impossible to ignore the truth of that, because the Blue Crab Bistro's brick-walled courtyard, softly lit by gas sconces, was one of the most romantic spots in all of St. Caroline. Countless marriages had begun with a proposal right here.

She hoped Jack wasn't aware of that particular fact.

The waitress led them to a table near the back. Most of the tables in the courtyard were big enough for only two people, and spaced far enough apart to allow for private conversation. Jack pulled out Becca's chair for her, then the waitress handed them menus.

Jack looked around before opening his. "I've never been back here. Can you believe that? It's … quaint. I feel like I should be plotting the overthrow of the crown."

They ordered drinks—white wine for her, a beer on tap for him. The waitress brought out a basket of warm bread and butter. They ordered their meals—salmon salad for her, the pecan-crusted trout for him. Then Becca held her breath in anticipation of the awkward silence she was sure was about to happen. The hospital gala? That was an arranged date. Kayaking this morning? Fun, but hard to converse with one person sitting behind the other in a boat. Right now? This was the most date-like date so far. She feared that, once he realized how date-like this really was, he'd see better of the whole idea. The two of them dating? Two people who weren't planning to stay in St. Caroline forever? It was a crazy notion. What made sense was a good old-fashioned summer fling, a fun romp between two people that would end on Labor Day.

But a summer fling was out of the question for them.

The awkward silence never came, though, because Jack jumped right into the breach. "How long are you going to end up spending on that quilt my mom made?"

"Your wedding quilt?"

It was faint—oh so faint—but Becca detected it. The sudden pink tinge to Jack's cheeks.

"Yes. How much of your time is that taking? I'm just curious, that's all."

"Probably twenty, maybe twenty-five hours. Your mom wanted outline quilting—meaning it just follows the seams. So I don't have to spend time marking the quilt top."

"Becca, you don't have to do that. Seriously."

She shrugged. "If I weren't quilting yours, I'd be working on another one. It's all the same to me. I enjoy quilting." She sipped at her wine. "Really, don't feel bad about it. But don't startle me again or you're going to end up with little dots of blood all over it."

The waitress brought their meals.

"So what happened at the nursing home today?"

"Kitchen fire," he replied. "Some damage to that part of the kitchen. But we had to evacuate everyone and then get them all back inside after the fire was out."

"How many people was that?"

"Fifty, roughly. One of the little old ladies copped a feel on my ass, though."

Becca clapped a hand over her mouth to keep from spitting white wine all over the table. "You're kidding."

"Nope."

"What did you do?"

"Nothing. Although I thought about sending her Matt's way."

"You sure it wasn't just an accident? Maybe she lost her footing and grabbed for something and …" Becca pressed her lips together to keep from laughing too hard. "Your ass was handy."

"Yeah, I'm pretty sure I can tell the difference between an accidental grab and a grope. I can demonstrate it for you later, if you'd like."

Becca looked down at her plate. The idea of Jack's hands on her ass was not exactly an unpleasant one. But that was a place they couldn't go.

"How's your mom doing?"

He shrugged and popped the last bite of salmon into his mouth. He swallowed, then said, "Well, she's not getting better. There's only one direction for this to go."

"I'm sorry."

He nodded. "Her spirits are good. Better than mine would be, for sure. But it seems like just breathing tires her out."

The waitress removed their dinner plates and returned with dessert menus. Jack gave Becca a questioning look.

"Maybe we could split something," she suggested.

When the fancy dessert dish came out, they dug into the scoops of creamy amaretto gelato. Becca reflected that this was probably the nicest date she'd ever been on. Her nicest date and it was in her hometown. *Didn't see that one coming.* Dates with Brandon had been sports bars or Chinese restaurants, a movie or hanging out with his friends while they watched sports on TV. It wasn't that the Blue Crab Bistro was over the top fancy or anything—and compared to the tuxedo he'd worn to the hospital gala, Jack's shorts and golf shirt were very casual.

But it was nice.

Jack was nice.

Becca had just swallowed another cold spoonful of gelato when an older, fiftyish woman approached their table.

"You are the spitting image of your mother," the woman said to Becca.

Becca frowned involuntarily. She looked nothing like her mother.

"You're Penny's daughter, right? I went to school with her here, before my family moved away."

Jack was frowning now, too. But Becca knew what was going on. Penny was her biological mother. Michelle's younger sister.

"Oh. Thank you."

"What is Penny up to these days?"

Becca felt Jack's calf brush hers beneath the table, a gesture of support. From the expression on his face, he looked ready to jump into the conversation, too.

"She passed away when I was a toddler, actually," Becca said quietly. "I was raised by my aunt and uncle." *Aunt and uncle.* She had never really thought of Michelle and Dan Trevor that way. They were simply her parents. They had adopted her, in any case, so legally that's what they were.

"Oh my word." The woman laid a hand on Becca's shoulder. "I am so sorry. I had no idea."

"It's okay. I don't remember her."

"So sorry!" The woman rushed off.

Becca was quiet for a moment.

"Are you okay?" Jack asked.

She nodded. "I've never had that happen before. And I don't know why. Obviously, there are people in St. Caroline who grew up with my mother. No one's ever brought it up, though."

"Maybe they respect your parents too much to do that. Your real parents."

She gave Jack a wan smile. "They are my real parents."

CHAPTER 22

*J*ack reached down and suavely unclicked Becca's seatbelt, then slipped his arm between her and the seat back, gently pulling her over to his side. His other hand reached up and around the back of her head. No gentle pulling was required for this. Before he knew what was happening, Becca's own hands were on his head, her fingers threading into his blonde hair, her lips crushing his with a fierceness that sparked a tiny moment of fear before it was washed away by a tidal wave of lust.

The gear shift pressed into his thigh as he tried to get her closer. Suddenly the gear shift gave way and they were in the back seat of the SUV, still kissing. Damn, he was good. He'd gotten them out of the front seat and into the back without even breaking the kiss. Come to think of it, he wasn't even really doing the kissing. He was being kissed. Ravished wouldn't be an overstatement. His lips were being ravished, plundered, the whole nine yards. Bet Mattie's lips had never been plundered by a woman.

Becca's lips were hungry on his, nipping and sucking, her sweet breath tasting of amaretto and sugar. So much sugar. She was pushing him onto his back and the windows were fogged up with all the heat they were generating. He let her push, let her plunder ... hell, he'd let her do whatever she damn well pleased. Because this felt so damn good. Amazing. He'd never been this turned on with a woman. Never. The urge to break her kiss and move on to second base was overwhelming, but for once he was in no hurry. No hurry at all. He was perfectly content to just lie here and let her ravage him. His hard-on wasn't going anywhere, of that he was certain.

Her lips left his and kissed their way down his jaw. He turned his head slightly to allow her unfettered access to his neck. Just before he closed his eyes in ecstasy, he saw it. That damned sock monkey. What the hell was it doing in here? He glanced around to confirm that they were, in fact, in his car. Yes, they were. He closed his eyes. Maybe he was hallucinating. Yeah, that was it. Ninety-nine percent of the blood in his body was now concentrated in one spot, leaving nothing for his brain. That would cause hallucinations, right?

He opened his eyes again. The sock monkey was gone. But so was the back seat of his SUV. And Becca. The only thing that remained from that insanely hot make out session was the brain to penis blood ratio tenting the sheet he was lying beneath on Matt's sleeper sofa. He shifted his hips. It was hot as hell in his brother's cabin. Matt had no central air conditioning, just those window units that made enough noise to wake the dead.

He lay there, letting his mind drift back to the dream. No, more like trying to force his mind back to the dream. If only he could fall back to sleep and resume things right where they'd left off. Right where he was about to get laid by a plundering, ravaging Becca Trevor.

None of that had happened last night. Not in his conscious mind, anyway. After dinner, he had driven Becca home, walked her up to the front porch of her parents' house—like a gentleman!—and chastely kissed her. Okay, so it hadn't been totally chaste. He held her close, kissed her long and good, enjoyed the feel of her slender body beneath the lightweight fabric of her dress. They were on the front porch of her parents' house, so he couldn't go any further than that. Dr. Trevor probably wasn't a shotgun-toting kind of father—and Becca was twenty-five years old anyway. But he could maybe stick Jack with a needle shot of tranquilizer or something.

Still, he had walked back to his car with his body's blood distribution in the exact same state it was now.

Why Becca Trevor? Why was she having this effect on him? Was it just because he hadn't gotten laid in eons? Was it because they were both just home for the summer? They could have a no-strings-attached summer fling and then walk away unscathed? He didn't know, and the sound of his brother turning on the shower distracted him from the need to find an answer.

He kicked off the sheet and sat up. He was trying to help out his brother around the cabin, in exchange for living here this summer. Making coffee in the morning was an easy enough trade —and moving around the kitchen, dumping yesterday's grinds in the trash and pulverizing fresh beans, had the added benefit of returning his blood ratio to normal levels.

BECCA HEARD her phone buzz with a text. She leaned back toward the nightstand to glance at the screen. Jack. She poked the quilting needle into his wedding quilt to secure it, then reached over and picked up the phone. She swiped at the screen. *Had a great time last night. And yesterday morning.* She touched a finger to her lips, which still felt just-kissed twelve hours later. And there was still a hot, tingling spot on her stomach where his erection had pressed into her. She wasn't surprised that he was too much of a gentleman to do anything about it. Brandon, on the other hand, would have tried to persuade her to sneak him into her parents' house and upstairs to her room. He would have whined and nagged, and then gotten mad when she refused. But Jack had simply said "goodnight" and walked back to his car.

A part of her was still a little disappointed by his impeccable manners. A larger part of her was beginning to feel even more disappointed that dating Jack Wolfe was something that couldn't go anywhere. Not long term. She texted him back. *Me too.* A split second later came his reply: *We should do it again sometime.* She was about to type *We should,* then thought better of it. *Don't lead him on.* She set the phone down beside her on the bed and went back to quilting his wedding quilt. Somewhere out there in the world was a very lucky woman who was going to get this quilt one day—and the man who came with it.

It just wasn't going to be her.

That was yet another reason to rue the stupid choice she had made on the night of the graduation party. She finally had a good, decent man—a good, decent man who was wicked sexy, too—interested in her, and he was totally off limits. *Story of my life. Everything thing good is just the flip side of something else bad.*

Her phone buzzed again. She dropped her eyes to the screen, expecting to see Jack's name. But it wasn't, and her breath caught at the sight. *Shari Weber.* The woman who had adopted Jacqueline Michelle. The last time Becca had heard from Shari directly was years ago. The adoption had been open, but she didn't want to insert herself into a family she didn't belong to. They were "friends" on Facebook—nothing more than that. She tapped open the message.

Hi Becca, hope all is well. Went by your apartment today but you don't live there anymore? Can you give me a call?

She sat there for a moment, staring at the message. What reason could Shari possibly have for wanting to talk to her? Becca tapped on the tiny phone icon and listened to it ring.

"Becca! Hi! How are you?"

"Good. I'm good." She stared at the tiny stitches running across the top of Jack's quilt.

"You moved? I went by your old place."

"Um, yes. I'm staying with my parents. For the summer."

"Oh? On the eastern shore? My parents love that area."

"They do? That's good. That's nice." Becca wondered where this was going.

"Well, I wanted to have this conversation face to face but over the phone will have to do, I guess."

Becca began to get a bad feeling. "Is … nothing's happened to …" She couldn't even force out the words. *Please let nothing have happened to Jacqueline Michelle.*

"No, no. Jackie is fine. Wonderful, in fact." Shari paused. "It's me something has happened to. I was diagnosed with breast cancer three years ago. It was in remission, but now it has come back." She paused again, to let the words sink in.

Becca wasn't sure what to say, just like she wasn't sure what to say to Jack about his mother. But Shari continued.

"I'm not getting better. The doctor says I have probably a few more months."

Becca could barely breathe. Shari was dying? And …

"What about …" She remembered to use the name Shari had. "Jackie?"

"That's why I'm calling, Becca. I need to make arrangements for her. My parents love Jackie and Jackie loves them. But they're both seventy-five years old. My father has had one heart attack already. I'm afraid they might not be around another ten years to see her through high school. *They're* afraid they won't be. I have a cousin and a few friends I could ask to be Jackie's guardian and adopt her. I'm confident one of them, at least, would say 'yes.' But my first choice would be you."

Becca pressed her free hand hard into the mattress as her body wavered. The idea that she might faint floated through her mind.

"Me?" Her voice came out as barely more than a squeak. *The woman who gave her up the first time?*

"Yes. You are still her mother."

"But I—"

"Becca, you impressed the hell out of me seven years ago with your strength and your steadiness. You didn't waver, not even once. I never told you this, but I had an adoption fall through five years earlier. The girl changed her mind when the baby was born. I was heartbroken and it took me those five years to get up the courage to put myself through that again."

"But I gave—"

"You gave her up because you were too young."

Shari didn't have to finish that thought. *You're not too young now.*

"I see a lot of you in her," Shari added. "She has a backbone of steel."

"I look at her pictures sometimes, on your Facebook page. But I didn't realize you were sick."

"I don't post anything about it online. It's not how I want people to remember me." She was quiet for a long minute, and Becca sensed she was trying to get her emotions under control. "You don't have to make a decision right this instant. But it would put my mind at ease to know that she was with you."

"How much does she know?"

"She knows that I've been sick. There was no hiding that. She doesn't know the full seriousness of it yet, though. I want to try and make arrangements for her care before I do that. I don't want to add that uncertainty on top of all this. I want her to know that she'll have a place to go, someone to take care of her."

Becca stared at the stitching swirling round and round on the quilt on the bed. The stitches mirrored the thoughts in her brain, questions and barely-articulated fears circling too quickly for her to grab onto any one of them. Adopt Jacqueline Michelle? A child she hadn't seen in person since the day she was born? Be her mother? As often as Becca had thought about what her life would have been like if she had kept her baby, she was having trouble picturing it now.

"At least consider it, Becca. Please."

She forced her eyes to track the stitches on the quilt, follow them one by one across the fabric. Her mind began to still.

"I think Jackie and I should meet before any decisions get made," Becca ventured. "Maybe I can come out to Ohio for a weekend." She could get time off from Skipjack's. Mike might not be happy about it, but he'd do it. Her mother would give her time off, too. But she would have to explain why she needed to return to Ohio. She closed her eyes, unable to picture that conversation either. Was she even seriously considering this?

One step at a time.

"Why don't we come there?" Shari offered. "My father went to the Naval Academy. He and mom love that area. The four of us can come, and Jackie can see the town."

"Do you have the energy for a trip like that?" She thought of what Jack had told her about his mother. *It seems like just breathing tires her out.*

"With my parents along to help, I can do it. I've stopped chemo. I don't want to spend the rest of my time sick from that."

"Where would you want her to live?" There were so many questions to be answered, if this were to happen. And Becca wasn't even sure the idea was a good one, for her or for Jackie. What did she know about being a mother? "I wasn't really planning on coming back to Ohio."

"Wherever you want to live, Becca. I know I can't dictate what happens after I'm gone. My parents are close to her, but they understand that she might not be in Ohio for much longer. The cousin I have in mind lives in Chicago so ..."

Chicago. Becca couldn't imagine being a kid in a huge city like that. She couldn't even really imagine being a kid in Columbus, Ohio. Childhood to her meant St. Caroline. The water, the shore, boats, crabs. That was silly, she knew. Plenty of people grew up in cities. Still … St. Caroline had been a good place to grow up. And the thought of a seven-year-old girl being raised by seventy-five year olds … *you're really considering this.* Even though it would blow her world to bits. What would her parents think when they learned they had a grandchild? What would her sisters think of her? The Wolfe family?

Jack?

Jack. She'd have to tell him.

"Are there any weeks that are better than others?" Shari's voice yanked Becca back into the moment. "Sooner being better than later, obviously."

"Any week is fine."

Jack will be furious. He'll never speak to me again. Which is what I deserve.

"I'll talk to my parents then and let you know. Thank you, Becca, for being willing to consider this. It would ease my mind so much to know that she was back with you."

They ended the call, and Becca let the phone drop onto the bed. *I'm not ready to be a mother. What if Jackie doesn't like me? What if she doesn't like St. Caroline?* So many questions, so many concerns. She was crazy for even thinking about this. Shari's cousin was probably a better option. *But how can I not consider it?*

It was her daughter.

It was Jack's daughter.

There came a light, tentative tapping at the door.

"Can I come in, Becs?"

"Sure, mom."

The door swung open and her mother slipped through. "You know, you were the only one who never locked her bedroom door."

Becca flashed her a smile, hoping it covered up the shock she was feeling from the phone call with Shari. "I remember you always told us that if the house caught on fire, the firefighters wouldn't be able to get us out if the door was locked."

"So you left the door unlocked so the firefighters could get in?" An amused smile played around the corners of her mother's mouth.

"No, so the firefighters wouldn't ruin the door by kicking it in. I was the only one who showed any concern for you and daddy's personal property."

"Speaking of firefighters, how was your date?" Her mom waggled her eyebrows, then pretended to look under the bed. "You didn't sneak him up here, did you?"

Becca rolled her eyes. "He was the perfect gentleman. And dinner was nice."

"What did you have?"

"The salmon salad."

"Oh, that's good. I order that a lot there. Did you eat outside, where it's *très* romantic?"

Becca rolled her eyes a second time. "Yes, we did."

"Was that Jack you were talking to on the phone? I didn't interrupt, did I?"

Boy, her mother was full of questions.

"No, it wasn't Jack. A friend from Ohio." She wasn't ready to talk to her mother about this yet. She needed to settle her own thoughts first.

"Did you have dessert?"

Dessert.

"Yes, we split one. But a weird thing happened while we were eating it."

"Oh yeah? What's that?"

"This woman came up to the table and said she went to school with …" She stopped. She was about to say "my mother," but Michelle was her mother.

"With me and dad?" her mother filled in the sentence.

Becca shook her head. "No, with … Penny."

"Oh. Oh Becs, I'm sorry. You're upset by that."

Becca shrugged. "It's never happened before, that's all. And I wondered why not. I mean, it's not like there aren't people in town who knew her. And they know who I am. I always felt like everyone was looking at me, when I was younger, and thinking about that."

"I think people don't mention it because they know you don't remember her. You were so young, sweetheart. Who was the woman? Did you recognize her?"

"I didn't. She said she no longer lives in town. She didn't offer her name and I was too flustered to ask." She looked at her mom. "She said I looked like her."

"You do. Sometimes I'll look at you from across the room and for a split second, I'll think it's her." Michelle touched her hair. "She and I barely looked like sisters."

"Do you have any pictures of her?"

She felt her mother's gaze on her, appraising, wary. "I do. Sit tight."

Minutes later, Michelle returned with a large cardboard box. Becca moved Jack's wedding quilt aside so her mother could set the box on the bed. Michelle folded back the flaps.

"I've been waiting for the right time to give this to you." She began lifting things from the box—a photo album, high school yearbooks, a small flat jewelry box. "I think now is that time."

Becca picked up the photo album. Inside, the pages were filled with photographs of Penny as a young child, as a teenager, as a young woman — and as a new mother holding an infant. Becca realized that she had never seen a picture of herself as an infant. Hot tears stung her eyes, as she turned back to the pictures of her mother. Yes, there was an unmistakable resemblance.

"My sister loved you," Michelle said. "But she wasn't able to be a mother to you. She was battling too many demons."

"Is it true that they were both drug addicts? That's the impression I've gotten over the years."

"I don't know about him, exactly. Honestly, we never had much contact with him. But they dabbled in it, certainly. Then after you were born and he left, that was when it became a bigger problem for her. I begged her to come stay with us, but she wouldn't leave Ohio. She was always waiting for your father to get his life together and come back to her. To the two of you."

"That was probably never going to happen, even if she had lived."

Michelle shook her head, sadly. "No, I'm certain it wouldn't have happened. Choose the father of your children wisely."

Too late for that advice.

"And write a will," her mother added. "It was a mess, trying to adopt you. We had to get you out of foster care, track down your father, and ask him to relinquish his parental rights … " She shook her head and took a deep breath. "But she was young. When you're young, you never think this is going to happen to you."

CHAPTER 23

$\mathcal{J}$ack found the door to his parents' house unlocked, his father already on his way to the station. You could do that in St. Caroline, leave your house or your car unlocked. Well, maybe the wealthy summer residents couldn't. Or shouldn't, at any rate. He took one last huge breath of fresh air before pushing the door open and stepping inside. The smell of sickness punched him in the gut.

Can't you fix this? Almighty, all powerful—and you can't make the air in here smell normal?

"Jack?"

His mother's voice was weak and he sprinted through the hallway to get to the sunroom quickly.

"Mom, are you okay?"

She sat, knees up, on the sofa. The ever present cotton blanket was wrapped around her. A shiver convulsed her body and the blanket slipped. Her fingers struggled to pull it back up. He hurried to the sofa and sat down next to her, tucking the blanket in around her shoulders.

"Do you need me to call dad?"

"No. He just left. I feel fine, Jack. No worse than yesterday."

No better either. He filled in her unspoken words.

"I'm a little sad today, that's all," she went on. "It's to be expected."

How could his mother be so calm about this when all Jack wanted to do was hurl things and beat his fists against a wall until they were a bloody pulp?

"Can I get you anything?" he asked.

"A cup of hot tea would be nice. If your cooking skills encompass that." She managed a mischievous smile and Jack forced himself to smile back. Putting out a raging fire was easier than hiding how upset he was when he was around his mother. The sheer force of will required left his stomach muscles in knots for hours afterward.

"I think I can handle that," he answered. "But you're lucky it's me and not Matt here right now."

"How are you two getting along?"

He adjusted her blanket again and then headed for the kitchen, ten feet away. "We haven't killed each other yet."

Her laugh was barely audible over the sound of the water splashing into the tea kettle. "If I hadn't been there when both of you were born, I'd swear one of you wasn't mine."

"Maybe someone switched me at birth." He flashed his own mischievous grin back at her. "Took the better looking baby instead." He opened the wooden box that held his mother's tea bags, all neatly slotted by color and type. "Which kind of tea do you want? Jasmine, orange pekoe, darjeeling, Earl Grey?"

"The darjeeling, I think. I can't taste the difference between them anymore anyway." He opened the tea bag and draped it over the rim of a mug. "You might not look like a Wolfe, but I can see that you're mine," she added.

He felt her eyes on him and he knew what she was seeing. Or rather, whom she was seeing. Not only had he inherited his uncle's name, but he had gotten his height from his mother's family too. When he got in his car to drive over here, he'd had the vague notion that today might be the day he confessed to her about working in the fire department. He didn't want that lie between them. It would haunt him for the rest of his life, he knew that. But her spirits weren't good enough for that today.

The tea kettle whistled and he snapped off the gas burner. He poured the water into the mug. "Strong or weak, mom?"

"Weak is fine, Jackie. Mostly I just want the heat."

Do you have to take away even the simplest pleasures from her? The taste of tea? Really?

He pulled out the soggy tea bag and dropped it into the sink.

"Here you go." He handed her the mug, not letting go of it until he was certain she had it.

"How was your date last night? Where did you end up going?"

"Blue Crab."

"Oh, that's nice. Your dad and I were there a few months ago." She blew on the hot tea.

He tried not to think about the fact that it was the last time she would ever eat there. Barring a medical miracle. *Which you could pull off, if you cared to. Evidently you don't.*

"Do you remember her biological mother?" he asked.

His mother looked up with a start. "Of course. When we were children. I don't think I ever saw her again after high school. Why?"

"Someone came up to our table last night and said Becca looked like her mother."

"Well, she does. Penny was always a bit of a spitfire, too."

"Becca has calmed down since high school." He was beginning to wonder whether that really meant beaten down, by whatever her life had been in Ohio. She was good at changing the subject when that came up.

"She's a nice girl. Are you planning to ask her out again?" His mother sipped at the tea she couldn't taste.

"I was going to call her later today and see if she wanted to come over to the cabin for dinner. Since my cooking skills do encompass more than tea."

"Kicking your brother out of his own house?" That mischievous Wolfe smile played around her lips.

"He's headed to Ocean City with some buddies after he gets off today."

"Ah … so no chaperone."

"I can't win here, can I? Kick my brother out or invite a girl over unchaperoned? Which is worse?" He knew his mother was joking, of course.

"Just busting your chops, Jackie."

His mother looked happier than she had when he arrived. For that, he'd happily be the butt of as many jokes as possible. His phone buzzed with a text. He pulled it out of the pocket of his shorts. It was one of the guys from the station. *Can you be on call tonight?*

Yes, Jack texted back.

"Who was that? Becca?"

He looked up at his mom. "No. Someone from California?"

"Someone from work?"

He shook his head, his own spirits deflating at the lies that were piling up one after another. "No, just a friend."

"When do they need you back at your job?"

He shoved the damned phone back in his pocket. "Not yet." He knew this was the perfect time to come clean, but he had just gotten her cheered up. He couldn't dash her good spirits now. Not yet.

BECCA HAD INTENTIONALLY DRESSED down for dinner with Jack— white denim shorts, a loose peasant blouse, flip flops—just to avoid the very situation in which she found herself right now. Lying beneath Jack on the couch in his brother's cabin, their bare legs tangled up together, Jack's lips exploring the curve of her neck.

On the other side of the one large room that served as the living-dining-kitchen area lay the remains of the dinner Jack fixed for her. The room was still redolent with the aroma of lemon from the chicken piccata. She couldn't even blame alcohol this time around. A bottle of white wine was in the refrigerator, unopened. Jack was on call for the fire department so he couldn't have any—and Becca wanted all her wits about her in the face of Jack's overwhelming ... maleness. Attractiveness. *Sexiness.* She tried to hush that voice in her mind.

And the bitch of it? He wasn't even trying to be God's gift to sexiness. He just was. The way he had moved around the small, poorly-equipped kitchen, wiping his hands on his tee shirt instead of an apron ... and then stripping the dirty tee shirt right off over his head with a *Can you excuse me for a minute? I need to powder my nose.* Thirty seconds later, he was back in a fresh tee shirt and plating their meals. Chicken, wild rice, glazed carrots. Delicious *and* healthy.

A woman could used to it.

But she couldn't get used to it, even as his lips nuzzled her jaw and evidence of his arousal lay heavy against her hip. Because he wasn't staying in town forever. Because she had something to tell him, something he wasn't going to take well. Something she wasn't going to tell him tonight—not before she told her own family and got their advice. She spent the morning poring over her mother's—Penny's—photos and her yearbooks. Tried on her jewelry. Spent her entire shift at Skipjack's watching kids puff up their chests and order their Monster Claw and Crabby Lady non-alcoholic drinks—and steeling herself each time for the way her heart collapsed with longing at the sight.

On her break, she went for a walk outside in the sweltering heat so she could look at Facebook privately. And something had broken free in her chest. She had spent years trying not to think of Jacqueline Michelle. There had been no point in torturing herself or entertaining "what ifs." But now she was desperate to see her in person.

She wanted to meet her daughter even though she knew no good could come of this. Her choices were awful all the way around. If she said "no" to Shari's proposal, could she live with that on her conscience for the rest of her life? If she said "yes," Jack would hate her. It might break up the lifelong friendship between their parents. Helping Shari and Jacqueline Michelle would upend so many other lives in the process.

Of course. She was Becca Trevor, and that was the way her life had always worked.

Jack's lips found hers again. His fingers were in her hair, and it just felt so damn good. *Might as well enjoy it ... this is the last time.* But then Jack's pager sounded and he broke the kiss with a start.

"Seriously?" he muttered.

"Rethinking your choice of profession?" She smoothed her hair as he pushed himself off the couch and into a standing position. "You could go back to being a lawyer."

"Then I wouldn't have been here at all." He checked the page. "I'd still be in the office, burning the midnight oil. I've got to go. Sorry." He leaned over and dropped a quick kiss on her lips.

"No worries. I'll clean up the kitchen before I leave."

"You don't have to do that," Jack said, already across the room and pushing open the screen door. It closed with a loud "thwap" before she could answer. She heard his car start up outside, and then he was gone.

It was for the best. Things were getting out of hand on the couch. Things that she was enjoying far too much. Jack had been turned on. She was turned on, more than she'd ever been with Brandon. Or anyone, for that matter. In the kitchen, she rinsed their dishes and loaded the dishwasher. She even located a broom and dustpan to sweep the floor. Then she turned the lock on the back of the doorknob and let herself out.

CHAPTER 24

Three days later, Becca was still a distracted mess of confusion and indecision. On top of that, she couldn't stop thinking about Jack—and he wasn't helping matters any by texting her sweet nothings all day long and turning up at Skipjack's to sit at the bar and nurse a beer for an hour. Yesterday, she screwed up three separate drink orders because she couldn't keep her focus on any task at hand. Today, he had swung by Quilt Therapy to ask her out to lunch. Her distraction was evident even to him.

"Are you okay?" he had asked, over deli sandwiches and iced tea.

No. Nothing is okay.

"Just tired."

She spent the rest of the day working at the quilt shop. Behind her, Cassidy was closing out the register and Natalie was wiping fabric dust from her scissors. Becca sat down at the big quilting frame and ran her palms over the quilt that was stretched on it. It was a traditional Amish-style quilt, a Diamond in the Square pattern, and pieced by a customer who then donated it to the shop. Becca loved Amish quilts—their simple geometry and rich, dark colors. They also provided a beautiful backdrop for Becca's meticulous hand quilting skills.

A spool of quilting thread and a packet of tiny quilting needles lay on top of the quilt. Becca deftly threaded a needle and set to work, willing the in and out rhythm of her hand to calm the storm of thoughts in her brain. She heard the lights click off upstairs, then one by one the shop's staff—including her sisters—left. Only her mother remained behind. Becca felt her gaze. A moment later, her mother sat down next to her at the quilting frame.

"What's wrong?"

Becca shook her head. "Nothing." *Everything.*

"I know you better than that. Is it Jack?"

"No. Things are fine."

"Where'd you go to lunch?"

"Just the deli."

"So what is it?"

Becca was silent, even as she knew her mother would wait her out. And why not spill the beans right now? Shari was planning to come to St. Caroline. Becca had agreed to it. Sooner or later, she was going to have to tell people. In fact, it really had to be sooner rather than later.

"Will you tell me if I promise not to be upset?"

"You're going to be upset. No way you won't be."

"Try me?"

Becca took a deep breath as she rocked the needle through the fabric. When she pulled the thread through, her mother covered her hand to still it.

"When I moved to Ohio after graduation ..." She took another deep breath. "I was pregnant."

She glanced sideways, to find her mother's brown eyes filled with shock. "I ... that's not what I was expecting to hear."

She watched as her mother struggled to regain her composure.

"Why didn't you tell me? Was it Alan's?"

Alan had been her on-again, off-again boyfriend in high school. More off than on. "No, it wasn't his."

"Then whose?"

Becca looked back down at the quilt, dreading the word she was about to say. "Jack."

"Jack? Jack Wolfe?"

Becca nodded.

"But you two weren't dating in high school."

"No." Becca's voice was low. "It happened at a party after graduation. Just that once. But once was all it took"

Her mother tugged at Becca's arm to make her turn and face her. "Why didn't you say anything? And leave town? Jack would have done right by you."

Becca looked her mom straight in the eye. "That's why I didn't tell anyone. Because his parents would have pressured him to marry me, and then he would have been stuck here in St. Caroline. He was all set to go to Cornell and then to law school ..."

"He could have gone to Talbot College."

She shot her mom a withering look. "You know that's not the same, mom. He got into the *Ivy* League. If he had stayed here, he wouldn't have become a lawyer." *He didn't become a lawyer anyway.* She ignored that little voice.

"Well then maybe he should have kept his pants zipped up."

"It was as much my fault as his. We both made a mistake. But I took care of things. I had the baby in Ohio and arranged for the adoption—"

"You did all that by yourself?"

"Yes, I found a woman who wanted to adopt. She's a single mom with a good career. It was an open adoption. She's been a good mother, better than I could have been as an eighteen-year-old."

"I don't doubt that, sweetheart. But for you not to even tell us about it ... I assume Jack likewise didn't tell Angie and Tim?"

Becca closed her eyes. "He doesn't know."

"What do you mean? Doesn't know ... about the baby? At all?"

Becca shook her head. "Shari—Shari Weber, that's the woman who adopted her—she found a friend to claim paternity. No one checked beyond that."

Her mother sucked in a sharp breath.

"I know it was wrong! Okay? I know that." Becca picked up the needle and began rocking it through the quilt again, searching for calm—or maybe wisdom or a time machine—in the stitches. A time machine would be helpful. The shop was dead silent. If she dropped the needle on the floor at that moment, they'd hear it clear as a bell. "But what were my choices? Ruin his life?"

"I wouldn't say that his life would have—"

"Mom, we weren't even dating! You said that yourself. If we had gotten married, we'd be divorced by now. We'd hate each other's guts."

"You don't know that—"

"Oh come on, mom. If he'd had to give up going to Cornell and law school to marry me, he would absolutely hate me by now." *Instead of asking me out. Instead of making my body feel things no one else ever has.*

Michelle stood up from the quilting frame and walked across the room. "You could have made the decision to adopt together."

"And what if that ended up not being the decision that got made? You and dad are close friends with the Wolfes. Their son gets your daughter pregnant, and they're not going to push for him to, as you put it, do right by me?"

"And so you're thinking about this now because you're dating Jack."

"I'm not sure you can say we're dating, exactly. I mean, he *is* planning to go back to California." *To his job not being an attorney.* "But there is more to it than that."

Michelle waited for her to elaborate. Becca took a deep breath and dropped the other shoe.

"Shari called me the other day. She was diagnosed with breast cancer a few years ago. And it has come back, and her prognosis is not ... good. She's asked me to take Jacqueline—Jackie—back." She let this sink in with her mother for a moment. "She's a single mom, as I mentioned, and her parents are too old to raise a grandchild. They're worried they might not be around until she finishes high school. Shari has a cousin and some friends she could ask to be Jackie's guardian, but she would rather I adopt her back."

"And how much contact have you had with this little girl?"

"None since she was born. I'm friends with Shari on Facebook, but other than that ... I didn't want to be lurking in the background of their lives all the time." She reached the end of the thread, knotted it, and popped the knot through to the batting inside. "And it was too hard for me."

"Oh Becs. I wish you had told us. You didn't have to do all that by yourself."

"I caused you enough trouble when I was younger."

"You just weren't as good at not getting caught as your sisters were." Michelle picked up the spool of thread and threaded a needle for herself. "So do you think this is a good idea? Adopting her back?"

Becca drew in a long, deep breath. "I don't know. I haven't decided yet. Shari and her parents are bringing Jackie to visit."

"Either way you have to tell Jack, you know. Let him decide what he wants to do, as well."

"I know."

But she could already guess what Jack would do. He'd never want to see her again—which was exactly where they would be right now if she had kept their baby in the first place. And he would leave St. Caroline again—because he had options, options

211

Becca had given him seven years ago. Even now, it was still hard to see any other path than the one she had taken.

"JACK, can you stop by the house on your way home? Check on your mom?" His father looked up from his desk as Jack leaned in to say goodbye, his shift over. It was nearly nine o'clock, the fading light outside the station's open bays soon to be just a shadow behind the day.

"Sure."

He heard the low, tortured keening the instant he opened the front door to his parents' house. He rushed up the stairs to find his mother rocking back and forth on the bed, her legs kicking weakly to free themselves from the tangled sheets.

"Mom! Are you okay?" He tried to unwind the sheets from her thin legs, his arms dodging each kick of her feet. "Are you in pain?"

That elicited a slightly louder moan, and he jabbed his hand into the pocket of his shorts to get his phone. He dialed 9-1-1, then went back to unwinding the sheets. The wait for the ambulance was interminable, his sense of helplessness intensifying with each passing minute. *Where are they?* Summer traffic could get heavy in St. Caroline, between summer residents and day trippers coming for the shops and restaurants. *Make the lights all green. You could do that, you know?*

He held his mother's hand. She had been thin and frail looking when he arrived home at the end of May. Now it was July and she was even thinner. Weaker.

"Mom, how are you doing?"

But she was slipping in and out of lucidity. He heard car doors slam downstairs. He knew the EMTs would just come right in; they knew this was Chief Wolfe's house and that his wife was ill.

"Up here!" he called to them. Footsteps pounded on the stairs. Seconds later, his parents' bedroom lit up with activity as the EMTs attended to his mother. Jack stepped back to make way for the stretcher.

"Mom, we're taking you to the hospital, okay?"

Her eyelids fluttered weakly. He wasn't sure whether his words had registered or not. Something vibrated against the palm of his hand, and he was surprised to discover that he was still holding his phone. He tapped on the screen to read the message from his father: *Heard the call. Meet you at the hospital.*

Jack followed the EMTs as they carefully carried the stretcher and his mother down the stairs.

"I'll follow behind in my car," he told her as they slid the stretcher into the back of the ambulance. "Dad's on his way." But her eyes remained closed. If she heard him, she gave no indication.

Not today! Jack turned the key in the ignition and his SUV roared to life. He realized his mouth was open. Had he just shouted that out loud? *Not today!* Yeah, he just did. He watched as the ambulance crossed the intersection ahead, right before the traffic light turned yellow. He slammed on the brakes. *Oh come on!* He fumed as the taillights of the ambulance disappeared from view. *I want to be there when they take her in!* Maybe his father would get there first. *Cut us a break here!*

Yelling at God was earning him a one-way ticket to hell, he was sure. *But hey, upgrade me to first class at least!*

He saw his father's car pull into the hospital parking lot just behind the ambulance. *Thank you!* His father had no doubt driven like a bat out of hell to get here that fast. It wasn't like the police were going to pull *him* over for speeding. Jack parked and sprinted to the hospital's emergency entrance. Inside, he looked around but the EMTs and his father were nowhere to be seen. He collapsed into an uncomfortable chair in the waiting area, along with all the other worried people, and proceeded to stare intently at the scuffed linoleum floor.

Why? Can you at least tell me that? What did I do? I've never committed a crime. Not even so much as a speeding ticket. Okay, a few parking tickets in San Francisco but parking sucks there. I've never cheated on a test, ripped someone off, shoplifted. Yeah, I got my brothers in trouble a few times when we were kids but they repaid the favor many times over. I've always been a gentleman around women. I hold doors, pull out chairs, respect that no means no. Okay, so not many women have said no to me. But if they did, I would respect it! Yeah, I hear you. I wasn't a gentleman that time with Becca. But she didn't say no! This is way out of proportion for that!

The hospital's public address system crackled and a barely-intelligible voice came on. Jack didn't bother paying attention. *I hate the smell of this place, too. And the way the house smells. Nice if you could do something about that. Just if you have the time, you know. If it's not too much trouble.*

He felt his father's hand settle on his shoulder. He would always recognize his father's touch, just like he would always remember his mother's. Some things are just imprinted on you. Like family.

"Hey son." His father sat down on the chair next to him. "Why don't you head home and get some rest?"

Jack nodded numbly. He vaguely remembered that he was dead tired. "Do you need anything before I go? Coffee or something to eat?"

"Coffee would be great. Two creams and a sugar?"

'You got it."

Jack trudged the halls of the hospital toward the cafeteria. He hoped it was still open this late. He wondered why hospitals always felt so empty even though they were always filled with people. He wished he could go back to the day he ran into Becca here, the day he had carried the fundraising quilt for her. That seemed like eons ago.

He liked Becca. Liked her a lot. Too much. In less than two months, everything here held memories of her. The swamp, Oliver's boat, the Blue Crab, Skipjack's, Secret Beach. He'd been going to those places his entire life and now he couldn't think of them without her in the picture. He'd never be able to go to the fireman's carnival without thinking about their ferris wheel ride together. Hell, he might not be able to get on any ferris wheel anywhere with anyone and not think of her.

Even this damn hospital made him think of her.

And now every night, he had to pull out the sleeper sofa in Matt's cabin, the very sofa where he had kissed the everloving hell out of her. Where would things have ended up if he hadn't been paged for a call? For a backyard fire pit that was out by the time he got there. Homeowners finally found their fire extinguisher in their garage.

He walked up to the cafeteria counter and ordered two coffees for his dad.

"Cream and sugar?" the woman behind the counter asked, unsmiling. Not that Jack faulted her for that. What was there to smile about in a place like this? Maybe over in the maternity wing, people were surely happy. But nowhere else.

If you really cared about any of us, there wouldn't even be a need for hospitals.

"Four creams, two sugars. Thanks."

He paid for the coffee and trudged back to the waiting room. He swore he could feel the weight of his heart banging against his ribs with every step. *Where's the hospital wing for broken hearts? Eh?* Jack's was so broken, he couldn't bring himself to even care whether it ever healed. There were only two things that made him forget about the pain. Going on a call for the fire department.

And Becca.

When he got back to the waiting area, his father was deep in conversation with a white-jacketed doctor who looked barely older than Matt. Jack was too far away to hear what they were saying, but the expression on his father's face said it all. The miracle he'd been begging God for—threatening God over, even —wasn't happening. From across the room, he could see his father's chest heaving with the deep breaths he was taking to keep himself calm.

Why was he even entertaining the idea of falling for Becca Trevor—when all this was going to be over soon? His days in St. Caroline this summer were numbered. Leading her on wasn't fair to her. Nor was his own heart in any kind of shape to withstand it.

But ten minutes later, sitting in his car in the dark hospital parking lot, all he wanted to do was drive straight to the Trevor house and let her wrap herself around him. Beg her—if need be— to wrap herself around him, hold him, pick up the pieces of his heart.

CHAPTER 25

"*How* ow is Jack's mother doing?" Mike set a case of
bottled beers on top of the bar. It was half past
eleven, Skipjack's closing time. Becca was helping Mike clean up
and prep for the next day. There was a large wedding scheduled
for the day after tomorrow at the Inn, and they expected the
restaurant to be busy as guests began arriving. She opened the
flaps of the box and began handing bottles to Mike for him to
restock the bar's refrigerator.

"Not good. Her condition was downgraded."

"Oh." After a pause, he said it again. "Oh."

What else was there to say, really? There were no words to fix
the unfixable.

"How's Jack taking it?" Mike added.

The clinking of one glass bottle against another filled the
empty restaurant.

"I don't know. It's been a few days since I heard from him. My
parents have been over to the hospital to see Mrs. Wolfe. They
said the entire family is there pretty much around the clock."

"Do you know how much time …"

"A few weeks is what the doctor said, apparently."

Mike took in a long, deep breath. "I wouldn't know what to do if that were my wife."

Just then, the fire alarm began blaring and the emergency light on the wall flashed red.

"You've got to be kidding me," Mike said. "We were almost done here too."

"Let me finish these up while you shut down the computer. It's probably nothing."

"It never is. Like that kid who pulled the alarm in the locker room."

They closed up and headed out just as the fire trucks pulled in. Becca watched as Jack hopped down from one and followed the rest of the firefighters inside. He wasn't at the hospital tonight, apparently. Maybe the reason she hadn't heard from him was partly because he didn't want to see her again. He was friend-zoning her. That was for the best, anyway. It would make telling him about the baby easier, too, if their emotions were less involved.

Still, she did need to talk to him. Even though this was a terrible time for him, it would be worse if he were to just see Jacqueline Michelle—Jackie—without any warning. Shari wanted to make the trip to St. Caroline next week so she had next to no time to spare.

Jack spotted her as soon as he came out of the building. He jogged toward her, his fire helmet dangling from his hand, his blonde hair dark with sweat.

"Hey there," he said.

Why does he have to be so insanely hot?

"What happened?" She nodded toward the inn.

"Guest was smoking in bed and fell asleep."

"Are they okay?"

An ambulance pulled into the inn's driveway. "Guess not," she added.

"The guy has some burns on his arm. Could have been a lot worse."

She shuddered at the thought of herself asleep while the quilt shop was on fire around her.

"Sorry I haven't called," he said. "I've been ..."

"I know." She touched his arm. "I'm sorry."

He took a deep breath. "It's what we were expecting."

"Doesn't make it easier."

"No. It doesn't."

Someone called Jack's name and he held up his arm as if to say, "wait."

"My shift is up. Do you want to go get something to eat? I just have to swing by the station and put my gear away."

"It's late."

"The Burger Barn is open until two in the summer."

"True." She didn't want to eat there, though. She needed to talk to Jack in private and this might be her only chance for awhile. "How about if I stop by there on my way home and you meet me at the house?"

"Sounds like a plan." He leaned in and dropped a quick kiss on her lips. "I'll give you a better one after I clean up," he whispered.

Doubtful, she thought as she watched him jog back to the waiting engine and climb inside. *Not after what I have to tell you.* He waved to her as the truck pulled away.

Forty-five minutes later, they were sitting side by side on the back patio of her parents' house, eating burgers and fries. It was nearly one o'clock. Her parents had long since gone to bed. The lights on the patio were off but even in the scattered light leaking out from the kitchen window, she could see how exhausted Jack looked. If only she could put off this conversation to another day ... but who knew when she would have Jack alone like this again? She had to maintain her resolve. *You screwed all this up. You have to fix it.*

Then he threw a monkey wrench into her plans. An exploding monkey wrench.

She felt his fingers trace the curve of her cheek, and it felt so good. So damn good that she never wanted it to stop. She wanted those fingers tracing lines and drawing pictures all over her body.

"I'm falling for you, Becca. You know that."

His fingers brushed over her lips, so lightly it almost felt like air moving over her skin. She was pretty certain her heart had stopped beating entirely. *My life sucks. Really, truly sucks.* She finally had a nice guy—a wonderful guy, a guy she could bring home to her parents—interested in her, and she had to smash the whole thing to bits. *And I have to do it right now before he kisses me.* Even though she wanted that kiss, one final kiss from Jack Wolfe, kisser extraordinaire.

She took a deep breath. She could do this. She had to do this. And losing Jack? Just one more thing that didn't work out in her life. *I should be used to this by now.* He was leaning in toward her. She captured his hand with hers and pulled it away from his face.

"I have something I need to tell you."

"Okay." Disappointment flashed over his face. He flipped her hand over and threaded his fingers into hers.

"I got pregnant." She wriggled her fingers free. He wouldn't want to hold her hand after this. Wouldn't want to even touch her.

"Oh. Okay. In Ohio?" He glanced down at her stomach.

She shook her head. "Here."

She watched warily as his expression went from surprise to confusion, finally settling into a worrisome poker face.

"Who was the guy?"

"You." She steeled herself for his reaction.

He frowned. "We haven't even …" Understanding took hold in his eyes. "That one time?"

She nodded. "We didn't use any protection." She glanced

away, unable to look him square in the face. "Because we were stupid, stupid kids."

"Is that why you left town?"

She nodded.

"Why didn't you tell me? I would have done right by you."

She hated that phrase by now. She clasped her hands tightly in her lap, digging her fingernails into her palms, trying to keep her emotions under control. "I know you would have. That's why I didn't tell you. I would have gotten blamed for ruining your life."

"Becca, that's ridiculous—"

"You know it's true. You would have been stuck here in St. Caroline instead of going off to the Ivy League and law school, and it would have been my fault. I would have been the girl who trapped golden boy Jackie Wolfe."

He leaned back onto his palms on the cool stone of the patio. His face was neutral, but she could see the tightness in his jaw, the set of his mouth. He was upset. Naturally.

"I'm sorry. I know you should have been told, but I did what was best for you."

"Thanks for deciding that for me."

Becca unfurled her hands. "Come on. We were kids ourselves. We would have been divorced by now and you'd resent me for the rest of our lives. You know that's the way things would have worked out."

"So … you had an abortion?" He stared out into the blackness of the back yard.

"No! I never even considered that. The baby was adopted by a woman in Ohio." She could barely breathe, waiting for his reaction to that news.

"You had the baby?"

"Yes. I'm sor-"

"Not exactly a baby anymore."

"No."

"Boy or girl?"

"Girl."

He closed his eyes for a long moment. When he opened them, he said, "I have a daughter somewhere. And you never told me." He turned to look at her, his face not so neutral anymore. Anger flared in his brown eyes. "So why tell me now? Guilty conscience?" He spit the words out like a bloody tooth.

"Her mother—the woman who adopted her—is ..." She paused, realizing for the first time the parallels with Jack's life right now. "... she has cancer. She's not going to make it." She waited for that to sink in, then continued. "She wants to name me as Jacqueline's guardian. She wants me to adopt her back."

"You named her after me? Or was that a coincidence?"

"Shari let me name her. It was an open adoption."

Jack snorted derisively.

"But I haven't had any contact with her since she was born."

He shoved his hands through his hair. "So are you going to do this? Adopt her back?"

"I don't know yet. They're coming for a visit next week."

"Do I get any say in this?"

Becca had no answer to that. It was a question she had asked herself over and over. Of course, Jack should have a say in it. But what kind?

"Do you want a say?" she asked quietly.

He sighed, then shook his head as if in disbelief. "I don't even know. I don't know what to even think." He looked at her. "This is about the worst possible time to drop this on me. I'm about to lose my mother and now you tell me I'm a father?" He stood up. "Not to mention, I barely have a job. Are you going to sue me for child support?"

"No! That never even crossed my mind." She stood and reached for him, but he shooed her hand away.

"Yeah right."

"Shari is leaving a trust to help with expenses."

He turned to leave.

"I'm sorry," she said again.

"Sorry's not a get out of jail free card, Becca."

She cleaned up the remains of their dinner as she listened to Jack's SUV start up and drive away. He was right. "Sorry" didn't fix anything. There was nothing that could fix what she did seven years ago. But her alternative hadn't been much better. If they'd gotten married back then, they would be divorced by now and Jacqueline would have parents who hated each other.

"Hey there." Her father had come downstairs and out onto the patio. "Jack leave?"

Becca was certain her father wouldn't have come downstairs if he didn't know that Jack was gone.

"Sorry we woke you."

"So you talked to Jack?"

"Yeah. It didn't go well. Not that I expected it to."

Her father sat down on the edge of the patio and patted the stone pavers next to him. Becca sat.

"If we had gotten married, that would have been a disaster," she started to explain.

"No doubt. I also doubt that you physically overpowered him and dragged him into the trees. So he is not blameless here, either."

"It might have ruined your friendship with the Wolfes."

"Maybe. Because I would have opposed the two of you getting married at that age. I see enough eighteen-year-old parents in my practice to know how well that usually works out. But *my* children are more important than any friendship I have. That's true for your mom, too."

"So what do you suggest I do now?"

"With Jack or with Jacqueline?"

"Both?"

"Well, I see single parents all the time. Quite a few who are less suited to parenthood than you are."

"That's damning with faint praise, dad."

"I didn't mean it like that. Besides, you won't be doing this by yourself."

"You say that like I've already decided to do it."

"Haven't you?"

She stared out into the dark. Near the bottom of the yard stood the big old maple tree that Jack's mom sat beneath at her parents' anniversary party, the tree beneath which Mrs. Wolfe had asked Becca to finish Jack's wedding quilt. Tonight, the tree's trunk and leafy branches were just shadowy silhouettes in the dark. Her father waited, quietly. That was Dr. Trevor. Strong, patient, gentle, and wise. As a pediatrician, he had to figure out what might be wrong even when the patient was too young to talk.

That talent had always extended to Becca, too. She and Dan Trevor weren't related by blood. Biologically, he was her aunt's husband. Becca was six years old when she learned from the school gossips that she was adopted. Dr. Trevor drove to school to pick her up early, because Becca wasn't able to stop crying. Even today, she could still remember the shock—and the shame —of that news. Not just that her parents weren't really her parents, but that everyone else in St. Caroline already knew it.

He, of course, had known exactly what to say.

"Do you remember the day when I learned that I was adopted?"

"Yes, I remember it like it was yesterday."

"You told me that we weren't related by blood. But we were related by love."

She felt her father's arm drape over her shoulder, heavy and comforting.

"You always said exactly the right thing. I don't think I have that in me."

He chuckled, and the movement vibrated through her chest.

"I'm sure sometimes I said exactly the wrong thing. You just don't remember all those times. I would bet my last dollar that if you asked Cass, she would contend that I always said the wrong thing."

"The Wolfes are going to hate me."

"No, they won't. Tim will be angrier with Jack for not keeping his pants on."

"Easier having boys than girls, huh? Less to worry about."

"Well, I don't have any sons so I can't speak to that. But I think Jack is probably the perfect example of how nobody really knows what goes on with other families' children."

"I did it for—"

"I know. Your mother told me. For what it's worth, sweetheart, I believe you did the right thing back then. Did it imperfectly. And I wish you had enlisted our help." He squeezed her tight against his side. "You didn't have to live out there in Ohio by yourself all these years."

"I did it to help Jack."

"Honestly? I don't care about Jack. But you did the responsible thing—found a person who could give your daughter a good life. And now she is also trying to do the responsible thing for her daughter. Of everyone involved in this ..." He searched for the right word, but Becca went ahead and supplied it.

"Mess."

"Well, I was trying to be more diplomatic. But she knows this little girl better than anyone else, and she thinks you are the most responsible course of action."

"Responsibility isn't exactly my middle name."

"On the contrary, you take responsibility for too many things, sweetheart. Things that aren't your responsibility to begin with."

"If you're talking about the insurance deductible—"

"That's one thing, yes. Mom and I are going to put that into a college fund for Jacqueline."

"You're supposed to use it to—"

He lifted his arm from her shoulder and turned to face her. "You don't get to tell us what to do with our money, sweetheart.

That's not your responsibility. Just like Jack Wolfe's life was not your responsibility seven years ago. Or now either. Even this little girl is not your responsibility any longer. Just because her mother thinks you're the right solution to her dilemma doesn't mean you have to be." The sternness left his voice. "But Becs, if anyone is responsible enough to take this on, it's you. Your sisters? I'm not sure I'd be sitting here offering the same advice to any of them." He reached out and tweaked her chin. "You inherited all the responsibility genes."

Becca looked back out into the night. There were so many things she didn't know about raising a child. Or about herself, for that matter. And certainly, she knew next to nothing about little Jackie Weber.

"You'll have lots of support here, Becs. Us, your sisters, Tim. I don't know what Jack will do. Of Tim and Angie's boys, he's the one I know the least. But Tim will be there for you. I'm sure of that."

He shook out his legs, stood, and reached his hand down to help up Becca.

"And you know, I've dealt with kids in my practice who have lost a parent. What these kids need is continuity in their lives, some things to remain the same, and the knowledge that someone understands their fears. We couldn't give that to you. By the time we got everything sorted out in Ohio, you'd already spent several weeks in two different foster homes. Because of the girls back here, we had to just bring you to St. Caroline right away. You were so young, Becca, and you had no idea who we were. It still breaks my heart, thinking about it."

"I didn't make it easy, did I?" she said.

"No." He squeezed her hand gently. "But your mom and I would do it all over again in a heartbeat."

CHAPTER 26

"**W**hy did you two break up? I thought you said things were going well." Matt lifted another slice of sausage-laden pizza from the carryout box. He took a large bite, his eyes trained on Jack.

"Things stopped going well." The pizza on his plate looked thoroughly unappetizing.

"How so? I know a thing or two about women, Jack. Maybe I can offer you some advice."

Jack resisted the urge to roll his eyes at his brother. He doubted Matt knew a thing or two about the situation Jack was currently in. *Hook up once with a girl you barely know at the very end of high school. She gets pregnant and leaves town without telling anyone. Gives up the baby for adoption without your permission. Then comes back to town the exact same day you do, makes you fall in love with her, and then tells you she might be adopting your child back.* Yeah, Mattie knew nothing about that.

On the other hand, he couldn't keep the situation a secret from his family much longer. Not if the girl was coming to St. Caroline soon. Jacqueline. His daughter. That blew him away. He had a daughter. He still wasn't sure what he thought of that. Or how he felt toward Becca anymore. He was angry, sure. Confused, definitely.

He also missed her. He was sitting on Matt's sofa, the one where they'd had that intense make out session. She'd gotten under his skin. Maybe she had gotten under his skin seven years ago, and it had lain in wait until this summer.

"Becca got pregnant."

"Come again?" A slice of pizza paused, mid-air, between the plate and Matt's mouth.

"You heard me."

"There are condoms in the bathroom. You could have helped yourself."

"Yeah, I noticed that you have a lifetime supply. I'm not talking about now, anyway. She got pregnant seven years ago."

Matt's expression was one of pure skepticism. "You two got together ..." Matt calculated the time. "... back in high school?"

"Just once. At a party."

He watched as understanding dawned on his brother. "Is that why she moved away?"

Jack nodded.

"Huh. Mom and Dad never mentioned that."

"They don't know."

"*Don't* know? As in still? Present tense?"

"I didn't know until a few days ago. Becca didn't tell anyone. She just went off, had the baby in Ohio, and gave it up for adoption."

"Damn."

The word hung between them for several minutes as Matt finished his slice. He popped open another can of soda.

"So when are you going to tell them?"

"I don't know. It has to be soon because the adoptive mother is bringing her for a visit."

Matt frowned. "*Why?*"

Jack realized he had left a lot out of the story. "The adoptive mother is terminally ill. Cancer. She wants Becca to take the girl back." Not "girl," he reminded himself. *Your daughter.* "Jacqueline."

"Jacqueline?" Matt shook his head. "Wow. I got no advice for you on that."

"That's a first. The one time I actually could use some advice, you come up empty."

~

THE HOSPITAL'S automatic doors slid open and Jack rushed head-long into the fresh air of the parking lot. He doubted he would ever get the smell of illness out of his nose. Every day brought the inevitable closer, like a train speeding out of control and Jack was tied to the tracks. All he could do was lie there and watch it happen. There was no escaping it, not even for a minute.

Becca had been an escape, a respite from reality, but now that was gone too. And really, he was probably making more out of their friendship than was really there. What had possessed him to confess that he was falling for her? Because was he? He came home on Memorial Day. It was now the end of July. Hardly enough time to fall in love with someone. Not to mention, there was no indication that she felt the same way. Sure, she was physically attracted to him—that much was clear. But Becca played her feelings close to the vest. He wondered whether anyone really knew her all that well.

Maybe all she had wanted was a summer fling, an escape from the reality of her own life in Ohio ... until reality intervened. That was probably just as well. Jack's own reality was upstairs in a hospital room. He had been "excused" by his father while a nurse tended to his mother.

He strolled around the corner of the hospital, through the small flower garden planted there, and back to the front entrance. Then he did it again, waiting for the text from his father saying that it was okay to return to his mother's room. On the fourth go-round, he saw a familiar figure crossing the parking lot toward the automatic doors.

Becca.

He picked up his pace to get there before she did, because the sight of a large bundle of fabric in her arms gave him a sinking feeling. *Oh hell no.* She got closer and closer to the door. How was it that she could cross a large parking lot faster than he could traverse a miniature garden? He began to jog.

"Becca!" he shouted and watched as she stopped in her tracks. Yep, that was his wedding quilt in her arms. Another complication. As if there weren't enough already. He slowed to a walk until he was standing in front of her on the sidewalk. Her expression showed her to be as wary as he felt.

"Hi." She hugged the quilt a little tighter to her chest, like a shield.

"What are you doing here?" In the back of his mind, Jack knew there had to be a more graceful way to start this conversation but he was too tired to find it.

"Your mother wants to see your wedding quilt." She bounced the bundle of fabric in her arms. "My mom was here to see her yesterday."

"You're not telling her about ..."

"Jackie is her name."

"Do your parents know?"

"Yes. I told them."

"I haven't told mine yet."

"You're going to have to do that eventually."

"I am aware of that. But it's hard to find a good moment these days, you know? You picked a great time for this."

"I didn't choose this timing, Jack. If it were up to me, I would wave a magic wand and Shari would be healthy. She would continue to be Jackie's mom. But that's not the way things are working out."

He reached out his arms. "Give me that. I'll take it up to her."

She frowned at him. "You don't trust me?"

He paused. Obviously, the answer to that question was "no."

Becca didn't wait for that answer. "I did what I did so you wouldn't get stuck in St. Caroline. So you could go to law school and get a big fancy job and have the wonderful life everyone thought you *deserved.* I did it for *you.*"

She shoved the quilt into his arms and turned on her heel. Ten feet later, she spun back around.

"And now here you are, in St. Caroline anyway," she yelled from across the hospital's driveway. "You dropped out of law school. There's no big fancy job, no wonderful life."

"What does that have to do with—"

"I moved away from my family for nothing! I've been lying to everyone for years for nothing! I gave up my daughter for *nothing!*"

Becca turned and headed back to her car, this time for good. Jack turned in the other direction, only to see his father standing in the open doorway of the hospital. His father's eyes dropped from Jack's face to the quilt in his arms, and then back up to his face.

"Care to share what that was about?"

Jack sighed. "I might as well tell you both upstairs. If you think mom can handle it."

"She'll probably handle it better than it appears you are. And if she's going to hear about this from someone, I'd rather it be you."

His father's voice was thick with disappointment. Jack had promised not to add to his mother's worries. On the other hand, his father did tell him that she wanted everyone to come clean about things. *No, mom, I'm not gay but ...*

They walked toward the bank of elevators, and Jack shifted the quilt into one arm so he could press the call button.

"I feel like I'm ten years old right now and being marched to the kitchen to discuss my behavior."

"More or less."

His father clapped a hand on his back, square between Jack's shoulder blades. Inside the wall, the elevator groaned and creaked as it made its way down to them.

"You're probably going to say that I'm acting like I'm ten years old."

"Nah. You seem to have come to that conclusion already on your own." The elevator door opened and Tim stepped inside, holding the door for Jack. "That was always what discussions in the kitchen were about. Getting you boys to see your own behavior. Mattie and Oliver were never quite as good at that as you were." He sighed. "Even though they had more practice than you did. Especially Matt."

"Matt had *way* more practice. Not a skill he ever did develop."

"Oh, I think Mattie sees his own behavior now. He just doesn't give a good damn."

The elevator doors closed and Jack felt that moment of weightlessness as the car began to lift them. When they reached the fourth floor, the car shuddered to a stop and they waited for what felt to Jack like an hour before the doors opened. He blinked hard as he stepped into the harsh, bright light of the hospital corridor. Jack immediately turned in the direction of his mother's room, but his father's hand halted him.

"Son, you were always a smart kid. Three steps ahead of your brothers. Your mom and I tried to protect those differences for you, so you wouldn't feel pressured to do what your brothers did."

They stepped aside to make way for a nurse pushing a man in a wheelchair.

"Instead, I felt pressured to do what you and mom wanted me to do." Jack watched the wheelchair disappear into a room.

"I see that now."

"And Becca evidently felt that she would be pressured to do what you and mom would have wanted me to do. And now

everything's a huge mess. Not that it's your fault, dad. I understand that parents do what they think is best at the time. You
probably had to wing it more with me than with Mattie and
Oliver."

Tim started to walk slowly down the hall and Jack fell into
step next to him.

"Honestly, Jack? When it came to you, I deferred to your
mom's wishes. Maybe that was a mistake."

"Please don't tell me it was just because she loved me too
much." Jack didn't want to hear that hoary cliché.

"She loves all of us too much."

They were nearing his mother's room.

"I did try it your way," Jack said. "I went to law school. I stuck
it out for two years. But I hated it from the beginning. I can't
stand being cooped up inside all day. And I need the instant grati-
fication of helping someone immediately."

The door to his mother's room was open halfway. They
stopped a few feet outside.

"Well, I always have a use for a smart firefighter. With your
mother's blessing, of course." His father laid his arm across Jack's
shoulders. "Not that Mattie isn't smart."

"Or smart ass," Jack replied.

Their laughter announced their presence as Tim pushed the
door all the way open. Jack's mother looked tired, as she always
did these days, but happy to see them.

"What's the joke?"

"The question of whether Mattie is smart or just smart ass,"
Tim answered.

"I'm not wading into that," she said. "I think all my boys are
geniuses, handsome, and fine men all around."

Her eyes lit on Jack's face, but it was his father's look that
burned straight through his skin. He set the quilt on the foot of
the bed, then leaned over and kissed her cool skin.

"About that, mom … I have something to tell you."

Behind him, his father cleared his throat.

"Several things, actually."

His father picked up one of the metal and vinyl visitor's chairs and carried it over to Jack. Yeah, that was a good idea—sitting down so he was at his mother's eye level. His father leaned over her and tucked in her blanket, adjusted the white pillows beneath her head. Today, she wore a bright red and yellow scarf printed with flowers. The scarf was happy and cheery, two emotions no one in this room could lay claim to—though his mother was certainly pretending.

Jack tried to collect his thoughts. Which of the several things he needed to own up to should he start with? Dropping out of law school? Joining the St. Caroline fire department? Getting the daughter of one of his mother's closest friends pregnant? Or should he start with a blanket admission of lying to everyone for several years?

Finally, it was his mother who spoke first. "How's Becca?"

"Good. I brought the quilt for you to see."

"Bring it up here. Let me see it."

He moved the quilt to her lap.

"Tim, can you—?"

His father moved immediately to help her sit up a little higher. "Good?"

Jack couldn't picture his father alone in the house, without the woman he'd spent his life with. Jack couldn't picture life for any of them without her in it. *Take me instead.* He helped his mother unfold the wedding quilt and watched as she ran her bony, spotted hands over the fabric. Her fingers traced the tiny stitches Becca had spent hours putting in. Like he could ever use this quilt now, not with what had happened. No way could he ever give it to his bride. How to explain that? *Here's my wedding quilt, made by my mother and the girl I carelessly knocked up when I was eighteen.* He wasn't that great a catch to begin with.

"She did a nice job," his mother said quietly. She looked up and smiled at him. "Nicer than what I was able to do for Oliver and Matt. Don't tell your brothers though."

He doubted his brothers cared, although Serena did use Oliver's wedding quilt in a guest room. Jack couldn't imagine even using his that way. It would always remind him of Becca. Quilting, in general, reminded him of the Trevor family.

He helped her fold the quilt back up.

"Michelle said you and Becca aren't seeing each other anymore."

His heart seized up at the thought of what else Michelle Trevor might have told her.

"Yeah. I mean, well ... we weren't really seeing each other to begin with. Just hanging out."

She rolled her eyes at him. "You're staying with Mattie. I'm surprised he hasn't taught you how to prevaricate better than that."

He took a deep breath and dived in. "Mom, I've been prevaricating about a lot of things."

"You're not working in the legal department at your company," she said matter of factly.

Jack knew he had just failed entirely at keeping the surprise from his face. "Who told you—"

"There's an employee directory on their web site. You're listed under security."

"That's true. I dropped out of law school last year. I'm not a lawyer. I'm a security guard." He took another deep breath. He needed the oxygen before dropping the final bomb. "And a firefighter."

Her gaze left Jack and fell on her husband. "Where?" she asked, still not looking at Jack.

"In California. And here. Dad put me on at the station. They're short-staffed."

He couldn't take his eyes off her face. She was struggling to stay calm and she made no effort to hide it from him or his father."

"I'm sorry, mom."

"You're a Wolfe." Her eyes returned to him. "For better or for worse." She took a long, raspy breath. "Well, if you're going to do it, I'd rather it be here with your dad and brothers."

Her words were equal parts acceptance and resignation, and he knew that working for his father was not much comfort to her. Tim Wolfe hadn't been able to save her twin brother—and his best friend. It wasn't a given that he would be able to save his sons either.

"I'm a good firefighter," Jack said quietly, then added, "better than Mattie."

That broke the tension in the room and brought a smile to her lips again. "I guess the real threat to your safety is the two of you living together."

"I promise not to kill him. Unless I absolutely have to."

"Jackie—" She gestured at the plastic tumbler of water on the hospital stand. He picked it up and held it to her lips. "Thank you. So why did you and Becca break up?"

"Becca got pregnant."

There was a look of alarm on his mother's face. "She is? Well, why would you break up?"

"Not is. Was. When we were teenagers."

His father sucked in a sharp breath.

"You two weren't even dating ..."

"It happened at a party after graduation. Just that once and ... once was all it took."

"Oh Jackie."

The disappointment in her voice made him feel ten years old.

"Why are we just now learning about this?" she asked.

"I just learned about it a few days ago. That's why she left St. Caroline after high school. She moved to Ohio and had the baby there."

His mother frowned. "I can't believe Michelle never said anything to me."

"I'm going out on a limb here and guessing that Michelle and Dan didn't know either," his father said. He looked at Jack for confirmation.

"No, they didn't," Jack confirmed it. "She didn't tell anyone. She went to Ohio and gave the baby up for adoption."

His mother flinched and he knew what she was thinking. *Grandchild.*

"Why would she do that? We would have made you marry her."

"That's why she did it, mom. So I wouldn't have to marry her. Fate worse than death, apparently."

A low rumbling sound came from his father's throat. A quick glance at him told Jack that his father had just made the connection to the conversation he'd overheard downstairs.

"Why are we learning about this now then?" his father asked.

If you're going to take me, now would be a good time. Just saying.

"The woman who adopted her—"

"Her?" his father said.

"Yes, it's a girl. Jacqueline." He paused a moment to let that bit of information sink in. Then he continued before his parents had the time to consider the other implications—in a family of boys, there was finally a girl. And no one knew about it. "The woman— her mother—is ill." Damn. He didn't know how to say this. *And you're making me do this in the freaking hospital!*

"Oh, sweetheart." His mother understood without him having to spell it out.

Thank you! Finally, a little help!

"She needs a guardian. She wants Becca to do that. To adopt her back."

"And is Becca going to do that?"

"She said she hasn't decided yet."

CHAPTER 27

$\mathcal{B}$ecca leaned on the bar and sipped at the glass of ice water Mike had poured for her.

"Nervous?" Mike asked.

She nodded. "A little." She looked over at the round table in the corner. Five chairs surrounded it, a shiny mylar balloon tied to one. "Okay, a lot."

Becca wasn't working that day. Instead, she was waiting for the Webers to show up—Shari, Shari's parents, and Jacqueline. Her daughter. She was still getting used to thinking that. They flew into Washington, DC, the day before and were on their way to St. Caroline now. Their arrival was expected any minute. Shari had texted her several times with updates.

Leaving DC.

Crossing the Bay Bridge.

Ten minutes out, I think.

"You'll be fine," Mike reassured her.

It wasn't really herself she was worried about. But what if Jackie didn't like her? What if Shari's parents didn't? Or—worst of all—what if Shari didn't? After all, it had been years since Becca and Shari had seen each other. She might see Becca as

238

unsuitable and change her mind about wanting Becca to adopt Jackie. Her parents and the Wolfes had done their best to keep the situation quiet but word was still getting around St. Caroline. Can't keep a secret for long in a small town. Not that she cared about what people thought. It was hard for her reputation to get much worse at this point. (*She went after Jack Wolfe? And now she's trying again? The girl has balls, you gotta say that.*) But the last thing Shari needed right now was to have to persuade a friend or cousin to spend the next eleven years raising Jackie.

Her parents had gone to the hospital to talk to Angie and Tim, who weren't angry the way Becca had expected. Becca had sent her apologies via her mother, but she was reluctant to go to the hospital herself. Much as she wanted to speak to Jack's mother in person, she didn't want to run into him again. He must be furious about people in town knowing he was the father.

Becca took another sip of water to calm her nerves. Their argument at the hospital was the last time they had spoken. Nor had she even seen him around town. That didn't surprise her though—all of the Wolfes were practically living at the hospital when they weren't at the station.

Inside her purse, her phone buzzed. She took a deep breath, knowing it was from Shari.

Just dropped off rental car with valet. Checking in. Be there in a few.

"They're here," she said to Mike.

He patted her on the arm. "Don't worry. You're going to get the best service Skipjack's has ever offered. Just be yourself."

Just be myself. That's what had gotten her into this situation in the first place.

She walked over to the corner table and pulled out a chair across from the one with the balloon. When she looked up, they were there—standing at the hostess station, Shari in a long-sleeved blouse and skirt, a patterned scarf covering her head and knotted stylishly at the nape of her neck. Her parents, Robert and

Alice Weber, looked like any other well-heeled guests of the Chesapeake Inn. Robert was dressed in seersucker Bermuda shorts, a yellow golf shirt, and leather-trimmed boat shoes. Alice wore a pale blue sleeveless dress and open-toed flat sandals, her silver hair short and chic.

Then there was Jacqueline, who coolly took in her surroundings, surveying the other tables, the bar with its smiling bartender, the black and white photographs on the wall. Lastly, her gaze landed on Becca. Becca gave her a smile, and hoped it looked more confident and at ease than she felt. The girl's cheeks quirked up in a quick smile and then she turned back to the Webers.

That was her daughter. *Right there. My daughter.* She couldn't believe it. It was hard to reconcile this tall young girl with the infant she had last seen in person in an Ohio hospital. She had hoped the memories of that day would fade, but they hadn't. She still vividly remembered being wheeled into the operating room for the c-section, Shari in a gown and mask walking next to her. She remembered the bright lights stinging her eyes and the blue screen blocking her view. Then a baby's hiccupped cry and a nurse handing a swaddled bundle to Shari. And the most unforgettable thing of all—the expression of utter joy and wonder on Shari's face, and her tearful "thank you" to Becca, who lay exhausted on the operating table and feeling suddenly more alone than she ever thought possible.

Now here was that baby again—only now she was seven years old and tall for her age. Her blonde hair was pulled back in a French braid and her arms and shoulders glowed tan in a sleeveless halter-style sundress. Her long legs ended in beaded flip flops on her feet. She looked like Jack ... and all of Becca's sisters. That was a good thing, Becca thought. Jackie would fit into her families here. No one would be able to look at her and immediately pinpoint her as the "new one," the way Becca had always felt in town.

Kylie, the hostess, smiled warmly at the Webers. Becca was glad that most of the other diners in the restaurant today were guests at the Inn and not locals. Only a few people glanced up at the Webers as Kylie led them toward Becca. Mrs. Weber walked slowly, leaning on her husband. Shari had mentioned that her mother fell and broke a hip a year ago. She could see why the Webers might not feel comfortable raising a young child.

When they reached the table, Shari wrapped her arms around Becca as though they were long lost friends. After the momentary surprise of that wore off, Becca hugged her back, feeling the boniness of Shari's ribs beneath her arms.

"Look at you!" Shari touched the ends of Becca's long hair. "Last time I saw you, this was so short."

Becca was hit with an image of herself as a pregnant teenager. She had let her dyed black hair grow out, and then chopped it off so only her natural color remained.

Shari turned to the table. "Mom, Dad, this is Becca."

They shook hands, then Shari introduced her to Jackie. The girl extended her hand for a grownup handshake, too. Shari had yet to tell her who Becca really was. Both she and Becca wanted to see how this visit played out first. As far as Jackie knew, Becca was just an old friend of her mother's.

"Nice to meet you." Her voice was clear and confident.

Becca felt her heart crack a little, at the knowledge of what lay ahead for her. How much of that confidence was going to survive? How much of it was really there now? Becca had always put on the tough girl attitude, even at Jackie's age, but it was all image. Nothing more. On the surface, she had dared people to mess with her. Underneath, she had been terrified that someone actually would.

Becca's favorite waitress, Janelle, arrived to take their drink orders.

"Oh look, dear," Alice Weber leaned over to show the wine list to her husband. "This is an excellent wine list. I'll have a glass of the Columbia River pinot gris, please."

Becca looked over at Mike and smiled.

"Do you have a local beer?" Robert Weber asked Janelle.

"We have a summer ale from the Brass Monkey Brewery in Annapolis. It's easily our best-selling beer."

"I'll take one of those, then."

Shari ordered sparkling water, and Janelle turned to Jackie.

"We have a special kids' drink today," Janelle said. "It's limited edition, just created this morning by our bartender, Mike. That's him over there." Mike gave them all a wave. "It's called the Pirate's Jewel. It's a sparkling peach lemonade with raspberry ice cubes that give it a little extra zing as they melt."

"Sounds good," Shari said.

Becca caught Janelle's eye. Mike was smooth. Becca had been working shifts all week so she could take a few days off while the Webers were here. Not once had Mike said he was creating a special drink for Jackie.

"I'll try one of those," she said. She leaned across the table toward Jackie. "This restaurant is famous for these drinks. They had them back when I was a kid."

Jackie weighed that information. "I'll try one, too," she said. "I like lemonade, Never had peach lemonade before, but I'm game."

It was hard not to speculate on where Jackie took after Jack, and where she might take after Becca. Becca remembered Jack as being precise and articulate in his speech, even in elementary school. But he hadn't been drawn to the new and unknown like a moth to flame—the way Becca was. Jackie seemed to have a little of each quality.

"Becca, I never knew you grew up in such a pretty little town," Shari said as they perused the menus. "Dad, you never told me how nice this area was."

"Well, I was a student back then. St. Caroline was a little quiet for young bucks like us." He smiled at Becca. "After the Navy, I moved to a landlocked state to be with the love of my life." He gave Alice a quick squeeze of the shoulders. "But I still miss the water."

"You know, I forgot how much I missed it too until I moved back here this summer." St. Caroline was starting to grow on her. She joked to Cassidy just last night that the town had changed so much since she was a kid. Becca knew the truth. It wasn't St. Caroline that had changed. It was her.

As they ate, the conversation meandered from boats and the weather to their day trip to Washington, DC, and what Jackie was looking forward to in second grade. They were just finishing dessert when Matt Wolfe entered the restaurant with Mason and Cam in tow. Becca wasn't sure how the Wolfe family really felt toward her these days. Her parents assured her that Tim and Angie were not upset with either her or Jack. But Jack's brothers might view the situation differently.

She hoped that Matt just wouldn't notice her, but the lunch hour was winding down, and not much obstructed the view between the hostess station and their table. Not enough for even a five year old. Cam spotted her and waved. Becca waved back, just as Matt turned to see what his nephew was up to. She was surprised at Matt's smile, and even more surprised when he and the boys began walking toward them.

Or not surprised, she thought, when Matt walked around the table to a spot where he could get a good look at Jackie. Mason introduced himself straight away to her. Becca introduced Matt to the adults. Pleasantries were exchanged and Matt wished the Webers a good visit.

But even Shari took note of his last long look at Jackie before pulling the boys away to a table across the room. She gave Becca a questioning look and Becca answered with a tiny shake of the head. As Robert and Alice pored over the check, Becca mouthed "brother" to Shari.

~

THE NEXT THREE days were a whirlwind of activity. A visit to the town's historic lighthouse and museum, shopping on Main Street, a cookout with Becca's family, a trip to a waterpark, a sunset sailing charter. It was the last that Jackie seemed to enjoy the most. Even Becca was tired by Saturday evening. She couldn't imagine how exhausted Shari must be.

Robert Weber had taken Jackie to see a Little League baseball game, with the promise of ice cream afterward. His wife was resting in her room at the Chesapeake Inn. Becca was sitting in Shari's room across the hall, eating room service sandwiches from Skipjack's.

"This has been a wonderful week," Shari said. "Your family couldn't have been nicer."

"They survived me. I think Jackie will be a walk in the park compared to that."

Shari laughed, but Becca could hear the rasp of her breath beneath it. Sitting on the Inn's big upholstered sofa, Shari looked tiny, like a strong wind might snap her in half. Or the air conditioning kicking on. She looked like Jack's mother—dark shadows beneath sunken eyes, sharp cheekbones where there hadn't been any before, her scarf not hiding the fact that there was no hair on her head.

"I'm really having a hard time picturing you as a difficult child. When we went through the adoption, you were as steady as a rock. You were a lot more certain about it than I was, to be honest. I wanted a child, more than anything, but I wasn't sure I'd be a good mother or not."

"You've been a terrific mother, Shari. I did the right thing back then. I wasn't ready to be a parent."

"And now?" Shari's expression was one of both hope and girding herself for bad news.

"Yes, I'm ready now."

"Oh Becca." Shari hugged Becca with what little strength she had left. "Thank you. Thank you." She released her weak embrace. "Thank you for loaning her to me these seven years. As hard as this is—" She waved a thin hand in the air, as if to indicate "everything." "It would be so much harder if I hadn't had the chance to be a mother. I feel like that's selfish because I know it's harder for Jackie to go through this. And eventually, she won't remember me much." Tears shone in her eyes.

Becca took Shari's hands in her own. "I won't let her forget you. You were her first mother." She gave Shari's hands a gentle squeeze. "I was so young when my mom passed away. I don't have any memories of her. But I won't let that happen to Jackie."

Shari frowned. "What do you mean? I thought we met your ..."

"I'm adopted. My mother is actually my aunt. You didn't notice that I look like exactly no one else in the family?"

"I did sort of notice that. But I chalked it up to recessive genes or something. Oh Becca, I had no idea." Shari smiled and wiped away the threatening tears. "This makes you even more perfect."

"I guess I don't really think about it much anymore. I did when I was a kid, though. Really, I pretty much didn't let anyone forget it."

"And now I adore your parents even more. And all your sisters ... I was an only child. I always wanted sisters. I'm sure the reality is different from my fantasies."

Becca shrugged. "It can be. But aunts are probably more fun than sisters."

"This is working out so much better than I even hoped for. I wasn't sure how your family was going to take this."

"They will help me if I need it." She rolled her eyes. "And even if I don't need it."

"Your mom said that you and Jack? Is that his name? That you two were dating again."

"We were, sort of. But not anymore. He's only here for the

summer anyway. He lives in California. I'm not sure how that's going to work out, honestly, since the rest of his family still lives in St. Caroline. I'm glad you adopted Jackie, but I made a huge mess of things here."

"Your mom said he didn't take the news well."

Becca let out a sigh. "No, he didn't. Nor should he have, I guess. I should have told him I was pregnant but I thought it would be better for him if I didn't. I mean, it *was* better for him but ..." Becca stood and began gathering up their plates for room service to collect. "... maybe it was only best for me."

CHAPTER 28

"Hey guys, help me out with the blanket here—" But Cam and Mason kicked off their flip flops and ran down to the water. "Or not," Jack finished his sentence. "Mason! Keep an eye on your brother!" he shouted at the boys as they crashed into the soft, lapping waves of the bay.

Serena wasn't feeling well again today. Jack had offered to get Cam and Mason out of the house for a few hours so she could rest. According to Oliver, this pregnancy was way harder than the first two had been. Jack started to wonder whether Becca's pregnancy had been hard or easy, then he stopped himself—the way he did every time Becca Trevor crept into his thoughts.

You're mad at her, remember?

He shook out the blanket and spread it across a patch of sand, then dropped the backpack filled with sunscreen and water bottles on top of it. It was Sunday morning and already Secret Beach was filling up with sun worshippers. He was about to point that out, but stopped that impulse too. He was done discussing things with God. God clearly wasn't listening. So screw it.

He looked toward the water and his heart stopped cold. The

boys were gone. He sprinted toward the water, then heard Cam yell, "Uncle Jack! We're over here!" He turned to see Cam stretched up on tiptoes and waving both hands at him. Mason was talking to a tall, blonde girl.

A girl Jack hadn't seen before ... but who looked exactly as he had imagined she would.

The moment he'd been dreading—trying like hell to avoid—was here. He couldn't take his eyes off his ... daughter. Matt was right. He had no plausible deniability here. If Jack Wolfe was going to have a daughter, that's exactly what she would look like. Tall and gangly like he'd been at her age. Blonde hair bleached even lighter by the sun. And—as her eyes flicked up to meet his—impeccable situational awareness. When he was a kid, everyone's perception of him was of a quiet kid whose nose was always in a book. But that hadn't meant Jack was oblivious to what went on around him. He was perfectly capable of reading and taking in his surroundings at the same time.

Like she was right now. She was talking to Mason, who was seven years old too, but her eyes kept returning to Jack. Seven-year-old girls used to terrify him when he was that age, and he was remembering why. Her gaze made him feel like she was peering straight into his mind—and she was not impressed by what she was finding.

He looked away from her only to find Becca's gaze skewering him too. She leaned over and spoke to the kids, who took off immediately for the water. They had been dismissed. Now it was his turn, evidently.

He walked over to Becca and the woman she was with—his daughter's adoptive mother, who was covered up head to toe. Long sleeve shirt, one of those long skirt things women wore at the beach, and a broad-brimmed straw hat.

"Hey," he said when he reached them.

"Hi there. Shari, this is Jack." Becca's voice couldn't have been any frostier. Obviously, she wasn't spending any time remembering ... he pushed that thought from his mind. *You're not supposed to be remembering either.* "Jack, this is Shari Weber."

Jack shook the older woman's hand. Her skin felt papery thin, just like his mother's. Up close, he could see a scarf peeking out from under the straw hat she wore. The dark shadows beneath her eyes were starkly familiar—just like his mother's.

Thanks for the happy day at the beach! No need to let me forget about things, not even for a few hours!

Shari Weber looked him up and down, then glanced toward the water where the kids were splashing in the shallows.

"Yes," he answered her unspoken query. "I'm the other half."

"Are those your boys? Your brother had them the other day. That's when they met Jackie."

"No, Cam and Mason are Oliver's kids. That was Matt you met."

"Oliver's wife is pregnant. She's been sick a lot with this one," Becca explained.

He watched the three kids play together. Two other girls joined them, all of them laughing and talking. Happy. He couldn't imagine what Jackie would go through, losing her mother at this age. He wasn't sure he was going to survive it himself. Oh intellectually, he knew he would. He'll wake up the morning after she's gone ... and then the next morning ... and the morning after that ... and every morning for the *entire damn rest of my life!*

But a piece of him would be gone. A piece of his family. He couldn't even begin to imagine holidays and birthdays in the future with just his brothers and father. The picture was fuzzy and indistinct—four men, two young boys, and Serena as the one female, the lone balancing force to all that testosterone.

"Can I ask what you've decided to do, Becca?" The question was out of his mouth before he even had a chance to consider how bad the timing of it was.

Becca looked at Shari, then back at him. "The plan is for me to adopt her. It's not going to happen overnight."

Shari jumped in. "I'm working with a child psychologist in Ohio. It's going to be a gradual transition as we prepare Jackie for what's ahead. I don't know how many more trips I will have the strength to make, but my parents will bring Jackie here. I will fly Becca out to Ohio for visits. You too, if you want."

"All of this is contingent, of course, on Jackie wanting to be with me," Becca hurried to clarify.

"But after this weekend, I don't think that's going to be an issue," Shari jumped in again. "And my parents are out with a realtor this morning, scoping out the real estate market here. They're quite taken with St. Caroline."

"They would move here?"

Shari nodded. "They never intended to retire in Ohio, but they stayed to help me with Jackie. And to be near her."

"She might live with them at first," Becca added.

"That would help a lot, if her grandparents were here," Jack allowed. It sounded like Becca had this all planned out already. *It's really happening.* His daughter was moving to St. Caroline. He watched as she turned cartwheels in the sand, then tried to show Cam how to do them too. "Her cousins seem to like her."

He wasn't sure what to feel about all this. Or think about it. It was hard to fathom that he and Becca—together—had created that little girl. Another person. And just like the first time, things were happening that he apparently had no part in.

HIS MOTHER'S eyes were closed when he slipped into the hospital room, and his heart stopped. It was doing that a lot lately and yet he was still here. He watched the slight form of her body beneath the thin hospital sheet, looking for the faint rise and fall of her breath. He didn't want to be the one who had to … he couldn't even articulate the thought. The doctor had said there was maybe a week left.

Just get me through this. Please. That's all I ask. Get me through this next week and I'll be a model citizen from here on out. Whatever you want, I'll do it. I'll help Becca with Jackie. I'll stay in St. Caroline. Anything. Just help me survive this.

"Jack?" His mother's voice was weak. "Is that you?"

"Yes, mom. How can you tell it's me with your eyes closed?"

"A mother's intuition." Her eyes opened. "Plus, your dad said you'd be coming by."

He smiled at her. At least, her sense of humor wasn't gone yet.

"I'm on call, but maybe nothing will happen in town today."

"There's a good chance of nothing happening. St. Caroline is nice that way."

"It's starting to grow on me, I'll admit." He sat down in the hospital chair that was always right next to her bed.

"So you think you'll stay?"

"Maybe. Becca is going to adopt Jackie."

"That's what Michelle said." She reached her hand out to him. "Have you forgiven Becca yet?"

He didn't answer immediately. The answer was "no." He wasn't sure he ever could forgive her. Becoming parents to a seven-year-old traumatized by the death of the only parent she's ever known? The odds of him and Becca screwing that up royally were pretty high.

His mother seemed to read his thoughts.

"You would not have made a good father back then," she said.

"I know that." His voice was soft.

"But I think you would now."

"I'm not sure about that."

"Becca has a good head on her shoulders. She did the smart thing."

"She didn't tell me about it though. She didn't even give me a choice in the matter."

"There's no perfect route through life, Jack. Pardon my

deathbed wisdom here. Becca took the path she thought was best at the time. What's done is done."

He leaned back in the hard, cold chair and stared up at the ceiling. "I don't know anything about kids."

"Nobody really knows anything about kids until they have them. And even then, every kid is different. Having Oliver and Mattie didn't completely prepare me for you."

"Do you want to meet her?"

"I do. More than anything. But I think it wouldn't be wise. She's already losing a mother. No need for her to lose a grand-mother, as well."

He patted the outline of the phone in the pocket of his shorts. "I have a picture."

"I would love to see that."

He pulled out the phone and tapped on the screen to pull up the photo he had taken of Jackie, Mason, and Cam at the beach. The three of them were squinting in the bright sunlight, sand coating their legs up to the knees, their wet hair plastered to their heads. He handed the phone to his mother, who studied it silently for a long while before speaking.

"You and Becca will have plenty of people to help you. You know that, right?" She handed his phone back.

Jack was beginning to nod agreement when the pager went off in his other pocket. He pulled it out.

"I've got to go, mom." He leaned in and kissed her cheek. "I'll be back later, okay?"

"What kind of call is it?"

"Car accident. I have to go right past it on my way to the station. Maybe it won't be bad and I can come right back."

But when he drove up on the scene, he saw immediately that it was bad. Very bad. The car was practically wrapped around a tree. Two police cars were parked in the middle of the road, blocking traffic. Jack would have to ask them to move one vehicle so he could get through. There was no other way to the station from here, and he needed to get his gear and get on a truck.

As he pulled closer, though, the car began to look familiar. He locked eyes with one of the police officers, who began running toward him, waving his arms. Jack realized why the car looked familiar. It was Serena's car.

He veered his car onto the shoulder of the road and threw it into park, cut the ignition. He called the station.

"Do not let Oliver respond to this call!"

Then he dialed Matt's number too, but it was too late. He ran full speed toward the fire engine as it pulled up, willing his legs to move faster as Oliver hopped down from the driver's seat, his face already frozen in horror and shock.

"Ollie, no!" Jack yelled as his brother began to run toward the mangled car. Out of the corner of his eye, he saw Matt launch into a sprint.

Oliver shook him off when Jack grabbed his arm. "Don't, Ollie. The EMTs are here." When he yanked hard on his brother's sleeve, Oliver gave him a hard shove. Jack stumbled backward into Matt.

"Stop him, Mattie."

They were wrestling with Oliver, who seemed to have gained superhuman strength all of a sudden. It took the arrival of their father to finally pry Oliver away from the car.

"I'm not leaving!" Oliver's words were sharp with anguish.

"No one's asking you to leave." His father was calm. "I'm asking you to stay out of the EMTs' way and let them do their job."

Oliver struggled against his father's hold but, even at fifty-five, Tim Wolfe was still as strong as a younger man. He turned his head to mouth at Jack and Matt, "Who's in the car?"

Jack and Matt looked at each other, the second part of their father's question all too clear. *Who's in the car besides Serena?*

Given the condition of the car, the possibilities were too awful to contemplate.

"I'll go try to find out," Jack said.

Two other firefighters were working on the car, painstakingly cutting away the roof. Jack gave them a wide berth. He approached the EMTs on the other side of the car. One was kneeling next to the shattered window, talking to Serena, trying to keep her conscious and calm. Jack leaned over to look inside, dreading what he might see.

Please let them not be in there. Don't take the boys too.

The back seat was empty. The relief was short-lived, though. The voice of the EMT talking to Serena was growing increasingly urgent, trying to keep her from slipping into unconsciousness. Jack couldn't look at her. It was hard enough when you didn't know the victim of an accident. In California, he never had. They were always strangers. The buildings were always unfamiliar.

He stood and backed away from the scene. That wouldn't always be the case in St. Caroline. There would be moments like the night the Trevors' quilt shop caught fire and he recognized the empty car in the parking as Becca's. Thank God for that damn sock monkey. It was hard enough standing outside while his brothers went in to find her. Something like this? It would take three grown men to drag him away too.

He strode back to where Matt and his father were still holding onto the eldest Wolfe son. He shook his head to let them know that Mason and Cam were not in the car. The phone in his pocket vibrated and he pulled it out. It was a text from Becca.

Charlotte has the boys. Serena asked her to babysit for a few hours.

He held the phone up so Matt could read the text. His brother nodded, then whispered to Oliver. Oliver gave no reaction, and it hit Jack. The boys weren't in the car but Serena wasn't entirely alone either. She was pregnant.

CHAPTER 29

*B*ecca slid a mug of coffee onto the bar in front of Jack. A drunk Jack. Understandable, given the events of recent days. His mother was dying and now his sister-in-law was in a hospital in Baltimore—in a coma, the baby lost.

"We're closing up. Drink this and I'll drive you home."

Jack lifted his face from where he'd been studying the lacquer on the bar for the past hour and a half. His eyelids were heavy. At least a day's worth of stubble shadowed his jaw. Under other circumstances, it would be the sexiest sight she could imagine. But tonight, he looked like a wreck.

He looked at the mug of coffee like he'd never seen such a thing before. He wrapped his hands around it. His lips parted to speak and Becca waited for him to protest the necessity of her driving him home. Instead, he said simply, "Thanks."

While he drank the coffee, she closed out her shift on the register and helped Mike finish cleaning up. Mike cocked his head toward Jack, who was staring into the mug like he was reading tea leaves.

"Are you going to need any help?"

"I don't think so. I think he's sixty percent exhausted, forty percent two sheets to the wind." At least Jack wasn't an obnoxious drunk. In fact, he was exactly the kind of drunk she'd expect him to be—quiet, lost in himself. Not the type to bother anyone else in the bar. Still, she felt Mike's eyes on her as she helped Jack stumble across the parking lot to her car. She gave him a wave as she pulled away.

Jack leaned his head back against the headrest and closed his eyes.

"You asleep over there?" she asked.

"No. Haven't slept in two days."

"I'm sorry, Jack."

He flicked his hand in the air. "Not your fault. My life just sucks right now."

Did he include her and Jackie in that judgment? Probably. She drove the rest of the way without saying anything else.

The lights were all on at Matt's cabin when she pulled into the narrow gravel driveway. She'd no sooner put the car into park when the door to the cabin burst open with so much force, she half expected it to pop off its hinges. Jack slowly unfolded his long body from her car. Matt set upon him immediately.

"Where have you been? I've been calling and texting you!" Matt was spitting mad.

Becca took note of Matt's red eyes and her heart sank. Jack fumbled in his pocket and came up with his phone. He squinted at the side.

"Sorry man. Somehow the ringer got turned off."

Becca followed Jack closely as he slowly navigated the three steps to the cabin's narrow porch—in case he fell.

"Everyone's been trying to find you! And nobody has the time to do that right now!" Matt stepped aside to let Jack and Becca through the door. But inside, he shoved Jack in the chest. Jack stumbled back, then caught himself and lunged at his brother. Becca grabbed at Jack's shirt. When her hand slipped off it, Matt's arm clipped her jaw.

"Hey asshole!" Jack went at his brother again. "Don't you touch my girl!"

"Didn't realize she was still your girl. Thought you dumped her."

"She's the mother of my child."

At the word "mother," all the fight went out of Matt and he slumped against the wall. "She's gone, man. That's why we've been trying to get in touch with you. She's gone." He ground the heels of his hands into his eyes. "She's gone."

Jack stormed out into the night, leaving Becca running after him.

"Jack!"

Even inebriated, he was faster than she was and she lost him to the dark. She walked back to the porch and sat on the edge. Behind her the cabin's door opened and then Matt was sitting next to her.

"Sorry. I shouldn't have said that in there."

She shrugged. "You guys are upset." Jack hadn't really "dumped" her. It hadn't been anything so official as that. Probably because they hadn't really been "official" to begin with. Not romance-wise, anyway. Officially friends. Officially parents of a little girl. But not lovers.

"Still." Matt rejected her excuse for his behavior. Matt might be the bad boy of the Wolfe family, but he was still a Wolfe. His parents' influence was strong.

"Where do you think he went?" Becca stared into the humid night, looking for some sign of movement.

"He'll be back. He used to do this when he was a kid too. Were you guys out tonight?"

She tweaked the hem of her navy blue Skipjack's skirt. "I was working. Jack sat at the bar all night."

"That's not like him."

"No."

She hopped off the porch. She understood why Jack ran off.

257

He was trapped in his head. Trapped in being "Jack Wolfe." His levelheaded nature was one of his strengths. If she were going to be honest with herself, it was that characteristic that had motivated her behavior at the graduation party. Climbing into the back seat of her car—any girl's car, for that matter—was as un-Jack Wolfe as one could get. She had wanted to see if she could lure "good" Jack Wolfe out of his head and into trouble with her. She succeeded—and that success, that one misguided whim—had tied the two of them together forever.

But some situations couldn't be thought through. Like losing a parent. And right now, Jack was out there in the night trying to be good and levelheaded, trying to contain a whole mess of feelings he wasn't comfortable having anyone else see.

"I'll go find him," she said to Matt and walked off into the dark.

She was going to lure Jack Wolfe out of "Jack Wolfe." And if luring didn't work, she would drag him out kicking and screaming.

He turned out to be easy to find. He was sitting by the pond behind Matt's house, his knees drawn up to his chin. She plopped down next to him.

"Hey," she said.

"Hey," he said back.

She sat there for a minute, watching the shadowy forms of dragonflies skim over the pond's still water. Lightning bugs blinked on and off in the trees on the other side.

"Are there snakes in this pond?" she asked.

"Yup."

"I don't like snakes."

"Most people don't. So you might want to go back inside."

"You have EMT certification, though. If a snake bites me in the ass, you could suck out the venom, right?" From the corner of her eye, she could see him biting the inside of his cheek to keep from smiling.

"I'm sure Mattie would be happy to do that."

"I'll go ask." She started to stand. Jack's arm shot out and pulled her back down.

"Over my dead body. Or his dead body, more likely."

"I'm sorry. About everything."

"Yeah. Life sucks."

"It does."

Across the pond, the lightning bugs were slowing down, going dark.

"I should be mad at you," he said.

"You should be. What I did was wrong."

"But what you did was right, too. I would have been a terrible father. Well, maybe not terrible. But not very good."

"And you'd definitely be mad at me now. Permanently mad. And she'd have that in her life, two parents who can't stand the sight of each other."

She listened in the dark for his breathing, but it was barely audible. Even though there were several inches of night air between them, she could sense how tightly the muscles of his body were clenched.

"I can't believe she's gone," he said after awhile. "Shit. I don't know how my phone got turned off."

Becca stood, then sat back down again—this time, behind Jack. She stretched her legs out alongside his, wound her arms around him, and rested her cheek against his back. There were no words for moments like this. She felt that, intuitively. She couldn't believe Angie Wolfe was gone, either. Couldn't believe Shari Weber would be gone within the year, as well.

She felt his back push against her cheek as he took a long deep inhale. She rode the movement up and back down again, as he let the breath pour out.

"I don't think I can do this," he said quietly. "It hurts too much."

She ran her palms along his bare arms, wishing she could

absorb his pain into her own body. After a moment, his hands covered hers and stopped them. He threaded his fingers into her fingers as his back began to heave uncontrollably beneath her cheek. She rode that movement out too, holding him as steady as she could while he let out the whole mess of feelings no one had any words for.

INSIDE, the sofa bed was pulled out and made up, a thin cotton blanket folded across the foot of the mattress. Jack had no idea how long he and Becca spent outside by the pond. Could have been hours, but probably wasn't. Either way, he felt better now. Purged. Empty. Light.

"Thanks, Mattie!" Jack called out.

"You're welcome," came his brother's sleepy reply.

"Mind if my girl spends the night?"

Becca was shaking her head "no."

"Whatever. Just don't make too much noise."

"You're just jealous."

"Yeah. A little." A beat later, Matt's voice came again. "Becca? Thanks."

Becca rolled her eyes at Jack. "You're welcome."

"Okay. Leave me alone now."

"You bet!" Jack couldn't resist getting the last word in.

Becca swatted his arm. "Stop," she whispered.

"What? It's my God-given right to harass my brother."

"Not when he's being nice to you."

"Yeah, even then." Jack toed off his running shoes and let himself fall back onto the pullout bed. Becca looked down at him, her features soft with exasperation and … something else he still wasn't ready to put a name to.

Alright! Affection! She feels some affection toward me.

LOL.

Jack frowned. *Did you just LOL me? You finally answer me and that's what you say? LOL?*

"Jack, are you okay?" Becca sat warily on the edge of the mattress.

"Please tell me I wasn't speaking out loud."

"Yeah … you kinda' were."

He closed his eyes. "Sorry. How much did I say?"

"Something about affection and LOL."

He groaned. "I'm hearing voices and … talking to myself."

"I think you're still a little drunk. And way beyond the point of exhaustion."

He opened his eyes and looked at her … looking at him.

That's more than affection on her face, son.

Jack bit down on his tongue to keep himself from answering.

"Do you need anything before I go?" she asked.

He rolled onto his side and grabbed her arm, pulled her onto the bed with him. "You. I need you."

They were face to face now, and it occurred to Jack that he was not a pretty sight at the moment. His eyes were surely bloodshot, his nose red. He didn't even want to think about the state of his hair. And yet, there was still that look on her face.

"Has anyone ever told you that you're insane?" he said.

Her expression softened even further. "No, but I'm sure plenty of people have thought it. They're just too polite to say it out loud." She grinned at him.

"Did you just bust my chops?"

"Your brother's wearing off on me."

"They're working on a cure for that."

"You need to get some rest."

He scooted over and wrapped his arms around her. Immediately, a soothing peacefulness flooded his veins. Yes, his life sucked right now. But when she held him out by the pond, he was in a place where it didn't suck. A place that might be waiting for him when he got back from the hell he was in.

"I'll rest better if you're here with me." When he loosened his arms, her amusement of a moment ago turned to hesitation. "We won't wake up Mattie, I promise."

She held up her little finger. "Pinky swear."

He hooked his finger in hers, gave a little squeeze, and lowered their hands to the narrow sliver of mattress between them. She fell asleep first, clearly exhausted by his histrionics. He listened to the soft hush of her breath in and out. He gently unhooked their little fingers and curled his entire hand around hers. He was bone tired. And yet, his body was stirring. He was turned on, hard as a rock, even though the rest of him felt like a giant blob of mush.

How many nights had he lain in this very bed, thinking about having her next to him? Pretty much every night—even after everything that had come to light. The fact that she had been pregnant with his child, given birth to his child ... why did that make her even more attractive to him? His brain was too damn tired to ponder that again tonight.

For tonight, he was content to just lie there next to her and enjoy the way her presence made his body feel, to allow himself to float along on a pleasant—but intense—current of arousal without the need to do anything about it. The bottom had just dropped out of his life, but he felt safe right here, with her. *It's called love, son.* He ignored that, closed his eyes, and drifted off to sleep.

CHAPTER 30

$\mathcal{F}$at drops of rain fell like tears onto the mourners in the cemetery, there to pay their final respects to Angie Wolfe. Even though the air was still hot, Becca shivered as the pallbearers—Tim Wolfe, Oliver, Matt, Jack, and two other firefighters—carried in the casket. They lowered it onto the metal frame, their faces tight with strain and grief. She had managed to get Jack out of his head the night his mother passed. When she woke up the next morning, he was wrapped around her like she was the only thing keeping him afloat.

But she hadn't seen much of him in recent days. Her texts to him had garnered only the briefest of acknowledgments. She tried not to take it personally. He was hunkered down with his father and brothers. She couldn't imagine what they were going through—she just wished she could be of more help.

Her mother seemed to read her mind, and squeezed Becca's shoulder gently. "Give him time," she said.

Becca nodded. Not that she had any other choice but to give him time. Maybe it didn't matter anyway. She knew what she had seen on his face in Matt's cabin, but he still hadn't said he was staying in St. Caroline. That wasn't his original plan. He came home to spend time with his mother. Then he would go back to California and whatever life he had out there. A life she wasn't part of. As far as she knew, he hadn't changed his mind about that.

The men stepped back from the casket, their crisp black suits dotted with rain. They all wore matching floral printed ties, apparently one of Angie Wolfe's requests.

Becca paid little attention to the words of the reverend. Her attention was reserved for Jack, who was so deep inside his head and his grief that she could tell he wasn't hearing anything either. Or seeing anything. His eyes were trained hard on the wet grass in front of him.

Thunder rumbled in the distance. As a child, she had loved summer thunderstorms—violent and visual, great streaks of lightning splitting the sky over the bay, the noise rolling in like nature's anger.

She closed her eyes when the reverend began to pray. When she opened them again, Jack was no longer standing with his father and brothers. She glanced around the cemetery as the mourners began to disperse, some stopping to shake hands with Tim Wolfe and then pull him into an awkward embrace. But Jack was nowhere to be seen. He was gone.

JACK STOOD at the sink in Matt's small bachelor kitchen. He'd spent the evening cleaning up the cabin, which could charitably be called a disaster. Takeout was all he and Matt were eating lately—and the proof of that was stacked all around the kitchen and on the coffee table. Pizza boxes, white Chinese rice containers, crushed fortune cookies, enough empty soda cans and water bottles to qualify the place as a recycling center. He had bagged up the trash and taken it outside. Loaded Matt's tiny dishwasher, then filled the sink with soapy water to wash what wouldn't fit.

HEARTS ON FIRE

Matt was staying at Oliver's house for the night, watching Cam and Mason. Oliver had driven straight from the cemetery to Baltimore to be with Serena, whose condition had not improved. Jack himself was drained. Mentally, physically, emotionally—he was nothing but a hollowed out shell. He could barely even remember being at the funeral home. Already it felt like something that had happened days ago, instead of just that morning.

He spent the afternoon at the post-funeral reception in the fire station's community room. The Trevors had organized it, marshaling donations of food and drink. If there was someone in the town of St. Caroline who hadn't stopped in for at least ten or fifteen minutes, Jack couldn't think of them. Every time he started to go look for Becca, someone else had waylaid him.

Eventually, he managed to slip away and follow her to the station's kitchen. He desperately had wanted to kiss her, but didn't—because how inappropriate would that have been? Now, however, he wished he had. Everything seemed inappropriate now anyway. A smile, a slice of cake, a hot shower. Anything done for pleasure. He couldn't even imagine experiencing enjoyment again. Ever. He felt utterly defeated.

You won. Happy?

He had apologized to Becca for his inattention in recent days. "I'm not fit company to be with." It was a lame excuse, but the truth.

And tomorrow she was leaving for the Virginia suburbs of Washington, DC, to meet with some businesswoman who wanted Becca to make quilts for her new office building. So he had missed his chance to spend a little time with her.

The last time had felt so damn good, sleeping next to her, waking up in the middle of the night to find her body snuggled up against his, wrapping his arms around her to hold her tight until dawn. It had felt more intimate than sex.

He scratched his thumbnail against a plate, trying to loosen dried-on something or other. Not that he didn't want sex with her again. He did. But there wouldn't be alcohol involved the way it had been seven years ago. The next time he had sex with Becca, they both would be sober.

The next time. Who are you kidding?

There wasn't going to be a next time.

Why not?

His thumbnail stopped its scratching. That wasn't his voice.

You can leave me alone now. Thanks.

He wanted a next time. Things had been going great with Becca before he learned about her pregnancy. It was easy being with her, and that was something he'd never been able to say about a woman before. When she was around, everything was clearer. Sharper. Right. That was it.

Being with her just felt right.

And they had a child together. There was that, as well. There were flimsier foundations for a relationship. So they were going about things ass-backwards. They started a family first and then fell in love.

You're overthinking things, Jackie.

The words were clear as a bell in his mind. But he knew they weren't his words.

The dish drainer was filling up with cleaned dishes. Two more plates, a saucepan, and a fistful of forks and he was done. But he paused, his hands submerged in the soapy water. Someone was behind him. He felt it as strongly as he'd ever felt anyone's presence.

The door to the cabin was unlocked, as it always was when he and Matt were home. No need to lock up in St. Caroline. So anyone could have wandered in. Tiny soap bubbles rose from the dishwater and fanned out around his head. He exhaled slowly, then spun around.

No one was there.

He pushed away from the sink and walked down the short hallway to Matt's bedroom. Empty. Ditto for the bathroom.

He was losing it, clearly. The strain of the past days was getting to him. Hell, the strain of the last few months. He wished Becca were here. She'd make him feel less crazy. Ground him. But she was working at Skipjack's tonight, and he didn't want a repeat of the other night—him leaned over the bar, two sheets to the wind. She deserved better behavior than that.

He finished the dishes and dried his hands on a dish towel. He collapsed onto the sofa, too tired to even bother pulling it out into a bed. On the chair in the corner was folded his wedding quilt. He stared at it for a long while. Had his mother known he and Becca would get together? Is that why she asked Becca to finish it?

Just a coincidence.

There was that voice again.

She's just the finest hand quilter I've ever met.

He was holding his breath. *I'm losing my mind.*

Let go of your mind, Jackie. Reach for your heart.

CHAPTER 31

*A*t the revolving door, Becca turned and took one last look at the soaring lobby of the office building. Six months from now, four large-scale art quilts would greet employees and clients as they strolled toward the elevators. Her own art quilts! Becca could hardly believe it. Not only did someone want to hang her quilts where hundreds of people would see them every day, that person even wanted to *pay* for them. Becca had a deposit for the work in her purse, a check for more money than she'd ever had at one time.

She pushed through the revolving door and then stepped aside to send a group text to her mother and sisters. *Got the job!* Immediately her phone was flooded with congratulations and, from her mother, *I never doubted you would.*

She dropped her phone back into her purse, sneaking another peek at the deposit check—just to make sure she wasn't dreaming this entire day. Six months ago, the idea of making her big, improvisational quilts for a business wouldn't have occurred to her. It wouldn't have occurred to her to even try.

Her phone vibrated again. It was another text from her mother. *And all that money is YOURS. You're going to need it.*

That was certainly true. There was so much to do in the coming months to prepare for the adoption. Shari had offered to cover her expenses but Becca had insisted on paying some of them herself. She put the phone in her purse again and zipped the bag shut. She tucked it protectively beneath her arm and started to walk toward the parking lot. The day was classic mid-Atlantic summer weather—hot as Hades and with humidity you could practically wring out of the air. The macadam of the parking lot shimmered in the heat. She couldn't wait to crank up the air conditioning in her car.

Three rows back, she turned left. It was easy to spot her modest white car parked among the luxury sedans and sports cars. Also, there was a man standing next to her car. A tall man. A very tall man.

Jack.

Her heart began pounding. She missed him and the intensity of that longing slammed into her all at once. She would have broken into a run if it weren't for the skirt and heels she was wearing. She had to settle for hobbling as fast as she could.

"How did it go?" he asked right as she reached the car.

"What are you doing here?"

"I asked first."

"It went great. I got the project."

"Congratulations. Though you probably had the project the minute you set foot in the building."

She shrugged. "Maybe not. I don't have a track record doing commissions. She's taking a leap of faith with me." Her eyes dropped from Jack's face to the bundle of fabric in his arms. "Your turn. What are you doing here?"

"Your father told me where you were."

"And what are you doing with your quilt? Did I miss a section?" She knew she hadn't though.

"I'm supposed to give it to my bride."

Becca was quiet, not quite sure where this was going.

"Well, technically," he went on, "we're supposed to get married, I give you the wedding quilt, we consummate the marriage, and then we have kids. But we have this all out of order anyway. So I'd like to give you the quilt now, and then we consummate things tonight. Or—" He rolled his eyes toward the street. "—as soon as we can get through this traffic back to the hotel room I took the liberty of booking."

"You're spending the night?"

He nodded. "Not alone, I was hoping."

Yeah, that was an over-the-top hopeful smile on his lips. He was so adorable right now, she'd consummate whatever he wanted. She knew she was grinning like a fool—and she didn't care.

"And then we maybe consummate it again in the morning, just for good measure," he added. "Or in case I'm too nervous tonight and end up being more like a fumbling teenage boy than the suave, sexy lover you deserve."

"Suave, sexy lover?"

"I might have some mad skills these days. You never know."

Grinning like a fool on steroids now.

"You've been living with your brother. I suppose he might have taught you a few things."

"*Please.*" He rolled his eyes. "But speaking of living arrangements, we'll need to get our own place. It'll make consummating easier in the future. Plus, Matt's pullout bed is not that comfortable."

"I noticed. But I think we only need to consummate once and then it's done." She bit the inside of her lip to keep from laughing. "Plus, I have another meeting tomorrow. With Sylvia, a child psychologist here. I want all the help I can get."

"Can I help you?"

"The meeting's at nine."

He shrugged. "I can consummate you by nine. Probably even eight-thirty, easy."

No amount of biting could prevent her from laughing now.

"I love you, Becca."

She took another step closer to him, until the edge of the quilt brushed up against her arm.

"What are you proposing here?"

"Love. Marriage. Kids. A lifetime of happiness and great sex. Which will lead to more kids."

"What about Jackie?"

"Our first child. See? We're already ahead of schedule." He shifted the quilt into the crook of his left arm. His right hand reached out to caress her cheek. "But more seriously, we're her parents. She needs us."

"Are you sure?"

He nodded. "Completely sure. More sure than I've ever been about anything."

She lifted the quilt from his arm and cradled it against her chest. "Then I accept the wedding quilt."

"And …?"

"And I love you, Jack Wolfe."

He bent over to kiss her tenderly, his hand snaking around her back to pull her closer. But there was the matter of the quilt, wedged in between them.

"Maybe we should put this in the car," he murmured.

She dug her keys from her purse and unlocked the car. Jack opened the door, then took the quilt from her and carefully— almost reverently—placed it on the back seat. He touched the headrest on the driver's side.

"Where's the sock monkey? Worried someone might break into your car and steal him?"

"No." She playfully socked him in the stomach. "I always had him in there because it was something familiar. Something to make me feel at home. But now I am home. Finally." It had only taken twenty-four years for her to feel like St. Caroline was home. Better late than never.

Jack closed the back door to her car. "Now where were we?"

"We were at 'I love you, Jack Wolfe.'"

He reached around and unsnapped the barrette holding her hair back. He tucked the barrette into the pocket of his shorts. "You can have that back later," he whispered just before his lips touched hers.

She felt his fingers push gently through her hair, cupping her head and deepening the kiss. She let her body relax into his and returned the kiss. As hot as it was outside, the fire racing through her veins was even hotter.

"If we don't get inside where it's cool, I'm going to spontaneously combust." The words slipped from her mouth into his.

"Not to worry. I know how to put out all kinds of fires." His lips kissed their way up to her ear. "I'm a Wolfe. I'm endlessly fascinated by fire. But I might let yours burn for awhile. A good long while."

EPILOGUE

*B*ehind Jack, the bay sparkled in the crisp spring sunshine, sailboats bobbing on the waves. Before him sat everyone important in his life. His father, in a black tuxedo, sitting next to Michelle Trevor in a pale green mother-of-the-bride dress. Next to her sat Robert and Alice Weber. To his left stood Oliver, Matt, and Mason. Lined up on the right were three of Becca's sisters—Cassidy, Natalie, and Charlotte. If he weren't mistaken, Mason was head over heels in love with Charlotte.

In the back, behind the rows of guests in pristine white chairs, Lauren Trevor sat at a white baby grand piano. And all around him, he felt the presence of his mother. His parents had gotten married here at the Chesapeake Inn thirty-two years ago—inside because of rain.

Jack and Becca were getting married beneath clear blue skies, not a cloud to be seen anywhere. All of his mistakes—the graduation party, dropping out of law school—had led him here, to this perfect day. The past eight months had been busy. Crazy, some might say. He and Becca had moved into his parents' house for now, to keep his father company and to save money for a home of their own. They'd spent one memorable weekend painting Mattie's old room pink. There were any number of childhood incidents that could be revenge for.

On top of that, his father was keeping him busy with training. His mother had extracted that promise from Tim Wolfe. Jack would be the best-trained firefighter the town of St. Caroline had ever known. He was already well on his way to being the most popular fire dog mascot in town history, certainly the tallest.

Becca had completed her quilt commission for the business in Virginia and now had several more, in addition to being a popular teacher at Quilt Therapy.

But at the heart of their new life was their daughter. Jacqueline Michelle.

The music Lauren was playing changed into a more light-hearted tune as Jackie and Cam appeared at the top of the aisle. Flower girl and ring bearer, they both took their duties seriously. Jackie wore a dress of pink eyelet that matched Cam's cummerbund and bowtie. From her hand swung a white wicker basket filled with rose petals. Tucked in among the petals was the small purple sock monkey Jack had won for her at an amusement park in Ohio.

There had been many, many trips to Ohio. But there wouldn't be many more. When the school year finished, Jackie and the Webers would be moving to St. Caroline.

Three sets of grandparents to spoil her. You're in so much trouble.

He smiled at her, his daughter, and she smiled back. It was an unusual situation, to say the least, but it was working. Maybe working too well, given Jackie's not-so-subtle hints about a brother or sister. Not that Jack had any objections to lots of "consummating," as Becca still jokingly called it.

When Cam and Jackie reached the end of the aisle, they split apart. Cam went to stand with his father, brother, and uncle. Jackie joined her aunts.

Jack's heart swelled with love for her. And pride. He hadn't expected that, to be so proud of her. She had been through so much—and more lay ahead—but she was a fighter. She was maybe more like Matt that way. Or Becca.

Lauren's music changed again, this time slower and weightier. And then she was there, Becca heading toward him on her father's arm, beautiful and lovely and gorgeous … there weren't enough words to describe the way Becca looked to him. Her dress was beaded and embroidered from shoulder to waist, where it practically exploded into a full skirt of filmy fabric. Her cinnamon hair was pulled up, with wispy pieces framing her face. He was going to undo that fancy hairstyle later, when they consummated their marriage. Officially this time.

Dan Trevor smiled broadly at Jack as he and Becca slowed to a stop. Becca turned toward Jackie and motioned for her to join them. Jack clasped one of Jackie's hands, and Becca the other. There was never any question about their daughter being part of the ceremony. He and Becca might be getting married today, but they were a family already.

THANK you so much for reading Jack and Becca's story. If you enjoyed this book—and want to read more about the Wolfe and Trevor families—you'll love TWO OF HEARTS!

One-click to start reading Matt and Cassidy's story!

Two committed commitment-phobes …

Cassidy Trevor is the backbone of her family's quilt shop, the one everyone relies on, the person who makes the trains run on time. She has a good life with loving parents and sisters, a job-for-life that she enjoys, and respect as a capable businesswoman

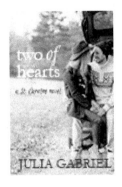

within the community. Still, she can't help wondering ... is there something more out there?

Matt Wolfe has spent his entire life living down to everyone's expectations. He's the body, the workhorse, the guy who always says yes. As a member of a fire-fighting family, he's also seen too many people lose everything they hold dear within the space of a heartbeat. He knows it's easier to let go of things if you never really wanted them in the first place.

... warned away from each other by their families ...

The Wolfe and Trevor families aren't the Montagues and the Capulets. Just the opposite. Both families have been close for years, but one love match between them is enough.

... strike a mutually beneficial arrangement ...

When Cassidy and Matt are volunteered to co-chair a holiday event, their working relationship slides into a secret friendship ... with benefits. Everyone gets what they want. Matt gets to sample the forbidden fruit he has coveted for years and Cassidy gets some much-needed stress relief from the pressures of running the family business while planning her escape from St. Caroline.

... and get more than they bargained for.

Cassidy has avoided commitment because she doesn't want anything tying her down. For Matt, a fling with Cassidy is perfect —the built-in expiration date means no messy breakup and no disappointment when expectations aren't fulfilled. But now the one person who "gets" her, who supports her dream to leave St. Caroline, is the one person Cassidy can't bear the thought of leaving. And, for the first time in his life, Matt is discovering expectations he wants to live up to ... his own.

One-click TWO OF HEARTS TODAY >>>

Turn the page for an excerpt from *Two of Hearts* ...

EXCERPT FROM TWO OF HEARTS

"Hey. You okay, buddy?" The guy standing next to Matt Wolfe at the hotel bar clapped him on the shoulder. Dave, the guy's name was. Matt had met him exactly six days ago at the nearby fire training academy. Matt was in Texas taking a week-long seminar. Today was the last day and everyone in the class was out to celebrate.

"Yeah. Fine," Matt replied, squinting harder into the hotel lobby's weird orange mood lighting. It made the space look like a science fiction movie set. Or like the whole place was on fire. Maybe that was why the fire training instructor had dragged them all here.

"Because you got a weird look on your face." Dave wasn't letting this go, and Matt really wished he would. It had been a long week. Matt wanted to drink a few beers to be polite, catch a cab to the hotel where he was staying, and fall face first into bed. His flight left early in the morning.

"I think the beer goggles have kicked in," he said.

"Oh yeah? Who you checking out?"

"I see a woman over there who looks like someone I know. From back home. But I don't know what she'd be doing way out here." It probably wasn't her. It was hard to tell in the orange light, and her face was turned down toward the phone in her hands.

"Which one is she?"

"The one in the pink dress, cowboy boots. Blonde hair. Glasses. Sitting alone in one of those big chairs." Big enough for two, he thought.

"Whoa. Not bad. Well, if you do know her, introduce me." He clapped Matt on the back again.

"If that's really her, she's an ice princess. I've known her all my life and no one has ever been good enough for her."

Dave laughed. "Well, I love a challenge. Let's head over there. You can either introduce me or we'll just introduce ourselves."

For a split second, Matt considered not following Dave over to the woman in the pink dress and cowboy boots. Chatting up women used to be one of his favorite pastimes. Or, as his brother Jack was fond of saying, his only pastime. But lately, nothing engaged his enthusiasm. His mother had succumbed to ovarian cancer the month before and his older brother's wife lay in a hospital in Baltimore, comatose from a car accident. It had been a rough year and Matt was frankly exhausted. Physically, emotionally, mentally. He was wiped out.

Dave took three steps with his long legs, then turned to look back at Matt. "You coming?"

Matt pushed away from the bar and followed. "Yeah, sure." He'd let Dave do all the talking.

As they got closer to the woman in the pink dress and cowboy boots, he saw that she was in fact the person he thought she was. Cassidy Trevor. One of the Trevor girls. The sister of his brother's fiancée. The daughter of his parents' close friends.

For all those reasons—and probably more that he was forgetting—Cassidy Trevor was forever off limits to Matt. All the Trevor sisters were. As Dave strode determinedly toward her, Matt wondered whether that prohibition applied to him too.

You're not Cassidy Trevor's keeper. Plus, she really was an ice princess. In fact, that should probably be in capital letters. Ice Princess. And maybe neon lights, just for good measure. She was going to shut down Dave's advances like nobody's business.

Then he reconsidered. Dave wasn't a local St. Caroline boy. Cassidy had always turned her nose up at the guys in town. As a teenager, she had spent summers chasing after the summer kids. The rich summer kids. Which had always seemed like a losing proposition to Matt, since the summer kids all went home at the end of the, well, summer.

Not that it mattered to Matt, of course. He had been under strict orders for years to leave her alone. That was fine with Matt. There were plenty of fish in the sea, and he was an excellent fisherman. Gifted, some might say. And by "some," he meant himself.

She looked up from her phone, seeming to sense their impending arrival. Confusion darkened her eyes for a moment, then she smiled one of those big Trevor smiles. Broad with blinding white teeth. He realized why he hadn't been entirely certain of her identity from across the lobby. Her blonde hair was done up in some curlicue hairstyle. He'd never seen her wear her hair that way. Usually, it was long and loose around her shoulders or pulled back into a simple ponytail. Occasionally, a neat bun. Once in awhile, a thick braid down her back. But never this loose, curly do. He wasn't sure whether he liked it or not.

"Matt. Hi," she said when he and Dave reached her. Dave immediately perched himself on the edge of the wide leather chair. The familiarity of the gesture rankled Matt. But Cassidy didn't seem to mind. She glanced at Dave, then looked back to Matt. "What are you doing here?"

"Training at the fire academy nearby. Since I'm taking over some of Oliver's duties while he's on a leave of absence."

Cassidy nodded somberly. "How's Serena?"

He shrugged. "The same. Ollie's too distracted to be at work right now."

"Understandable."

"Yeah. So what are you doing out here? All dressed up?" He looked down at her boots. They were a roughed-up brown leather, with pink flowers embroidered on the toes.

"My college roommate got married this afternoon." She smoothed her pink dress. "I was on bridesmaid duty."

Dave cleared his throat. *Oh right.* He wanted to be introduced.

"Cassidy, this is Dave. He's a firefighter from Kansas City."

Cassidy shook Dave's hand. "Nice to meet you."

"So you two know each other?" Dave was taking charge of the conversation. Matt was too tired to object.

"We grew up together in Maryland," she answered. "Our parents are friends."

That barely scratched the surface of their connections, Matt thought. Or maybe Cassidy didn't see them as being all that connected.

Dave reached over and lifted her drink from her hand. "Whatcha drinking?" He sniffed at the glass, another act that irritated Matt. He didn't exactly consider Dave to be a friend. It wasn't like they were going to stay in touch or anything.

"Just water," she answered, then trained a big flirty smile at Dave. "I think I had one too many pomegranate martinis at the wedding."

"Pomegranate martinis? That sounds either really good or really awful." Dave flirted back, his hand touching her shoulder for an instant. Her bare shoulder, Matt noted, since the straps of her bridesmaid's dress were so thin as to be nearly non-existent.

"They were pretty good."

"Hmm." Dave made a show of studying the bar. "I wonder if the bartender here will make us some?"

"You should go ask." Cassidy winked theatrically at Dave. "Hint, hint."

"I think I will."

Matt resisted the urge to roll his eyes. Dave was practically puffing up his chest at his success so far with Cassidy.

"You want one, man?" Dave asked Matt.

Matt held up his near-empty beer bottle. "Nah. I'm good." He watched as Dave threaded his way through the increasing crowd and back to the bar.

"So how long are you out here for?" Cassidy asked.

"I leave tomorrow morning. And what about you?"

"I'm renting a car and driving over to Austin and San Antonio. I'm going to spend a few days checking out some quilt shops. See if I can find any good ideas to steal for mom." She flashed that blinding Trevor smile at him again, which had the same effect on him now that it had when he was in middle school and she was the glamorous eighth-grader, the "older woman" a year ahead of him.

O Cassidy, Cassidy! Wherefore art thou Cassidy?

Yeah, he remembered a few lines of Shakespeare from middle school, too.

"So how was the wedding?"

"It was good. Fine. Fun. You know." She shrugged.

Was conversation with Cassidy always this awkward? It wasn't as though they didn't see each other back home. They were friendly, if not exactly friends. But right now, he felt like he was chatting up a woman he'd just met in a hotel bar. *Look for conversational openings.* He glanced down at her short cowboy boots with the pink flowers.

"Did you wear those in the wedding?"

She twisted an ankle back and forth, and he tried to ignore the slender length of tanned leg between the boot and the hem of her dress.

"I did. We all did." She laughed. "We're out of context here, aren't we? We're not in St. Caroline anymore."

"No, we're not, Toto." That made her laugh again. Cassidy had a big, hearty laugh. She was a girl who liked to have fun. *Not a girl. A woman.* There was a straightforward quality to her that Matt had always found appealing. "You look nice," he added. "That color's very pretty on you."

"Well now, Matthew Wolfe. Aren't you just the perfect gentleman?" Her voice was suddenly soft and flirty. "Though I have to say, you look like you've been rode hard and put up wet."

It was his turn to laugh now. "It's been a tough week. With the training and all." Matt was about to ask whether she was staying at this hotel, when Dave reappeared with two martini glasses.

"Yup. Bartender hooked us right up." Dave handed a pomegranate martini to Cassidy. "Let me know if these taste as good as the ones you had earlier. If not, I'll go give the bartender hell."

Cassidy took a small sip. "Mmm. Tastes exactly the same."

"Excellent." Dave clapped Matt on the back. "Tom over there said to tell you he wants to talk to you."

Yeah, right. Matt could tell from the bemused expression on Cassidy's face that even she saw through that ruse. Dave wasn't even trying to hide it. *But fine.* Cassidy wasn't giving off any signs that she objected to Dave's interest. And Matt wasn't her keeper, he reminded himself for the second time that night. And for probably the millionth time in his life. But who was keeping count?

"Well, see you two later then." Matt retreated to the bar and to Tom, who didn't seem surprised to see him.

"Ol' loverboy, eh?" Tom laughed.

Matt didn't share the laugh. *Too damn tired right now.* The week had been nonstop work at the training academy. He drained the rest of his beer and, against his better judgment, ordered another. The thought of sleep was enticing, but he'd stay awhile longer to say goodbye to Cassidy. He half-listened to Tom's mostly idle chatter and added a few comments where it seemed appropriate or solicited. He ignored the interested stare of a woman at the other end of the bar. When his beer was finished, he turned back toward the lobby.

Dave and Cassidy were gone.

Well, can't say you didn't see that one coming. And like the world-class idiot he was, he had even facilitated it. He pulled out his phone to text his brother, Jack.

Just ran into Cassidy out here.

A moment later, a reply came. *Oh yeah? Becca says she's out there for a wedding.*

Matt stuffed his phone back into his pocket. Of course, the Trevor sisters weren't off limits to Jack. Nothing was off limits to Jack. The sky was the freaking limit for his younger brother.

For Matt, the ceiling had always been about thirty-five thousand feet lower. He was the workhorse in the family, the body that could always be counted on when another body was needed. *Old reliable, that's me.* Not that he was complaining. When his father, the chief of the St. Caroline fire department, had asked him to take over some of his older brother Oliver's training and management responsibilities at the station, Matt had stepped right up. Being a firefighter was what it meant to be a Wolfe. His father, his uncle, both of his brothers—all firefighters in St. Caroline. He wasn't taking over Oliver's job permanently. As soon as his wife was out of the hospital, Ollie would be back at the station. And Matt would step back into his old job, where he'd been since college.

He knew people tended not to take him seriously most of the time. Yes, he liked to have a good time. And yes, he liked women. Why not? Interacting with the opposite sex had always come easily to him. Generally speaking, it had been his experience that he could have any pretty thing he wanted. As long as that pretty thing's name didn't have "Trevor" tacked on to the end.

~

One-click TWO OF HEARTS TODAY >>>

AFTERWORD

HEARTS ON FIRE is the most personal book I've ever written.

Like Angie Wolfe, my own mother succumbed to ovarian cancer in her fifties. I was 24. That year—1989—is still the single hardest year of my life. Grief is a complex experience. I have memories that are as vivid as five minutes ago—leaning against a wall in the hospital's hallway and weeping, or the phone call from my brother with the news that her condition had been downgraded to terminal.

My mother, Margaret Carson 1932-1989

And yet, I remember very little of the day of her funeral. Waiting for the funeral home's limousine. That I never took off my red winter coat in the funeral home. One of my cousins hugging me at the cemetery. That's it. Literally, just those three things.

I did most of the things Jack does in the book. Rage. Bargain with God. Cuss when bargaining didn't work. Offer myself up instead. I can't tell you how many times I cried during the writing of this book.

But none of my books would exist without my mother, Margaret Eileen Carson (1932-1989). And so I dedicate this one, especially, to her. She passed on her great love of reading and books to me, and through my books I pass on a bit of her spirit to you. — *Julia Gabriel*

A portion of the proceeds from this book have been donated to the Ovarian Cancer Research Fund Alliance.

MORE FROM JULIA GABRIEL

St. Caroline Series

Hearts on Fire

Two of Hearts

This Reminds Me of Us (coming July 2019)

Phlox Beauty Series

Next to You

Back to Us

The Senator's Wife

ABOUT THE AUTHOR

Julia Gabriel writes contemporary romance that is smart, sexy, and emotionally-intense (grab the tissues). She lives in New England where she is a full-time mom to a teenager, as well as a sometime writing professor and obsessive quilter (is there any other kind?).

If all goes well, she'll be a Parisienne in her next life. Her books have been selected as "Top Picks" by RT Book Reviews, and critics at RT Book Reviews, Kirkus, and others have called her work "nuanced," "heart-wrenching and emotional," "well-crafted contemporary romance," and "deeply moving storytelling."

Be the first to find out about new books, sales, and more by signing up for my email newsletter!

Say "hello" on social media ...